THE
HIPPIE HOUSE

THE HIPPIE HOUSE

KATHERINE HOLUBITSKY

ORCA BOOK PUBLISHERS

National Library of Canada Cataloguing in Publication Data

Holubitsky, Katherine, 1955-
The hippie house / Katherine Holubitsky.

ISBN 1-55143-316-8

I. Title.

PS8565.O645H66 2004   jC813'.54   C2004-901024-

Library of Congress Control Number: 2004101755

Summary: Summer 1970. When a local girl is found murdered, the freedom and innocence
of "youth" are forgotten and, for fourteen-year-old Emma, things will never be the same.

Orca Book Publishers gratefully acknowledges the support for its publishing programs
provided by the following agencies: the Government of Canada through the
Book Publishing Industry Development Program (BPIDP),
the Canada Council for the Arts, and the British Columbia Arts Council.

Design and typesetting: Lynn O'Rourke
Cover Artwork: Karel Doruyter
Printed and bound in Canada

Orca Book Publishers
1030 North Park Street
Victoria, BC Canada
V8T 1C6

Orca Book Publishers
PO Box 468
Custer, WA USA
98240-0468

08 07 06 05 04 • 6 5 4 3 2 1

Dedicated to Mike with affection.
And to the memory of my grandparents,
Frank and Mary James.

—Katherine Holubitsky

1

B<small>Y THE SPRING</small> of 1970, the dusty old shed that sat in the woods down by Fiddlehead Creek was known as the Hippie House. My father built it when we first moved to Ruddy Duck Farm seven years before. At that time he claimed it was to "duck out of the sun" when he was working in the fields. But as I grew older and began to notice that the only time he didn't use it was when he was working in the fields, I came to suspect that this had not been the truth at all.

For one thing, the shed was not even close to the fields where he worked. It stood at the southwest corner of the farm, closer to Uncle Pat's property line, and although it was in the woods, it was most easily reached from the main road. No, my brother Eric and I decided, it had nothing to do with getting out of the sun. Our father had built it to get away from Mom and her "blessed cigarettes."

This was not an unreasonable assumption because our mother spent the better part of each day parked in a brocade chair, inhaling murder mysteries as greedily as Pall Malls. Eric and I were convinced that one day we would step from the school bus to see—not our familiar old farmhouse at the end of the long lane, but a giant pile of ash, as if God had been smoking an enormous cigarette and carelessly, in passing, dropped the butt over our tiny piece of the world.

The truth was, Mom did not like large animals or mucky open spaces. In fact, she had never liked the out-of-doors at all. It was all too messy with variables beyond her control. Mom liked order; she liked polished silverware, precisely set tables and neat, well-behaved children. I knew she loved Eric and me. But I often wondered if she would have loved us even better if we could have been starched, folded and tucked into a drawer.

So it was with some persuasion that she had agreed to sell our comfortable home in Toronto and move to the country when Dad retired at forty-six. The sale of his busy hardware stores, along with a large inheritance left to him by my grandfather, had allowed him to do this. But Mom knew how my father loved the country. As they toured Ruddy Duck Farm, she'd watched his face shed ten years as he imagined the possibilities: the pond he would stock with rainbow trout, the large workshop, and the perfect field for a hangar and airstrip—for Dad was an expert pilot. And so she had agreed to the move.

For his part, if Mom was generous enough to let him spend his days with his ducks and geese and woodworking projects and farm machinery, he could certainly handle a bit of smoke.

My mother and father had an accommodating relationship and although they bargained a lot, they rarely argued.

The shed became the Hippie House the spring Eric turned seventeen and converted it into a studio for his rock band. My father had more or less abandoned it at that point and was only too happy to turn it over to The Rectifiers, to get Eric and his guitar out of the house and into the farthest corner of the farm where even a rutting moose could not be heard. Not that he wanted to discourage Eric from playing. Dad didn't discourage any activity if he detected a budding passion. But that particular one, he confided in me, needed a lot of growing room.

So at the end of April, every day after school for a week, and with our dog Halley bounding alongside, Eric and I hopped on the tractor and drove up the gravel lane that wound around the barn past the airplane hangar. We continued down the soft slope past the duck house and through the gate into the cool woods where patches of snow still clung stubbornly to the hollows in the ground.

Gravel turned to dirt, and after turning a bend at the end of the lane, we splashed across the creek by way of a concrete sluiceway to reach the Hippie House on the other side. After parking the tractor, we unloaded brooms and paint from the trailer and pushed open the sagging door.

Dad had not used the shed for some time, but it still smelled like him; an earthy blend of sawdust, machine oil and old metal tools. We began the task of cleaning up by packing the tools in boxes and stacking them beneath the workbench. We swept down cobwebs, and while I fed stacks of tattered yellowed newspapers into the stove, Eric began painting the walls purple with red trim. I pretended to be annoyed at having to help him. This was, after all, The Rectifiers project, not mine. But at almost fourteen, I was secretly delighted to have any connection with a rock band. Even if it was only my brother and his friends.

As we began our work, Eric told me about the amazing guitar player he had seen at an outdoor rock festival the year before.

"He was so cool, Emma, he blew everyone away. He talks with his guitar. It's like his voice. All you have to hear is one note and you know it's Buddy Guy."

"Is that what you want to do?" The fire snapped as I fed it another stack of papers. "Talk with your guitar?"

My brother thought about this. "I want people to listen to what I have to say."

Once the room was painted and we had cleared the floor to accommodate a drum set, I sewed curtains for the two windows. A large one next to the door provided a view of Fiddlehead Creek. A smaller one, thick with road dust, faced the main road. Eric stapled posters of Jimi Hendrix, Jim Morrison and Santana to the walls. He harnessed electricity from Uncle Pat's barn. Although blocked by the woods, it was still the closest structure to the shed.

Eric had me snap a publicity shot: the tangle-haired Rectifiers, brothers Miles and Malcolm Fritz, Jimmy Bolton and Eric, wearing T-shirts and grinning widely, posing with the instruments they could barely play in the doorway of the twelve-by-sixteen-foot shed. I gave myself a photo credit. I signed "From the studio of Emma Jenkins" in the lower right corner. Eric then had the photograph blown up and tacked it to the center post along with photocopies of their upcoming gigs. Actually, it was several copies of one gig—my grade eight graduation dance.

So that is why Uncle Pat jokingly began calling the shed the Hippie House. It was also Uncle Pat who'd given Eric hair clips and curlers for his birthday. They had been tucked in with his real gift, the first calculator we had ever seen. My mother's brother, Pat McEachran, had been responsible for encouraging my father to buy the farm adjacent to his property when he'd retired. But unlike Dad, Uncle Pat actually farmed for a living, along with my hardworking Aunt Alice. My cousins, Megan and Carl, had been born and raised on the farm.

Megan was fifteen, a year and a half older than me, and was very aware of boys, especially the lead singer of The Rectifiers, Malcolm Fritz. How very convenient that he was spending so much time at Ruddy Duck, practicing with the band. I had strict instructions to phone her whenever The Rectifiers organized a practice, and when they did, she invented all kinds of reasons why we should just happen to be down by Fiddlehead Creek.

Specifically in the vicinity of the Hippie House, where Malcolm might catch a glimpse of her. Despite all her efforts, Malcolm never did seem to notice her, although Eric did. I heard about it after dinner one night. I was embarrassing him in front of his friends. Quit hanging around!

The debut of The Rectifiers at my graduation dance was sensational. This was despite the fact that the band was really terrible. Malcolm, the singer and harmonica player, had the voice of a hinge, and Miles, the drummer, trashed "Proud Mary," having absolutely no sense of timing at all.

Their audience didn't care. We had ironed our hair, frosted our lips and dabbed lemon-scented perfume behind our ears. There was a revolution going on and until then we had been too busy growing up to enlist. But now high school waited at the end of the summer, and with The Rectifiers and their screaming guitars among us, we were involved.

JULY OF THAT YEAR was a seamless stretch of sticky afternoons spent sprawled at the opposite end of a canoe from Megan. Slathered in baby oil, we floated between the three islands on the farm's pond, working on our tans. From the direction of Fiddlehead Creek drifted the sounds of my brother's band, which practiced daily, while over our heads droned the engine of my father's Maul Rocket as he dusted the neighboring crops.

In the cooler evenings, when the trout began to rise and the shadows of the American elm trees lay long and dark on the laneway, Megan and I would often catch a ride with whoever was making the ten-mile trip into town. We'd sit cross-legged on old sofa cushions in the back of my father's van between the large oil drums. Or we'd squat in the back of Uncle Pat's pickup truck with our bottoms hovering a few inches in the air to prevent our backbones from being jarred as we traveled over the gravel road. If Eric agreed to take us, we would cram between

the instruments bound for the drop-in center where The Rectifiers often played.

The drop-in center was a long, open room above the ice arena.
With the exception of a few broken hockey nets, it had sat empty
for many years. Earlier in the spring, Mr. Gillespie, who owned
the local Dairy Bar restaurant, had suggested to town council
that it   ght make the ideal space for a teen drop-in center. It
was a suggestion that raised eyebrows, primarily because Mr.
Gillespie was known as a very conservative man. But when he
had council imagine an indoor theater of sorts to entertain the
large number of idle teenagers the warm weather had drawn to
the streets of Pike Creek, it was an image they could appreciate
and the proposal was quickly passed.

Notices were posted at the high school and strapped to telephone poles lining the main boulevards.

I was not yet in high school, so, unlike Megan and some of
my friends, I was not officially extended the invitation to drop
in. That was okay. I had my own ticket in. If I helped Eric haul
the band's heavy equipment up the dusty, narrow staircase, I
would be allowed to stay. At least for a couple of hours. Until
Eric decided that the climate was no longer good for my health,
when he would wave the threat of what my parents would say
and shoo me out the door.

The door to the drop-in center opened off the gravel parking
lot at the side of the arena directly onto a small foyer at the
bottom of the stairs. The stairwell had recently been painted,
and although this temporarily masked the odor of moldy wood,
it had done little to hide the scuffs and lacerations of more than
fifty years. A single lightbulb in a broken cage lit the way to the
second floor. Chesterfields and chairs dragged from musty base-
ments were donated for the comfort of those who dropped in. At
one end of the room, a stage was created with sheets of plywood
and concrete blocks.

Maurice Kaplan volunteered to oversee the drop-in center. Maury was twenty-eight years old and owned the only trendy clothing and miscellaneous-cool-stuff store in Pike Creek. He had emigrated from Detroit a year earlier to escape being drafted to fight in Vietnam. Wide-wale corduroy flares, thick leather belts, elongated Pepsi bottles, bubble shirts, loops of silver and packets of colored beads competed for space in his store. In addition to this, if he was pressed by the right customer, big, red-bearded Maury would bring his collection of incense burners and pipes from the back room.

Maury's policy of administration was not to discourage what he did not see. This meant that he discouraged very little, as much of his time was spent entertaining the older girls at the entrance to the second floor.

A strobe light spread dappled light across the mellow crowd while The Rectifiers played. Here and there, a match flared, a joint was lit and passed freely only to be stubbed and hidden in the palm of whoever was in possession of it when Constable Wagner made his nightly tour.

The door to the drop-in center remained propped open on those summer nights. People gathered in the parking lot. They drifted up and down the stairs, milling in and out of the large, smoky room. They would be listening to or ignoring The Rectifiers as they played. The band had no program to follow, no set to get through, and the audience simply came and went on the night breeze.

Often, young people from larger cities, passing through Pike Creek on their way to Georgian Bay, would stop at the intersection where they were to turn north. Attracted by the music they would pause for an hour. And Maury never challenged their right to join us. It was, after all, 1970, a time of unquestioning acceptance. It was the cool thing to do.

Toward the end of July, I became aware that this open-armed policy did not sit well with my parents. By then they knew of

my arrangement with Eric, and it was not that they didn't trust
me or my friends or probably any of the young people they knew
as the children of their friends. It was this new, casual attitude
that allowed anyone into our midst that concerned them. I knew
nothing different and so, echoing Megan and after tiring of
waiting for Eric and hitchhiking home one night, I told them that
they would have to accept it. It was just the way things were.

This, of course, got me a week confined to the farm. In addition, my privileges allowing me early entrance to the drop-in
center were revoked. I would have to wait until September,
when I was officially in high school, before I would be allowed
to return.

Despite its social limitations, the month of August passed
quickly. I spent several days sweating in the hot fields, helping
my father bale hay, then several more comforting him after he
ran over our blind old Persian cat, Lester, who had followed him
into the field.

My birthday on the tenth was devoid of the anticipation and
excitement of previous years. My parents gave me the jacket I had
asked for, and Eric presented me with ten dollars wrapped in a
series of boxes, a standard for the past three birthdays. My mother
baked the same double chocolate cake she baked for each of us on
our birthdays. It was decorated with fourteen pink candles and
Happy Birthday, Emma written in Mom's flowery script. There
were no surprises. It was a day much like any other. It was now all
so predictable. At fourteen, my days of being a kid were far behind
me. One thing was for certain, I needed a more sophisticated
name. Emma Jenkins—what were my parents thinking?—it was
so mundane. I asked them how to legally change it.

"What's wrong with Emma?" they both asked.

This exclamation was followed by Mom suddenly widening her
eyes to catch my attention. With one corner of her linen napkin
she patted her mouth in a demure, but rather dramatic way.

"It's an old woman's name. It belongs to someone who wins ribbons for her fudge at county fairs. I want something with class. Something that doesn't suggest I fell off the back of a turnip truck. I was thinking along the lines of Faye or Sophia."

Eric's eyes fell to my chest and he began to laugh.

"Dad!"

"Alright, alright. I'll tell you what. Rather than change it," said Dad, "why don't you try one out for a while." He winked. "Sophia, would you kindly pass the cream?"

I passed the cream. As I did, Mom's eyebrows shot up again. She dabbed furiously at her mouth in another attempt to catch my attention.

"Mom, would you quit making those faces? What are you trying to say?"

She sighed. "Emma—"

"Sophia," I quickly corrected.

"Sophia. You have broccoli caught in your braces. You may be excused from the table to clean your teeth."

A few days later, attention turned to Carl. Not an unusual occurrence as Carl often attracted attention for what he did. This was because my cousin, a tall, doughy eighteen-year-old, possessed a rather simple mind. Carl's attention span was brief and his actions were largely motivated by impulse. Forethought and consequences seemed incomprehensible to him. Carl was known to stress machinery until it broke. He had once started a fire in the hayloft and he had destroyed many good paddles attempting to discover the amount of force needed to drive them into the mud at the bottom of the pond. My father had found them waterlogged and ruined in the long grass beneath the weeping willow next to the spillway where the current eventually deposited debris.

But over the years, the damage he inflicted on Ruddy Duck paled in comparison to the grief he had caused Uncle Pat.

Despite this, and in no small part due to the patient guidance of Uncle Pat and Aunt Alice, Carl had graduated with a vocational diploma at the end of grade ten. For several months he had been working at the Pike Creek Dairy. Every morning he loaded gallons of milk and pails of ice cream into trucks.

On this August day, he had accidentally locked Mr. Chisholm, owner of the Pike Creek Dairy, in the walk-in freezer. The mistake occurred after Carl had emptied the extra pails of ice cream and chunks of ice from his truck around noon. Squatting to wipe a shelf clean, Mr. Chisholm was hidden by a pallet stacked with butter when Carl locked the freezer door and went home.

Three hours later, Mrs. Chisholm dropped by the dairy to ask Mr. Chisholm's opinion on wallpaper. If it had not been for the fact that there was a sale on and she needed a decision immediately, Mr. Chisholm might have become as solidified as the Neapolitan that day. Finding no one in the office, she followed the faintest knocking, only to realize that someone was trapped in the freezer! Mr. Chisholm was rushed to the hospital where he spent the night recovering from hypothermia and agitated nerves.

Carl was given a week's vacation for his mistake, most of which he spent well out of Uncle Pat's sight at Ruddy Duck Farm.

So it fell to Dad to ensure that Carl's time away from work was spent wisely. Several times I caught sight of him with a reluctant Carl in tow, recruited to repair a fence or clean the cattle trough. My father also had him stringing soda pop cans together to create a sort of security alarm. The string was draped around the base of the large fuel drums we kept on our farm. Over the summer there had been several instances of gas thieves raiding the farms in our area during the night. Just the week before, our neighbors to the west, the Frasers, had their fuel drums drained and they hadn't heard a thing.

Poor Carl, that week had to be very difficult for him. I knew how much he would have preferred to be occupied in one of his own games: shooting his BB gun at the weather vane on the tractor shed or pushing Uncle Pat's old tractor to its limits, driving erratically across the field.

Eric helped occupy my time by assigning me sewing projects, like a vest with beaded fringing—exactly like John Mayall's on the cover of *Blues From Laurel Canyon*. He also wanted a pair of flared jeans with satin inserts. You know, for on stage.

My brother would sit behind me and watch his order being created. He was so good at so many technical and mechanical things, but I don't think it ever ceased to amaze him how a piece of cloth could become something he could wear.

One evening I returned home from Brampton where Megan and I had seen the movie *Wait Until Dark*. Susy Hendrix— Audrey Hepburn's blind character—being stalked by a killer in her apartment had been more than either of us could stand. Shivering close together in the back of Uncle Pat's truck on the way home, we'd had very little to say.

"I thought Roat was dead after she stabbed him," Megan whispered.

"So did I," I said.

"He was so good-looking."

"Yes, he was," I agreed.

When they dropped me off, the lights were out in the farmhouse and nobody was at home.

"Better turn on some lights," Uncle Pat cheerfully advised me.

It seemed so casual a remark in a world inhabited by murderers—until I realized that Uncle Pat had not seen what Megan and I had seen.

"I will." The words just barely escaped from the back of my throat.

Megan scrambled into the cab as Uncle Pat waved a big hand and they drove off.

We did not lock our doors when we went out, and I never yelled hello when I entered the house. Except at that moment. There was no answer. Armed with Halley, I took Uncle Pat's advice and walked stealthily through the house, flicking on every light in every room. Further hoping to chase away images of long knives and men leaping from dark corners while I waited for someone to return home, I sat down to work on Eric's vest at my sewing machine.

"Is there some reason you want the roosters up?" Eric, who had wandered in from the Hippie House, innocently asked.

Guiding a seam at full speed through the machine, I jumped. My foot came down hard on the pedal at the same time as I jerked my hand. The needle drove through the cuticle at the edge of my index finger. Shocked, and with my finger still pinned to the machine, I tried to tug it out. Realizing what I had done, I let out a howl. Eric quickly turned the wheel to set me free. Taking my hand, he studied the hole the needle had left clear through to the other side.

"Cool," he announced.

"It is not cool," I said, pulling my hand back. And for some reason, at that moment, his failure to sympathize unleashed the fear I had managed to keep in check over the last two hours. "And don't you ever sneak up on me again!" After whacking a surprised Eric, I began to cry.

In late August, the mounting traffic up and down the asphalt lane separating the pond from the farmhouse became a concern. Eric and the members of his band and friends of the members of the band would follow the lane up past the barn and park next to the tractor shed. From there they would walk down through the airfield, past the duck house and into the woods to the Hippie House. As the summer progressed, the band was joined by musicians from outside of Pike Creek who had heard The Rectifiers at the drop-in center and come to jam. Then there were the friends of these musicians, driving over the heated asphalt, scattering our flock of domestic geese. One carload of visitors, swerving to avoid my father's prized pair of white Chinese geese, left a rut in Mom's rose garden.

This rut was their final error.

There was one reason Mom went outside. Once a day, after donning a broad-brimmed hat, she would pocket pruning shears and clip down the lane to tend to her beloved rose garden, which tumbled against the stone retaining wall. It was these daily trips, in fact, that had prompted my father to pave our lane. A luxury and expense that most farmers would consider extravagant, paving the lane had been a worthwhile investment in my father's mind. It helped tame the mud and dust my mother so detested. It had been another attempt to help civilize her life on the farm.

Until the rut in the rose garden, Dad's annoyance had given rise to only a few pointed warnings. But now the growing traffic could no longer be ignored. Dad approached the topic after *The Ed Sullivan Show* one Sunday night, using the moment to also voice his concern about the type of people visiting the Hippie House. Some of them, he suggested, appeared far too old to be in school. What were they doing hanging around with seventeen-year-olds when they should be making something out of their lives?

Eric didn't know. Anyway, what was he supposed to do? Embarrass himself and his friends and everybody else by telling them to get lost?

Dad shook his head. "I'm not asking you to do that. It just seems to me like you're gathering a lot of hangers-on."

"Dad, it's not your problem."

My father thought for a moment, but he didn't reply. Clearly, Eric was not denying that it was a problem—it just didn't belong to Dad. He would give Eric time to deal with it in his own way.

So it was decided that The Rectifiers and their friends and all their acquaintances would have to park along the county road next to the woods. Never mind that the cars risked being pelted by gravel and dust. That was the price my father attached to his hospitality.

This made far more sense, anyway, because the walk from the main road to the Hippie House was short. Eric's friends could come and go and, with the exception of the noise level, we wouldn't even know they were there.

Tired of tanning, anxious for the last few days of summer to be over, Megan and I sat on the steps of the stone porch, leafing through the Eatons catalog, choosing winter coats and boots. We both adored a three-quarter-length suede jacket with zip-out lining. It came in tan, chocolate and, my favorite, dusty rose.

As we turned the pages of the catalogue we noticed that the sounds drifting through the woods from the direction of the Hippie House were becoming fragmented. Disjointed. A frenzied drumroll, an incomplete guitar riff, the wheeze of the harmonica suddenly cut short, and Malcolm's voice, too determined in its imitation of Jim Morrison, start and stall. All of this was nearly drowned by the hum and shouts of a crowd independent of the band.

Curious, Megan and I wandered down toward the Hippie House. As we drew closer, we could hear outbursts between the scraps of music. Malcolm was accusing Miles of playing so loudly that he was drowning out his voice.

"Well, listen to you! Marvin Gaye does not begin 'Grapevine' like he's being castrated. Can't you just sing the song and shut up!"

This prompted Malcolm to loudly and explicitly suggest what Miles could do with his drumsticks.

Now within sight of the Hippie House, it occurred to Megan and me that we recognized few of the bodies looming in the doorway and leaning against my father's shed. It frightened us that the strange men playing a strange game—throwing knives at each other's feet—did not ignore us as we were used to being ignored by the members of the band.

But they were not like the members of the band. Their hair was not long like my brother's, but short and slick. They wore black pants and black boots when everyone else wore cutoff jeans and leather thongs.

When they grinned and asked us to cross the creek, Megan and I made every excuse not to stay.

Eric began to arrive at the farmhouse in a bad mood, lock himself in his room and wail on his guitar, often while the party continued down at the Hippie House. He had not found a way to deal with the hangers-on.

ON LABOR DAY, my father shut it down. The Hippie House was, from that day forward, off-limits to anyone with the exception of the original band.

The following day I started grade nine in a newly renovated school. It was a sprawling, state-of-the-art school built to serve a small town and a large farming community. Fifteen school buses waited along the maple-shaded street when school dismissed at three o'clock. I was amazed that any school, but particularly my school, would have a theater with padded seats, two gymnasiums, a band room, carpentry and automotive shops, and, most impressive to me, a sewing room with all Bernina machines. Strolling through the wide halls with my friends, I felt that I had been promoted—that I was a part of something very big. By the end of the second week I had joined the badminton club and volunteered to sew costumes for the drama department's production of *Oliver!* that year.

My circle of friends widened as I began to socialize with people not just because we found ourselves in the same classroom, but because we shared the same interests. I became friends with several of the actors in the play. One of these friends was a girl named Hetty DeSousa, who played one of the "ladies of the evening." She had gone to the one other public school in Pike Creek, but she lived only two miles south of Ruddy Duck Farm.

Hetty lived in a castle, although she was not a princess; her father sold pharmaceuticals and her mother was a potter. Mr. and Mrs. DeSousa were the most recent owners of the castle, which had been bought and sold regularly since the original German architect had died. The castle had changed hands often mainly because prospective buyers would get caught up in the romance of the fairy-tale surroundings. They did not consider what a nightmare it would be to furnish the drafty interior and turn it into a cozy home. It was a small castle by German standards, but it did have a turret with winding steps and a room at the top that was Hetty's mother's studio.

I liked Mrs. DeSousa, who preferred that we called her by her first name, Ruby. I particularly liked it when she sat on the red vinyl couches in the enormous living room and laughed with us about current TV shows and boys. Within three weeks of our meeting her, Hetty's mother had taught Megan and me how to tie-dye T-shirts and silk-screen scarves. She'd taught us the correct way to apply makeup, explaining how certain colors either brought out our natural skin tones or made us look like we'd stepped off the set of *The Twilight Zone*. Ruby and I could discuss fabrics and pattern design for hours, until Hetty, feigning death from boredom, would roll her eyes back in her head and collapse on the goatskin rug.

Ruby had ideas and imagination; she had colors, textures and symmetry whirling around in her head. She could turn emotions and moods into something tangible. I was fascinated by her potter's wheel in the turret and the kiln in the stand of aspen behind the castle. It amazed me that she could turn a single lump of faceless clay into a vase more beautiful than the rose it held.

Hetty's older sister had recently moved away from home. Tanya DeSousa worked as a nurse's aide in Pike Creek's only senior citizens' home. She lived in a small apartment, three blocks past the ice arena, with another nurse's aide, Katie Russell. Katie was the older sister of Donny Russell, who was cast as the evil Bill Sikes in the production of *Oliver!*. Tanya and Katie were eighteen.

Because his sales job took him all over North America, Mr. DeSousa was away far more often than he was at home. For the most part, Mrs. DeSousa kept busy with her crafts and her pottery and decorating Tanya's apartment. But sometimes in the evenings she would light the candelabra above the massive stone fireplace and with Leonard Cohen echoing throughout the castle, she would dance all alone.

"Your mom is great," Megan commented one day. "I can't even imagine my mom listening to someone as cool as Leonard Cohen." When Hetty didn't answer, Megan added, "Don't you think?"

Hetty shrugged. "I guess. I don't know. She's just my mom."

One week into school, Carl was fired from the dairy. This happened when his ledger proved that he was consistently losing money, a discovery that did not come as a surprise to either Eric or me. Just past three o'clock each day, Carl's milk route took him past the high school. After stocking the refrigerators in the school cafeteria, he would gleefully pass out chocolate milk and ice-cream bars to "friends." Megan ignored what he was doing. She had long ago distanced herself from her brother, who failed to realize his celebrity was a result of his foolishness and that he was laughed at behind his back.

Each day Carl glowed in his fifteen minutes of popularity. He had not had many friends growing up; in elementary school there were few boys who shared his interests. There were fewer still in junior high when he was already two grades behind those his age. So in his mind, the attention he was receiving far outweighed any consequences. Besides, it wasn't like he hadn't taken a little heat in the past. He could handle it. So he continued to distribute frozen cups of ice cream with wooden paddles despite Eric's efforts to get him to stop.

The Monday following the week Carl was let go from the dairy, Aunt Alice instructed him to polish his shoes. He did this on the back porch while she typed up his resume at the kitchen table as she waited for the bread dough to rise. Uncle Pat began circling jobs in the classified ads. He drove Carl to interviews, not because he didn't trust him with the truck, but for the chance to impart some last words of advice, suggest answers to interview questions and ensure that he arrived on time.

When his day wasn't organized for him, Carl began to hang around the pool hall in town. At ten o'clock in the morning he broke balls with other young men who were out of work and out of school. I knew two of them, Ross Nash and Lyle St. Vincent. I knew them because of the many times they had slowed their car while driving past Megan and me, lifted their eyebrows and showed us their nicotine-stained teeth. It was well-known that Ross had done jail time in the spring for causing a disturbance and willful damage to the playground equipment in Queen Mary Park.

Carl adopted their style of dress: black pointed-toe boots with cleats, black jeans and a dickey beneath a white shirt. His hair, which he had always worn short, shimmered beneath layers of Brylcreem. He wore it sculpted into a sort of pompadour—a whopping crest at the front, a ducktail at the neck. And should one hair get out of line, he packed a rat-tail comb in the pocket of his shirt.

He began to cruise around Pike Creek and the vicinity with Ross and Lyle in the Dodge Charger they had customized by painting flat black. Never mind that it burned oil and the engine clattered—it had the look. Uncle Pat was not happy that Carl was spending his time with these "less desirables," but he could hardly continue to supervise a grown man.

It was one Saturday in the middle of September, almost too cold to be riding a bike, when I set out for Hetty's castle. My fingers had already turned red by the time I'd reached the end of our lane and turned onto the county road. I had the whole road to myself so I could follow the hard-packed tire tracks rather than keep to the shoulder where the gravel was loose and the ditch was deep on either side. I turned south. From the road I distinguished a metal pipe nearly camouflaged in the twisted canopy of the woods—the chimney of the Hippie House. The peak of the roof poked just above a small stand of spruce trees and underbrush. Hearing a car come up behind me, I veered to the side of the road. A station wagon with nose-smeared windows and three tail-wagging dogs in the back passed by me. Long before she reached me, the driver had slowed so as not to pelt me with gravel and dust. Once she was ahead of me, Mrs. Fraser waved in the rear-view mirror.

I was haunted by an image and I was always careful riding my bike. Several years before, while I listened, horrified, Megan had told the story of a girl about my age—about ten at the time— who was knocked down as she drove between farms on her bike. She became tangled in the wheels of the car that hit her, the car that had not bothered to stop. The following morning, after a frantic search for their daughter, her parents found her torn remains spread over many miles of country road.

As I rode, I imagined my parents finding pieces of me, my left foot clad in my new suede shoe outside our gate. And a little farther down the road, perhaps beneath Pat and Alice McEachran's mailbox, my right hand with the mood ring my grandmother had given me for Christmas. The stone would most definitely be black. But when it came to imagining the expressions on their faces, it brought tears to my eyes. In the cold, they stung my cheek.

Another car came up behind me and I moved to the side of the road again. Hearing it slow, I waited for the car to pass. When it didn't pass, when it continued to follow close behind me for many yards and made no attempt to pass, I turned around. I should have guessed by the smell of burning oil in the air. It was a flat-black Dodge Charger, and although I avoided eye contact, not wanting to acknowledge their presence and encourage conversation, I knew it was Ross Nash and Lyle St. Vincent in the front seat. I steered my bike to the opposite side of the road, but they followed me. I crossed the road again and they followed me back. Lyle stuck his head out the window. "Hey, honey, why don't you dump the bike and come for a ride with us?"

I tried to ignore them. I continued to pedal straight ahead and hoped that they would give up and go away. I quickly realized they were not going to give up and they were not going to go away. Ross continued to follow a few feet behind me. He revved the engine, and if I'd stopped suddenly right then, I would have been flattened beneath the wheels. As my heart thundered inside my chest, I clutched the handle grips as if my fingers were burned into them and even a tire iron could not pull them apart. I kept my bike as close to the edge of the road as possible without falling into the ditch. I thought about speeding ahead, but I knew I could hardly outrun their vehicle even in its dilapidated state. I also thought about dropping my bike and trying to make it across the field, but if they followed me there was far less chance someone would happen to come along than if I stayed on the road.

I was now on the side of the driver. Ross took the opportunity to pull up next to me.

"Come on, sweetie," he patted his lap, "you can sit right here and I'll teach you how to drive."

I continued to pedal. I continued to try and ignore him.

"All you need to do is grab onto the stick shift and—vroom, vroom—I'll do all the rest."

They laughed. And because I thought I distinguished a familiar voice intermingled in the laughter—because I thought I heard the delayed response of a mind slow to catch on—I finally looked directly at the line of leering faces. My cousin Carl sat in the middle of the line. My easily swayed, probably not-all-that-sure-what-he-was-guffawing-at cousin. The one I had patiently taught to tell time when I was seven and he was past ten. I was at once a little relieved to see someone I recognized, but furious with him for taking part.

"Carl!" I growled, my fear overridden by anger. "Tell them to get lost or I'm going to tell Uncle Pat."

A little surprised, Ross glanced at Carl. "You know her?"

"Yeah, sure," he shrugged. "That's Emma. She's my cousin."

Ross looked to Lyle, then back at me again. He stepped on the gas and sped away.

Enveloped in a cloud of foul-smelling air, I leaned forward on my handlebars and breathed a sigh of relief. It took many minutes for my hands to stop trembling and my heart to stop pounding, but when they did I wanted to grab one of the bloated paddles my father had found floating in the pond and whack some sense into Carl's half-witted head.

ONCE SCHOOL STARTED, The Rectifiers continued to practice, but the practices were sporadic and rarely did all the band members show up. There were now too many other things to do. Malcolm played hockey, Miles had a steady girlfriend and Jimmy took a part-time job at the Texaco station on the edge of town. Only Eric seemed interested in continuing the band.

And then on the eighteenth of September, Jimi Hendrix died. When Eric did not pick up his guitar for a week, Dad remarked that there was a chill in the air. Perhaps it was time to rescue the equipment from the Hippie House before it was damaged by frost. If Eric wanted, Dad would help him set up a room in the basement where he could continue to practice.

Eric's mood was complaisant as we drove down the gravel road on our way to the Hippie House. He was enrolled in ground lessons over the winter and he was now looking forward to getting his pilot's license. My father had coached him in the cockpit since he was young, but in the spring he would take control on his own.

The wind sock was blowing south and my ears stung in the cool air as I bumped up and down in the trailer behind the tractor. A flock of Canada geese shouted overhead, but they were not ours. Dad would wait until the pond froze before he herded our domestic flock into the barn. I turned and looked backward toward the Frasers' fields. In the distance I could see they were erecting a new building. I wondered what Mr. Fraser was up to now.

Perhaps ten years younger than my parents, he'd inherited the land from his father. His father and grandfather had been well-respected farmers in the area, but this Mr. Fraser had never been content to just farm. He did run a modestly successful cattle and chicken operation. But I think it was always his hope that one of his many other business ventures would take off and someday get him off the farm. He'd dabbled in many things including importing toys from the Far East and raising chinchillas for fur. On occasion he'd approach my father to invest in one of his interests. Dad might contribute "a neighborly amount." He called them Grant Fraser's entrepreneurial adventures. My mother had another name for them—she called them pipe dreams. But it was true that none of them had met with much success. The Frasers had no children. Mrs. Fraser had no time, my mother informed me. She worked hard to support her husband's numerous schemes.

I turned around. Eric drove the tractor past the duck house. He turned into the woods where large patches of gray sky were now visible through naked branches, and the soft hum of insect life had disappeared with the summer heat. Wet from an early morning frost, crimson leaves adhered to the tractor tires, and partially frozen clumps of earth turned soft beneath our weight.

Our mission was to clean the Hippie House before it snowed. Even before we entered the shed we retrieved swollen cigarette packages and bottles filled with dirt, trapped in the masses of roots along Fiddlehead Creek. Following Eric along the short path, I pointed to the spot where wild strawberries had once flourished. Along with the blackberry bushes, they had been trampled flat. Eric merely shrugged. We reached the shed, where I saw that someone had painted a large peace sign on the upper half of the door. Eric pushed it open.

I was astonished. The once purple walls were all but obliterated by graffiti: band sets, pictures and slogans, idle musings. The word *War* was scrawled in black ash across half a wall.

What is it good for?
Absolutely nothing!

The band equipment had all been removed and so what was left was general trash which we stuffed in the bags we had brought along. While Eric brushed ashes from the workbenches and coiled the remaining extension cords, I swept up broken guitar strings, a couple of roach clips, and withered French fries from the floor. I had not worn gloves, and with my fingers aching from the cold I did not do a very thorough job.

Eric's breath came in small clouds as he told me it was a bit of a drag, but probably just as well. When it came right down to it, their styles were so different they probably never would have been tight as a band. I didn't know whether to believe this; my brother's words were always chosen to cover what he was truly feeling. Only lately, when he picked up his guitar, did I think I may have seen a glimpse of what was going on inside.

I stood in the doorway and took a final look around. The curtain I had sewn for the window facing Fiddlehead Creek had been replaced by a Canadian flag. The one covering the window facing the road drooped in the center. The pocket for the curtain rod was coming apart. It needed to be stitched up again, but it would now have to wait until spring. I glanced at my jeans and pulled a needle from where I'd stowed it in the denim just above my knee. It was normal for me to have a few pins and needles embedded in my jeans. I'd discovered that as I was sewing they made a convenient pincushion. I wove the needle into the corner of the curtain to hold the fabric in place.

When we closed the door of the Hippie House for what was to be the last time that fall, we left only the idle musings of the summer scrawled across the walls—and the tattered reminders of my grade eight graduation dance stapled to the center post.

2

B Y THE END of the second week of October, the leaves of the American elms lining the lane had turned yellow, and many had already fallen. The rest waited to be set free with the next breath of wind from the north. It had snowed twice and melted twice. A week earlier, the plowed and rumpled earth still held enough warmth to absorb a light snow, but a thin collar of ice had formed on the perimeter of the pond now, and with the temperature sinking as the week wore on, it was doubtful it would leave.

Thanksgiving dinner was held at Ruddy Duck that autumn. My mother had started her campaign early. It was back in August, in conversation with Aunt Alice, that I had heard her glibly toss in a bid to hold the dinner at our house that year. Accustomed to my mother's not-so-subtle ways, my aunt had immediately countered that Mom had held dinner at Easter— Thanksgiving would be her turn, it was only fair. But even she must have known that she was wasting her breath. When given a chance to pull out all her finery, my mother was a defiant adversary. Not even Aunt Alice had the muscle to disarm her.

My father was in a grand mood, as he always was when standing at the head of the table before a Canadian goose that he himself had shot. He whistled softly as he sharpened his carving knife on the steel. Mom sat at the opposite end with the vegetables in their chafing dishes gathered before her, waiting for him to pass the first plate to be filled. Carl sat to her right, with Aunt Alice between him and Megan. Eric, Uncle Pat and I sat on the other side.

This arrangement did not suit Megan, who would have preferred not to sit in the dining room at all. In fact, she had asked for permission to eat in the kitchen. She didn't care that she would be by herself. She would eat dinner in the barn—where she would risk having her eyes pecked out by the geese for the murder of one of their own—as long as she didn't have to look at her brother's face.

Uncle Pat and Aunt Alice were not making much of an effort to talk. The truth was, they were not in very good humor. They had dealt with the crisis Megan was raging about shortly before leaving home. It seemed that Megan had used the washroom immediately after Carl, and in doing so she had found a pornographic magazine he had left behind. She was disgusted beyond words and Carl had crossed the line. Not only was he an imbecile, but now, after hanging around with those so-called friends, he was a pervert! Were her parents not going to do anything about the moral fabric of their son?

"Apparently not," she'd told me just before we sat down to eat. "They tell me it's normal. That I should be more tolerant and Carl should use more discretion. Can you believe it? My parents are as perverted as him!"

As we waited for our plates, I looked between Uncle Pat, whose attention seemed fixed on the light switch and Aunt Alice, who sighed every now and again while her hands lay folded primly in her lap. They still appeared quite respectable to me. Although, at that precise moment, they did strike me as two people who were hoping that if they ignored us long enough, we might all just go away.

"A little of everything, Alice?" Smiling brightly, Mom held Aunt Alice's plate in limbo while waiting for her reply.

"Huh?"

"Sweet potato? Brussels sprouts? Dressing?"

"Uh-huh," Aunt Alice answered, before returning to her thoughts again. My mother passed the plate to Carl, who set the food before her. "Oh, yes, thank you, dear."

Dad handed me Megan's plate with its specified "tad" of goose. After passing it down to my mother for the vegetables to be added, I looked across at Megan, who watched the proceedings closely.

"Megan—sweet potato?"

"No."

Megan's lack of manners seemed to rally Aunt Alice. "No, thank you," she interjected.

"No, thank you."

"Brussels sprouts?"

Megan shook her head. "Uh-uh."

Aunt Alice sighed. "Not uh-uh. No, *thank* you. Megan, where are your manners tonight?"

"*My* manners? My bedroom's next door to a psychopath's and you're worried about whether I use the word please?"

Throughout the meal, Eric had a very difficult time trying not to laugh. He focused on his plate, looking up only now and again. When he was not chewing, his lips were pressed tightly together, and when he did look up, I noticed his dewy eyes avoided mine. It had certainly happened in the past, during a solemn occasion, that just a glimpse of humor smoldering on one another's faces was all we needed to make us laugh out loud.

But Eric was already in a particularly buoyant mood. He had a new girlfriend that fall and by Thanksgiving he was in love.

She had been over to the house several times and I had often seen him standing with his arms around her, pressed against her in the courtyard at school. She was very pretty with blond, waist-length hair, hazel eyes and a wide smile. And she had so many gorgeous sweaters—it was the sweaters that Megan and I noticed the most.

"She just looks so good in them," Megan told me. "And she's just the perfect height, not too short, as in your case, or too tall, as in mine. She reminds me of Peggy Lipton in *The Mod Squad*. If I could look like anyone at school, I'd like to look like her. Wouldn't you?"

Her name was Angie Lucas, and after a week or so I decided I didn't like her very much at all.

For one thing, she got in my way. She would be sitting on the chesterfield, purring close to Eric, making me uncomfortable when I wanted to watch TV. I would try to sew, but I could hear them laughing in his room with the door closed, then long silences broken only by the start and stop of my machine.

She wasn't Eric's first girlfriend; he'd had a few, particularly since joining the band. But none had made him go stupid the way that Angie did. I hadn't heard him pick up his guitar in a month. He had missed two ground lessons, and because he began to go to Angie's after school, as a favor I'd done his chores for him four days in a row. And now, if I would continue to do them, he said he would pay me.

Eric had no time to play Risk or Monopoly or drive down to Brampton and see a Saturday matinee. He never wore a T-shirt a second day in a row and he spent hours in the bathroom perfecting his face and hair. Should he leave the sideburns or trim them back a bit?

"I don't know," I told him. "And what do you care what I think anyway? Ask Angie. Now would you give someone else a chance in the bathroom? You're not the only one who has a bus to catch."

Angie was good at gymnastics; she'd won provincial competitions. And she was good at complimenting Mom on her cooking and the way she set the table with "such class."

"What a delightful young lady," Mom commented to Eric at dinner one night. "And the manners. She certainly has been brought up right. Emma, you would think, by now, that you would know that is your dessert fork. You should be using the one to the left of your dinner fork. No, put it above the plate— above the plate with the tines pointing to the right."

Angie played the piano beautifully, and that fall she earned her grade ten Royal Conservatory of Music standing. On the day she passed the practical exam, she blushed a soft sunrise pink following Eric's announcement at the farm.

"Isn't that wonderful," Mom congratulated her. "I've often thought Emma should learn to play the piano. What do you think? Would you like Angie to teach you to play, dear?"

"No," I said, gritting my teeth, "I would not like Angie to teach me to play the piano. I don't have time." My eyes drilled into Eric. "My life has become one great big long chore."

When dinner was over, I took the stairs two at a time. Once in my room I fell across my bed, where I began to cry so deeply and so wrenchingly that if I'd walked into the room, I would have felt sorry for myself. I was convinced that there was no chance in this world that I would ever be even half as ravishingly beautiful and talented as Angie. That I would never make a boy go stupid the way that Eric had. That I would never turn a boy's head as I walked by, the way I had seen some of the girls at school do. That I was too short and that, when I ate, my manners were so vulgar and offensive that even a cow would be embarrassed to take me out on a date.

"Look at me," I sniveled to my dad. Shortly after I'd slammed the door and flung myself across my bed, he'd knocked softly, and after receiving no answer, walked in. "It looks like I fell into a roll of metal fencing and couldn't get up again. I hate these braces. I want them off my teeth!"

"Emma, you know that would be a mistake."

"But they make me look so ugly. And my hair. It's so thick and ratty. I iron it over and over again and I still can't make it straight."

"Hmm." Having no idea of current fashion trends, yet not wanting to belittle my need to follow them, my father was at a disadvantage. He thought for a moment, considering what in his world would work as a solution to my problem. "Well, if you come up to the workshop we could try the soldering gun. How straight does it have to be?"

And suddenly I began to laugh nearly as hard as I had cried.

He smiled, obviously relieved. "Emma, you can only be who you are. Don't ever try to change that; but make the most of it."

They were such simple words, but I've never forgotten them. I only wish I had begun to follow them at that moment. But I didn't know who I was at that moment, so it is probably not remarkable that I didn't follow them, not for many more years.

Angie broke up with Eric shortly after Halloween. He did not tell me the circumstances, but I think it had just run its course. He didn't appear overly devastated, but again, my brother was so very good at keeping his feelings inside. Eric reverted back to his old ways, combing his hair once a day and, in a pinch, wearing whatever he found on the floor. He did his chores and occasionally even offered to do mine. Tired of studying crosswinds and radio communication, wandering around the house in no particular direction on a Sunday afternoon, he stuck his head in my door and asked me if I wanted a game of Monopoly.

I was teaching myself to install this great new invention—an invisible zipper that was sewn in a sort of inverted way. I had already sewn it in wrong. I was ripping it out, anxious to do it the right way and curious to see the end result, but I hesitated only a moment before setting the seam ripper aside. "Alright, I'll have you a game."

Eric leaned against the doorjamb. "By the way, I need you to fix the pocket on my red and white shirt. I caught it on a nail in the tractor shed."

"Okay. But not until I get this zipper in right."

"I'll go set up the game. What do you want to be—the usual?"

The usual when we played Monopoly was the thimble. Eric was always the car.

"Yeah. No, you know what? I think I'll be the horse this time."

"The horse? Okay, if you want." He turned to leave, but a thought seemed to bring him back. "One thing about Angie—she couldn't sew."

It was not said with any particular distaste, but rather, it seemed to strike him as a curious fact.

"Oh really?" I said. Although I didn't think it the mystery that Eric obviously did. I'd never thought of it as a particularly glamorous or difficult thing to be able to do.

But he continued to stand there. "Yeah. She couldn't even sew a button on a shirt."

"Well, maybe she just didn't like it. Lots of girls in home ec think it's boring."

"Yeah, maybe," Eric said.

MEGAN AND I WERE at the castle when we first heard that Katie Russell had disappeared. Ruby was teaching us to macramé. As the snow blew outside and a fire spit and crackled in the mammoth fireplace, we sat on the rug gathered around her while she demonstrated the double half hitch. Hetty had just dropped *American Woman* on the console stereo at the same time as the telephone in the kitchen rang. Ruby left to answer it. Hetty lowered the volume while Megan and I fumbled through a couple of double half hitches on our own.

From where we sat we could hear Ruby's concerned voice. She was obviously talking to Hetty's sister, Tanya, attempting to calm her down. Hetty turned the record player off and we listened. It seemed that Katie had not come home the night before and Ruby was agreeing that it was certainly not like her not to call.

Pike Creek was hardly a dangerous place, but as Hetty quietly informed us as we listened to her mother's side of the conversation, Katie and Tanya had always let one another know where they were out of courtesy.

Ruby tried to get Tanya to remember if Katie hadn't said something that she might have forgotten, a date that might have slipped her mind. But judging from Ruby's end of the conversation, Tanya must have been quite positive that Katie had not mentioned going anywhere. Yes, Tanya had contacted the seniors' home where they both worked, and Katie had completed her shift, which had ended at ten o'clock. Tanya had also called Katie's parents, who had not seen her and could not guess where she might have gone. And now they were frantic. No, she had not packed anything, taken anything—for heaven's sake, her insulin kit was still there. Tanya knew Katie had not come home and gone out again because it had not been disturbed. Ruby ended the conversation by assuring Tanya that she would be right over.

"I'm sorry," she apologized, collecting her car keys from the hall table. "We'll have to finish another time." After donning her coat, she stopped briefly before the door. "Now, where could that girl have gone?"

It was said without fear, but with true curiosity. Because, indeed, in Pike Creek, where could Katie have gone? Hetty wanted to accompany her mother, so Ruby dropped us off at Uncle Pat's farm on their way into town.

Aunt Alice was in the kitchen, where she had just hung up the telephone after speaking with Mrs. Fraser. Apparently the last person to see Katie was Mrs. Bolton, Jimmy's elderly grandmother who lived at the seniors' home. Unable to sleep, she had been sitting alone in the common recreation room watching the late-night news on TV. Three days earlier, police had raided the hideout of the FLQ members responsible for the murder of Quebec's minister of labour, Pierre Laporte. Only one of the members was arrested; the others had managed to escape. The whereabouts of British trade commissioner James Cross, who had also been kidnapped, was still not known.

Mrs. Bolton recalled that she was watching the terrifying images of tanks and military troops rumbling through the streets of Montreal when Katie walked into the room.

"The whole world has gone crazy," she'd told Katie when she stopped to give her a hug on her way out.

"Only outside of Pike Creek," Katie had answered. "You and me, we're just fine. See you tomorrow." And she'd headed out the door.

Once she had told us this, Aunt Alice sat down at the kitchen table. "I wonder where Katie could be?"

It was the second time I had heard the question asked in the space of half an hour. But this time it was asked in a much more apprehensive tone. This, I thought, was due to the diverse nature of the two women I had heard ask it. Ruby, who thought in the abstract, who I considered to be carefree and probably, as a young woman of eighteen herself, more likely to follow a whim on her way home from work late at night. And my aunt, who organized her life in accordance with the demands of the farm: crops to be sewn when the weather was good, and people and animals to be fed at specific hours. My aunt, who used a map no matter where she was going because she did not have a speck of time to waste driving around.

"Maybe she met up with friends," Megan suggested. "Maybe they asked her to a party and she ended up staying overnight."

But Aunt Alice had known Katie's mother for many years. "I doubt it," something made her say.

The telephone rang. It was my mother, who was worried because there was no answer at Hetty's house and I had not yet come home. She asked to talk to me. Yes, she knew all about Katie Russell's disappearance. Eric had told her and she had given Jimmy's mother a call. Wasn't it odd, and just where did we girls think Katie might have gone?

For the rest of the afternoon, Megan and I stayed close to home. We understood that it was difficult for the adults to know what to do. For Katie was a capable adult of eighteen and not an innocent child.

Dinnertime came. In our need to channel our nervous energy we collaborated on making a pizza. The air in the kitchen smelled wonderful, all warm and doughy, but once we had pulled the pizza from the oven we discovered we had little appetite, so Carl devoured most of it on his own. The evening passed and still there had been no word.

Hetty and Ruby spent the night at Tanya's apartment along with Katie's mother. The next day, Tanya moved back to the castle. It was temporary, she told Hetty—until Katie came home again, or—she didn't know.

On that second day following the disappearance, restrictions were placed on our movements. If I was going somewhere with Megan, we were to phone upon arriving. If I was going out alone—well, it just wasn't allowed.

Because of the age difference, Megan and I did not really know Katie Russell. We really only knew of her, and in fact, in trying to remember her, we recalled seeing her only a handful of times at a distance the previous year. Yet we quickly became part of the strange atmosphere of uncertainty and conjecture that settled over the town during the next few days. Everyone seemed to have a theory. Some of these were quite creative. I discovered this as we discussed her disappearance in the smoking area at school.

Mandy Green, who dramatized everything since landing the part of Nancy in *Oliver!*, suggested that maybe Katie had just had enough of Pike Creek. The place couldn't be more stifling. "After all," she said, taking a last drag off a cigarette before flicking it to the pavement, "wouldn't any of us split if we were given half a chance?"

"Huh, well maybe," Megan answered. "On the other hand, it could be amnesia. It could have been something as simple as tripping at an intersection and bumping her head on the curb. It's been known to happen. Maybe she's wandering around somewhere right now thinking she's Natalie Wood or Grace Slick."

Mandy ground the cigarette butt beneath her heel as the school buzzer sounded, summoning us back inside. "Yeah, well if she's lucky, no one will set her straight."

Over the next few days, my parents and my aunt and uncle were involved in the search for Katie. They were only a few of the many people who spread across Pike Creek. Katie was an adult, but, as they would with any disappearance, Uncle Pat told us, it was best to rule out certain things. Working through grids, the search parties tramped across the parks and public grounds. They scoured the surrounding woods and the ditches lining the highways and secondary roads.

"What do you think happened to her?" I asked Eric after he picked me up at Hetty's one night.

"Spontaneous human combustion."

I looked at him. "What's that?"

"Her body chemistry was out of whack. For some reason she generated so much heat that she ignited and—poof!—she vaporized." Eric came to a stop at an intersection.

"I don't believe you."

"Okay, don't believe me, but there's at least three or four hundred cases reported in Ontario alone each year." He glanced to his right before making the turn. At the same time he took in my horrified expression. He must have suffered an unusual pang of guilt for teasing me because more quickly than usual he relented. "Alright, so it wasn't spontaneous combustion. But how do you expect me to know?"

Megan and I meant no disrespect considering the gravity of the situation, and we told each other so, but we didn't think Katie was very pretty.

"Her nose has got a ski jump and it's too big," Megan commented when we first saw her picture in the local newspaper. "I mean, not that it's her fault or anything like that."

"No, I think it's that her eyes are too close together."

"Maybe that's it. And her hair is so thin. I don't know how you could do anything with it. Maybe if you used a whole pile of Dippity-Do and rolled it in Coke cans for about a week."

"She's got a lot of freckles."

"They could still be there from the summer. Like Hetty's, the way she says they get way worse in the sun."

"Why would he pick her?" I wondered.

"Who?"

"Well, I mean, just say she was abducted. Say that some pervert was just driving around and picked her up and is keeping her as a sex slave. Don't you think if he had a choice that he'd go for someone really good-looking?"

Megan thought about this. "Like Angie Lucas you mean?"

And for a very brief moment I had a sympathetic thought for Angie. Maybe being amazingly good-looking did have its disadvantages. But it quickly passed. "Yeah, like Angie."

Megan shrugged. "Maybe there isn't a lot of choice in Pike Creek that late at night."

A full week passed. Katie had left without a trace, and hope was beginning to fade. Despite this, a few people continued to suggest possibilities, although after consideration, most of these were unconvincing. They simply lacked the conviction of those put forth in the first few days.

Perhaps it was a cult, suggested Mrs. Chisholm. Or perhaps she had been depressed and would soon snap out of it, someone else said. To this suggestion, both Katie's mother and Tanya vehemently protested, "Absolutely not." Katie was as happy as any girl whose whole life of starry opportunities glittered before her and who had just moved out on her own. Mrs. Russell became incensed that the police were asking so many personal questions. They should be concentrating their efforts on finding her instead of searching for flaws in her family when there were none to be found. Mr. Russell was emphatic that Katie was just not the type to accept a ride from a stranger. Everyone who knew her well agreed.

When another week passed and there was still no word from Katie, it was difficult to imagine anything other than the worst possible scenarios.

How awful it was to see her parents in town quizzing people, searching on their own for any whisper of Katie. How familiar we all were with the abduction and murder of Lynne Harper in Clinton, eleven years before.

On an afternoon late in November, I stayed after school to help my home economics teacher, Mrs. Suringa, take the actors' measurements for their costumes. I slipped the tape measure around Donny Russell's waist. As I did, I looked for some indication of how Katie's disappearance was affecting him—a gaunt, faraway expression, or maybe an uncontrollable facial tic.

But Donny only joked with me, contorting his face to show me how he planned to look when, as Bill Sikes, he hung from the flagpole at the end of the play. He did not let on how he felt about his sister disappearing without a trace.

3

My FATHER WAS very proud of our dog, Halley. Even in her old age he claimed she was the best hunting dog he had ever owned. This put Halley ahead of some very stiff competition, for Dad had always selected his dogs from excellent bloodlines. I knew nothing of the ability of Halley's predecessors to hunt, but my memories of the two white-muzzled black Labrador retrievers we owned when I was very young were fond.

Halley first distinguished herself simply by being a Clumber spaniel. Dad had read about the rare breed in a duck-hunting magazine. A low, heavily built bird dog, they were bred to crash through dense underbrush. Slower than most sporting dogs, they made up for this with unwavering persistence and a nose said to be second only to a bloodhound for keenness of scent.

"In addition to their hunting skills," I recalled my father reading aloud to us many years earlier, "they are even-tempered dogs with loveable personalities and not overly active when mature. They do have a tendency toward stubbornness," he continued with amusement, prompting Mom to interject that she did not want a dog that was not going to do as it was told.

"No, no, that's actually what you want. It's a good thing for a hunting dog. It means they won't give up easily."

"Oh," Mom replied.

Dad winked at Eric and me, drawing a hand across his forehead in a gesture of relief.

Halley turned out to be all of what the magazine said she would be and more. She was intensely loyal to all of us and very affectionate, winning Mom over the first time she pushed her head into her lap for a hug. Halley was given little reason to worry, but she could not stand being left out of any activity. She was eight years old in the fall of 1970 and although long retired from hunting, when sound asleep she would still lift her head at the sound of an airplane overhead, wondering if Dad had left her behind.

It was sometime around the second week of November that she began to act out of character. In the habit of taking long naps now, her sleep was easily disturbed. She would wake suddenly, roll to her haunches, look at us and whine. Or she would pace restlessly as if searching for something, talking to us like we should know what or where it was, before seeming to settle down again. She was anxious outside. She was never a wanderer, but she began keeping unusually close to us as we did our chores. Several times Halley glued herself to us so closely that we bumped into her as we turned around.

"Halley, what is it, girl?" we would ask.

Appearing glad to have finally been asked, she would run to the open barn door, then back to Eric or me, as if expecting us to take her somewhere.

One Sunday morning, Halley accompanied me down to the duck house. I was on my way to sweep out the old straw and spread a fresh layer on the floor. A heavy snow had fallen during the night, and after rounding the barn I stopped to gaze over the airfield, a marvelous ocean of white, pure and glimmering in the morning sun.

Here and there where the land rose and fell, snow had drifted in rhythm to the forces that moved it, swelling softly toward the woods, soaring halfway up the fence in places at the edge of the field. I stopped because it was a sight I was fortunate to observe. I was generally not quick enough. By mid-morning Carl would set out on Uncle Pat's snowmobile and this work of nature would be doomed.

For now the morning was soundless and still. The wind sock draped like an old balloon, but the gentle puffs of snow capping the fenceposts seemed somehow alert, reminding me of delicate birds paused in flight, waiting for the next gust of wind to carry them off.

The trail, of course, was hidden, and unintentionally I stepped in the ditch and sank a good foot down. Snow wedged into my boot beneath my pant leg and I knew I would have to live with the uncomfortable sensation of it sliding down to my ankle as a lump, then melting as I went about my work with one wet sock. Halley kept close, looking up at me often. She would not, as she normally would, be distracted by the scent of the field mice where they had tunneled beneath the snow. I noticed how beads of snow gathered in clumps and clung to her chest fur and the beautiful featherings on her legs. It could not be a much more comfortable feeling than having snow in your boot.

Looking straight ahead of us, past the duck house where the road curved into the woods, I thought how dark and mysterious, yet enticing in its strangeness, the snowfall had made the woods appear. I walked past the duck house simply to stand in its doorway. The branches of the fir trees bent low beneath the weight, and the birch and aspen, which were not silent once I was inside but full of complaint, shed snow from their branches so that it appeared that in the woods the storm was still going on. The snow was too deep to walk any farther, and by now Halley was whining incessantly, so I returned to the duck house to sweep the floor.

Once I had corralled the ducks into a pen, I let Halley follow me in. She would not stop whining or pacing. That morning she had no interest in the ducks—these particular ducks my father had trained her to ignore, although it went against her every instinct and it killed her to do it, so that now and again we would catch her chasing one when she thought no one was around. But that morning her mind was too occupied by whatever it was that only she could sense.

Insulated from the snowy world in the stuffy warmth of the duck house, I began to think of a story I had read in school. It was written by Guy de Maupassant and it was called "The Inn." It was about a caretaker who was snowbound for six months in an inn in the French Alps. Eventually he went crazy from cabin fever and loneliness. He cracked up when he heard his dog, Sam, howling outside the door.

"Halley! That's enough."

Spooked by her behavior, I returned to the house and tried to convince Dad to take her to a veterinarian. It didn't take much. After a week of her fitful pacing in the workshop where she normally dozed next to the woodstove while he drilled holes or stained wood, he was also convinced something was wrong.

The veterinarian could find no physical reason for her anxiety and, with the exception of a touch of arthritis, he declared her to be a very healthy animal for her age.

By the first week of December I had been assigned the costumes I was to sew for the production of *Oliver!*. I was to alter pants and a velvet jacket for Fagin. Mr. Wellington, the drama teacher, was always on the lookout at thrift and bargain stores for costumes for his department, and Fagin's jacket was one of his more lucrative finds.

In addition, I was responsible for Oliver's costume as a young boy as well as the skirts for the chorus of flower sellers. These would be quick to sew with their two simple seams and gathered waists.

But what thrilled me the most was to be asked to sew Nancy's dress—all that satin and velvet and crinolines and lace!—exquisite fabrics I had no reason to work with normally. I planned to save sewing her dress until the Christmas holidays, when I could devote all my time to it and I had the other costumes out of the way.

On a Saturday afternoon, sitting at my sewing machine with my back turned toward it, I pondered the deep blue jacket lying among the scraps of fabric on the floor. A mound of skirts, a chorus of color, lay across from me on a rocking chair. I had taken in the back and side seams of the jacket, ripped out the sleeves and reinserted them. I had then narrowed the shoulders to fit Fagin, who was also known as Adam Brown. I had done a superb job; Mr. Wellington had commended me. But—

I could not bring myself to do what he asked me to do next. This was to make the jacket look like the only piece of clothing owned by a nineteenth-century pickpocket who lived in the slums of London. Essentially, I was to trash the soft blue velvet, cut into its rich surface—Mr. Wellington may just as well have asked me to cut into my wrist.

"Don't be so dramatic," my brother commented when I told him this. "It's a lousy jacket bought at a secondhand store. Probably somebody got married in it and now they're divorced. It's not like Hendrix wore it at Woodstock. By the way, can you make me a white suede one with fringes like that?"

Eric was on his way down to the Hippie House, and because of this he was wearing tall boots and a heavy parka with the hood up. He did not wear any gloves. It was not cool to wear gloves unless he was doing heavy work or skiing, and every winter his hands suffered for it. The skin became so rough and cracked it bled. He was searching for a guitar strap he hadn't seen since September when we'd last closed the door. Maury was organizing a protest rally against the Vietnam War, to be held at the drop-in center on a Sunday in mid-December. The band had agreed to reunite for the day.

Halley, for the moment, was lying on the one patch of floor that was not taken by a fabric remnant. Eric called her over. Without lifting her head, she stared at him with her hazel eyes and tentatively thumped her docked tail. He called her over again. No doubt intimidated by his forbidding appearance, she gave one last thump and came over to me instead.

"You're too scary," I said, patting her chest.

Once Eric had left, I set the jacket aside until I felt more courageous. I would work on the flower sellers' skirts instead. Already I had folded the waists and run most of them through the sewing machine to create pockets for the elastic inserts. I finished four more, then I consulted my list of actors' measurements, measured and cut a length of elastic and after attaching a safety pin, I picked a skirt from the top of the pile—electric blue—and began to push the elastic through the waist. I remember this so clearly because I would recall it many times later. This is what I was doing when the back door to the kitchen opened and I heard the sound that would change our lives.

It was my brother—after bursting through the kitchen door, he was shouting for Dad, screaming for him in the most horrific voice, tortured and full of terror. Paralyzed by what I heard, I stopped what I was doing and listened. Eric was tromping back and forth in his heavy boots with "Dad" being the only word he seemed able to say. Setting my sewing aside, I hurried down the hall. By the time I reached the top of the stairs I could hear my mother trying desperately to calm Eric down—trying to understand what could possibly have upset her son, who was as even-tempered as his father, to the point that he could no longer speak. She was now at the bottom of the stairs.

"Emma!"

"I'm coming, I'm coming."

My heart hit my throat as I took the stairs two at a time. I slipped on the last tread. "What is it?" I asked, scrambling to my feet. I faced my brother, whose hair glistened with fine drops of melted snow, where he stood in the center of the room. Despite the cold, his face was pale and for a moment he reminded me of an angel. A small puddle was forming around his boots, and his chapped, gloveless hands—clenched as if in prayer—rose to his mouth and down again. But he was as unaware of this as he was unaware of anything else; although his eyes were on me, they remained fixed on whatever they had seen.

"Run to the workshop and get your father!" Mom ordered.

"But what's wrong?" I wanted my brother to snap out of his strange catatonic behavior. "Eric?!"

"Go!"

Already into my boots, I pulled on my coat while Mom attempted to guide Eric into a chair. "Emma, you come right back here with your father," she insisted as I flew out the door.

Fear for Eric's sanity carried me quickly to my father, who I was confident would understand whatever had put him in such a state and make everything well again. Halley ran several yards ahead of me. Dad looked up from his workbench when I opened the door. I had to catch my breath before I could speak, but it wasn't necessary. The look on my face must have told him something was wrong.

"Emma." He lay his tools aside. "What is it?"

"It's Eric. I don't know what, but something's happened."

Dad followed immediately and by the time we had arrived back at the farmhouse, Eric was seated in a chair with a blanket around his shoulders. He was trembling violently as though the shock within had worked itself to the surface. Tears clouded Mom's eyes and I guessed that by now she had some idea of what was wrong. Dad looked to her for some sign—some indication of how he should be approaching the situation.

She could barely speak. "Pat is on his way," was all she said.

Laying a hand on Eric's shoulder, my father bent down to speak to him. It was a body. In the Hippie House. A dead body strapped by what he thought was an extension cord to the center post. No, it was not a man. It was not a woman.

"A child?"

"No, a girl. Like Emma. Maybe a little older."

"Oh my god," my father whispered, dropping his eyes to the floor.

I didn't realize I was shrieking until Mom pulled me close to her.

"Do you know who she is?"

Eric shook his head. "I only saw her for a second."

Dad did not ask him anything more. Uncle Pat's truck could now be heard chortling up the laneway. After patting Eric's knee, Dad stood up and walked into the dining room, where he poured brandy into a tumbler. He returned to the kitchen and handed the glass to Eric. Eric shook his head.

"Drink it," my father insisted. He then told Mom to call the Pike Creek police before meeting Uncle Pat at the door. Halley tried to follow. "Emma, keep her in the house."

Halley resisted, but I held her by the collar as the door closed and I continued to hold her long after I had watched Dad and Uncle Pat hurry up the lane and disappear behind the barn. Mom was in the hallway. In a voice straining for control she was giving directions to the police over the telephone. Holding the empty glass in trembling fingers, Eric was staring at the floor. After a while, I lifted it from his hands.

"The door was open," he suddenly told me. "Just a crack. And when I pushed it—Emma, she was staring right at me."

I set the glass on the counter. And for a fleeting moment I wished I had seen what my brother had seen. I wished that I had shared in the horror of finding the body. Leaning over the sink,

I pumped a large amount of hand lotion into my palm. Taking one of Eric's hands in mine, I began to rub the lotion into the rough surface. It was not something I would normally do, and it was certainly not something he would normally let me do. But it was all I could think of to do at that moment and he didn't care.

"The police are on their way." Mom pushed tears from her cheeks, brushed her hands across her apron and dropped into a chair. She stretched her arms across the table. She squeezed Eric's hand—the one I had attempted to soften. Seeing that I was crying, she squeezed one of mine.

Dad and Uncle Pat returned, but for many minutes they stood outside the door. I could see them through the kitchen window. They did not talk, but stood apart and I somehow realized that as they straightened their shoulders, they were preparing themselves—regrouping against an unusually ruthless and savage opponent—one that had hit them blindside. I had never thought of my father as old, but I remember thinking at that moment how he looked every one of his fifty-three years.

We were not to leave the house. Aunt Alice, Megan and Carl were not to leave the house, and for his own peace of mind, my uncle drove home to pick them up and bring them all to Ruddy Duck Farm. We were to stay put until the police arrived and told us what to do.

We filed into the living room as Dad directed. We were full of questions, but at that moment the three who had been down to the Hippie House had nothing to say and the rest of us understood not to ask. Except Carl, who began grilling Eric. Never given to physical discipline, Aunt Alice quickly hushed him up with a cuff to the back of the head. Under normal circumstances, she and my mother would rush into the kitchen to prepare food when we were together. But today they ignored their instincts and listened only to my father and Uncle Pat.

Who is she? Who was she? Megan and I wanted so desperately to know. It was a small reassurance that Eric had not recognized her immediately.

"It's Katie Russell, isn't it?" Megan insisted.

"Yes—most probably," my father finally agreed.

My mother and Aunt Alice tried to calm us. But it was apparent in their eyes that they were as terrified as we were that a horror of this magnitude could be unfolding in our small corner of the world.

It amazed and bewildered us that we had heard nothing. That we had seen nothing. How could a crime so vile take place less than a quarter of a mile from us and we be oblivious to it all? How was it that we had not heard the violence or caught the scent of a struggle?

These were questions we not only asked ourselves, but that we would be asked by many people in the months to come. Not that they meant to place blame, but in trying to understand.

Dad positioned himself before the large window. Here he listened for the familiar crunch of gravel that could be heard before a car appeared on the crest of the hill as it traveled down the main road. I could not remember ever seeing my father's face so drawn. I had never known him to not at least attempt an explanation, smile reassuringly, or in a difficult situation, catch my eye and wink. He looked at none of us now. This was a discovery so unthinkable that even he had no experience to relate it to, and so, along with us, he waited for the police to arrive as though suspended in time.

Constable Wagner arrived with another police officer within twenty minutes. My father and Uncle Pat once again marched up the lane and down to the Hippie House, where they did not stay long. When they returned, my father and uncle looked very close to collapsing. The police officers were careful not to commit, but they also admitted the girl was likely Katie Russell. They were certainly not experts, they were quick to emphasize, but judging by the condition of the body they would estimate the girl had been dead at least a month.

Now they waited for detectives and forensic units to arrive from the provincial police department and the RCMP It was a day of many arrivals and few departures. By mid-afternoon our lane had become a parking lot, and the once snowy trail to the Hippie House had been trampled by so many feet it was muddy and worn. Men stood talking among the black-and-white cars while the photographer first walked through the Hippie House. A large area around the small building was cordoned off. No one was to enter from the road; a barricade was erected. The entrance through the woods, just past the duck house, was also blocked, as was a significant portion of the surrounding woods.

Dad was asked if he would be willing to take the photographer over the area for some aerial shots. Yes, he said, he would. It would require that he plow a strip of snow from the field, but between his neighbor, Grant Fraser, and brother-in-law, Pat, it shouldn't take long. The three men were relieved to be doing something useful and they worked quickly to clear a narrow runway. Cocking her head as if something wasn't quite right, Halley was the first to hear the engine of the Maul Rocket as it struggled, unaccustomed as it was to being dragged into the cold.

Once the plane was in flight, Uncle Pat plowed the trail down to the duck house, allowing the coroner's long dark vehicle to pass. It would be several hours before it would carry the body back to the main road.

The first reporters and cameramen began to show up very soon after the police. They continued to arrive from the larger and more distant cities all day. They took pictures and they filmed the house, the workshop and the frozen pond. With each snap of the shutter, anger rose inside me—who were they, these people tramping all over our farm?

Megan and I spent most of the day in the sunroom, which had the best view of the yard. We chattered on the edge of hysterics. Eric's friends drove up in Jimmy's pickup truck. For a few minutes they joined us in the sunroom.

Jimmy toyed with the change in his pockets as he blinked at Eric, who sat slouched in a chair. "What a drag, man, to find a dead chick in your own backyard."

Malcolm agreed. "And what sick head would do something like that?"

Staring across the pond in the direction of the Hippie House, Jimmy rubbed his head in disbelief. He turned and lay a hand on Eric's shoulder. "Are you going to be alright? Can we do anything—get anything for you?"

Mrs. Fraser and Ruby were two of the many neighbors from miles around who brought casseroles as if we personally had suffered a death. They did not know what else to do.

Once the police were in control, Mom and Aunt Alice were thankful to be in the kitchen, where they prepared sandwiches and served endless cups of coffee. They were women who thrived when given something nurturing to do. It was cold outside and there was no reason for the investigators to suffer physically along with everything else they had to see. Knowing that Carl would be nothing but an annoyance, they had relegated him to wash dishes so that no officer in my mother's kitchen would be forced to drink from a Styrofoam cup.

I did not know what role each of these people played, mostly men, but a few women, who worked well into the night with spotlights fixed on the Hippie House, the officers who took measurements and those who planted markers in our fields. But at some point I wanted them all to pack up and leave us alone.

The sunroom had doors to both the kitchen and living room. This allowed Megan and me to watch the activity outside as we strained for details in the conversations in both these rooms.

Late in the afternoon, Eric was interviewed in the living room by a man who had introduced himself as Detective Mather. From where I sat I could see a woman sitting off to the side in my mother's brocade chair. She did not speak during the interview, but she stayed after the detective had left, reassuring Eric in a comforting voice when he began to weep.

Eric told them why he had made the trip down to the Hippie House. He told them he had not actually entered it; he had done nothing but push open the door. He had last been down there about the third week of September. Yes, he would try and remember the exact day. He would ask his sister, Emma, she would know. Of course lots of people knew about the Hippie House. His band had practiced there all summer, which is how it got its name. No, today he saw nothing unusual outside the shed that he could remember, everything was deep in snow. No tire tracks, ski tracks, nothing. He did not have any idea who the girl was, although he knew Katie Russell was missing. To be honest, he had seen her for no more than a second and really only knew that her hair was black.

For now, Detective Mather had no more questions. As he stood to leave, his shadow fell across the door.

"How did she die?" my brother asked. I heard his voice break, but despite his fear, he wanted to know.

Detective Mather was obviously hesitant to answer him for he did not say anything right away. They would have to wait for the results of the autopsy, but it looked like she had been strangled.

"But there was blood," my brother commented. "A lot of blood. Around her neck."

"Yes. It appears the cord was pulled very tight."

Eric was silent a moment, but then he asked another question that I knew was not due to morbid curiosity but the kind of detail I would expect him to ask.

"What kind of cord was it?"

"Again, we won't know until the autopsy is performed. It's embedded quite deeply in the neck. But likely something quite fine. Like a piece of heavy gage wire."

"Or a guitar string," I heard Eric say.

Detective Mather's shadow grew huge as he put on his coat. "Yes. Or a guitar string," he agreed.

My aunt and cousins stayed over that night. Somehow it seemed best that we remain together. Megan shared my large bed, where we slept very little but spoke of our fears until dawn.

In the early hours of the morning I was returning from the bathroom when I noticed a light shining from beneath Eric's bedroom door. I knocked, but after receiving no reply, I walked in with Halley following me. Eric sat at his desk. Using an Exacto knife, he was carving the wings for a model biplane from balsa wood. It was a hobby from when he was a child, and I had not seen him build one for several years. The double-hung window was wide open. Even in the cold, Eric was careful to keep the room ventilated when he was using the dope needed to strengthen the tissue paper that would cover the frame.

Halley jumped on the bed and I sat down beside her. Eric did not look up from his work. For a moment, I looked at the many models lining his shelves and dangling from the ceiling, slowly circling in the air currents. I looked at the posters of musicians he had tacked on his walls. In one corner of his room stood an old radio he had refinished. Dad had discovered it in the barn when we'd first moved to Ruddy Duck Farm. Eric's guitar was propped against it. My brother's room was neat compared to mine, where thread and fabric chased dust from every corner. Only a paint-stained shirt and a braided guitar strap tossed beneath the window cluttered his floor.

"You found it," I said.

"What?"

"The guitar strap."

Eric shrugged, "It was under this pile of stuff on my desk." Having completed one wing, he set it aside and began working on another. "I'm never going back there," he said.

"I wouldn't either if I were you."

How strange it was to hear voices conferring, police radios crackling and car doors slamming outside our quiet farmhouse in the small hours on a cold winter night. How odd to have the dark sky washed in floodlights when we were used to only the small pool of yellow light cast from the lamp in our yard.

"Was it really awful?"

"Yes," was all he said.

"I wish I didn't know her."

"Yeah, well, you didn't know her very well. And anyway, it's not you. Or Megan. It could have been, you know."

The thought had already occurred to both Megan and me. "But the killer must be from around here. The killer must be somebody we know."

"Emma, nobody in Pike Creek would do that. Nobody that we know would do what I saw down there."

"But how else would he know about the Hippie House?"

Sighing heavily, my brother set the Exacto knife aside. "I don't know."

Eric didn't know, but he did believe that it was someone who had been out to the Hippie House. It was a thought that would torment him for many months to come.

4

IT WAS TWO WEEKS before the farm became ours again. By then, investigators had removed most of the floorboards as well as the center post from the Hippie House. This meant that if the building wasn't torn down, it would eventually collapse on its own. So for safety's sake, among all other reasons, my father and uncle pulled it down. It was a task they insisted on doing themselves and completed in half a day.

I was immediately relieved of some of my chores, those that took me out of sight of the house. Dad would take them over for now. I was instructed to stay close to the farmhouse at all times, and my parents would not allow me to walk down the lane to catch the bus on my own.

Trudging through a fresh layer of snow behind Eric one morning, I thought about how swiftly Katie had disappeared. She worked only ten minutes from where she lived, yet in that short time she had been abducted without a witness. It occurred to me how foolish I had been. I had never even considered the potential danger in what I'd assumed were normal activities. How many hours had I tempted fate by lingering on the road, alone, at the end of this lane? And during the summer there were the many times I had ridden between farms on my bike—spaces of time when I could so easily have been snatched like Katie, never to be seen again. At least not alive. In that moment, the vision I had of my life moving forward, unhampered, in a direction only I would determine, crumbled. Life transformed into something so fleeting and fragile it sent a shiver up my spine.

In the days following the murder, locks that had never been used were oiled and tested, and sales of locksets in hardware stores boomed. Dogs accustomed to lying on warm rugs in second-storey bedrooms suddenly found themselves expected to work, assigned to the cold linoleum next to a door. Lights remained on at all times, so that strangers driving through the area must have wondered what we were celebrating, why even in the early hours of the morning the farmhouses along the dark roads were ablaze.

Alarms and home security systems were not common at the time, so rudimentary ones were created. Sitting on the goatskin rug, Hetty and Ruby and I strung what seemed like miles of soda pop cans together. But miles of them were needed if they were to circle the entire castle where, hanging six inches from the ground, they would trip unwary visitors, alerting the people inside.

Not surprisingly, Katie's murder was the topic of discussion on street corners, in coffee shops, at local functions and in the halls at school. News reports and rumors were often combined, elaborated upon until the line between reality and truth became obscure. The body had been mutilated beyond recognition. Katie's watch—although some said it was a boot—had been stolen by the killer as a souvenir. Doug McCrae, who was playing the Artful Dodger in the school's production of *Oliver!*, told me the wire had been pulled with such force it had completely severed her head.

"Is that true?" I asked Eric, more horrified by the image of this than anything else I'd heard since the discovery itself.

"No, it's not, and why would you believe somebody who doesn't have a clue what he's talking about? Ask him this—was he there?"

Constable Wagner held a public information session at the high school in an attempt to ease our fears. Megan and I went together with Mom, Aunt Alice and Mrs. Fraser, who drove.

Aunt Alice sat in the backseat with us. "It's all these rumors flying around," she explained. "They've got everyone terrified. On the other hand, there's always a little truth in every rumor so I'm guessing Constable Wagner just wants to set us straight on what's true and what's not."

Detective Mather appeared confident, assuring us that the circumstances surrounding Katie's murder suggested that the killing was random. He also thought it was highly unlikely that the killer was from Pike Creek or that he was still in our midst. "Would he kill again?" Mrs. Gillespie wanted to know. Detective Mather hesitated, shifting his feet a little—until then the only hint of indecision. Finally he acknowledged that any answer he might give would, at best, only be a guess.

Katie had been raped, most likely in the Hippie House where she had died on the same night. The orange extension cord that had been used to tether her body to the post was a key piece of evidence. It did not belong to us, Uncle Pat or any of Eric's friends. However, the guitar string—an E—used to strangle her, tightened with such savage force it had cut deep into her throat, had once belonged on Jimmy's bass. He remembered the day he replaced it, tossing it to the floor after playing "I'm Goin' Home" four times in a row.

Mrs. Gillespie was probably not the first in town to suggest that Ross Nash and Lyle St. Vincent might have played a part in Katie's murder. She was just the first I'd heard discuss the possibility as if it were fact. I was eating chips and gravy with Megan in the Dairy Bar when I overheard her speaking to

Mrs. Chisholm. The two women sat in a booth across from us, dipping spoons into the whipped cream piled high on their banana splits. Mrs. Gillespie popped a cherry in her mouth. She told Mrs. Chisholm that she hoped the two hoodlums hadn't been ruled out as possible suspects. After saying this, she drew the cherry stem from between her teeth, leaving a large dab of whipped cream clinging to her upper lip. It wobbled as she continued to speak. In her mind, anyone who would set fire to the teeter-totter in Queen Mary Park was capable of anything.

I thought about what Mrs. Gillespie said. Ross was far from a model citizen, but the leap from public mischief-maker to psychopathic murderer did seem a very big stretch.

Ross and Lyle had been interviewed within the first twenty-four hours of the body being discovered, but so had the members of The Rectifiers along with many of their friends. Eric told me they had been asked little about their whereabouts on the night of November 9. The police were far more interested in people they may have recently become acquainted with from out of town.

Megan and I tried to recall what we were doing on the night of the murder.

"That was the day Eric and Jimmy drove us down to Toronto to see *Love Story*. Remember? And we cried all the way home. They kept asking us what we were blubbering about because they hadn't seen it. They'd gone to check out some music stores instead."

"That movie was so sad," Megan sighed. "The part at the end when they're in the hospital and Oliver lies down on the bed with Jenny, knowing she's about to die? Every time I think about it I still start to cry."

"I know. So do I."

"Oh my god! I cut past the barn and walked down the road right past the Hippie House on the way to your house that night! It could have been me that was killed!"

It seemed our whole world had been put on hold. Ordinary activities were impossible because of the restrictions, but they also brought little joy. It was difficult to get enthusiastic about going to a dance or buying a new record or a great pair of shoes when somebody so close to our age had died in such a mysterious and violent way.

Late one afternoon I passed Eric in the barn on my way to feed the geese. Tools lay spread on the floor around him where he kneeled on the dusty floor. He was tinkering with the snowmobile. Malcolm, Miles and Jimmy watched from where they sat, sprawled on bales of hay.

"My dad figures it was some freak on acid," I overheard Malcolm say. "Except he didn't word it like that. He said, 'It was probably some long-haired hippie high on LSD.'"

Malcolm's frumpy imitation of his father was so ridiculous even I had to laugh.

"Ever since the Tate murders and Charlie Manson and those crazy chicks were arrested, he figures every crime is committed by some long-haired hippie on LSD."

Miles stamped snow from his feet. "I don't know any long-haired hippies. Do you know any long-haired hippies, Jimmy?"

"Not that take LSD."

They all laughed a little. Except for Eric.

"Will one of you guys get this." he grumbled. "I can't support it and get the belt back on by myself."

"Hey, Eric, you've been so uptight since this thing happened. Try to relax, will you, man?"

I had never had such difficulty talking to Eric, who seemed to be living in a world separate from my own. He had trouble focusing. His homework was left undone and he missed ground lessons. When Dad suggested that he might forget them for the time being and start up again in the spring, he refused. More than anything else he wanted to continue to do what he was doing, and he didn't want anything to change.

It didn't matter what time of night I passed his bedroom, a light shone from beneath his door. Returning from the bathroom at three o'clock one morning, I quietly opened it. Light from the lamp on the bedside table fell across his face. He lay sprawled across his bed, tangled in a mess of twisted sheets. It appeared to me as though he had fought hard to free himself from their grip, but unable to escape, and exhausted from the struggle, he had fallen asleep.

I returned to my room, where I climbed into bed and began to think about the day Eric would no longer be at home. He was now in grade twelve. He had only one more year of high school and then he would be leaving for university. A strange and empty sadness came over me as I tried to imagine life without my brother around.

Two weeks after the discovery of Katie's body, my mother was tired of seeing photographs of Ruddy Duck Farm and the Hippie House in the newspapers. She had just about had it with curiosity seekers who drove past our farm, pointing fingers where they thought the Hippie House might have stood. She said she would just once like to go into town and not be stopped and asked if there were any further developments. How was she supposed to know? Did no one understand that just because the murderer picked our farm when he could have picked, say, Pat's, or the Frasers' next door, it did not mean she had inside information from the police! And if one more person asked her why we hadn't heard anything the night Katie was killed, she thought she was going to spit!

She began to smoke more than usual, if that was possible, and read much less, her concentration affected by her nerves. My mother bounced between chastising me for my foolishness and becoming giddy as she proclaimed how thankful she was that I was alive. One moment her dark eyes would turn and flare angrily. "And to think you hitchhiked on that very same highway last summer. Climbing in the car with people you didn't even know. What were you thinking, Emma Jenkins?!" The next moment I would be hugged simply for standing where I was.

A week before Christmas, Eric told us that Ross and Lyle had left town. "Mr. Blane won't serve them at the pool hall. Malcolm's dad said that no one else will come in if they do. They can't walk into a store or a gas station or even buy a hamburger without someone giving them a dirty look. They're being ostracized by everyone in town. I know they're just a couple of greasers, but they really don't deserve it."

"But maybe it was them. It's not like they've never been in trouble," I said, recalling Mrs. Gillespie's conversation with Mrs. Chisholm in the Dairy Bar. Although I still didn't believe it. "Maybe they're admitting their guilt by leaving town."

"It wasn't them. Besides, if it was that easy, don't you think the police would have arrested them by now?"

"Well, I wish it was them," Mom surprised us by saying. She jumped to her feet and began clearing dishes from the table.

Dad watched her frenzied movements for a moment. "Clare, you don't really mean that."

But my mother met him with shiny eyes. "Yes, I do mean it, John. Because then at least they'd be off the street and somebody could sleep at night. Somebody could let their children go to school without worrying that they're going to wind up dead."

My mother's reaction was understandable as fear turned to anger and frustration. I was seeing signs of it all around. I was beginning to feel it myself. When I had digested the murder long enough, replayed the discovery in my mind, discussed all the could-have-beens with my friends—I did not want to see one more picture of Katie Russell, this girl who had come uninvited to our farm. This girl with whom I had no connection but who had thrown our lives into chaos. This girl who had changed my father so that he seldom smiled.

We had heard nothing to alert us the night of the murder. How this could be possible ate away at my father like rust. He had always taken such care; he had never produced a diseased crop or raised an unhealthy animal. How could he have not known what was happening on his own land? How could he have not heard the girl scream?

It was the depth of the woods and the sound-insulating factor of the snow, Uncle Pat more than once assured him. Was that not the reason he had relegated the electric guitars to the Hippie House in the first place?

But in the winter the air is brisk and still, acoustically more obliging my father argued. And then there was the car.

John, my uncle would answer in his patient way, cars pass at all hours of the night, it is not an unusual occurrence. And even the scream of a woman could not be heard through the branches of the woods and then carry a quarter of a mile. And if, under perfect conditions it did reach his ears, it would be indecipherable, just another of the transient sounds of the night.

Yes, my father would say, nodding his head. Yes, you are right.

Dad would fall into deep thought at the dinner table while Mom slapped our food before us. I had seen him late in the evening, outside my brother's door, lift his hand, think again and move away.

It finally became necessary for me to see the site of the murder for myself. It was early in the Christmas holidays, but the day itself had not yet passed, and by then my movements around the farm were no longer as closely scrutinized. I was able to slip out without explanation while Mom was on the phone.

Halley led the way past the barn, where my heart sank at the sight of the muddied and trampled airfield. It had snowed only once since the discovery of the body and not long enough to conceal the ruts dug by vehicles and the tracks left by many men. These tracks spread widely down the hill and through the woods, and I thought how it was as if a troop of soldiers had swept down on the farm, leaving behind broken branches and primrose that would not flower again in the spring.

It was odd to round the corner in the woods and not see the familiar sight of the Hippie House ahead. Instead, through the branches I could see five hundred feet to the road where the barricade was still in place. Stopping on the bank of Fiddlehead Creek, I could hear the small trickle of water as it struggled beneath the ice. I looked across to where the Hippie House had stood.

My father and uncle had been thorough. There were no stray boards or forgotten shingles to be seen. The fresh layer of snow had left a twelve-by-sixteen-foot rectangle on the ground in the building's absence, and I believed that if I crossed the creek I would not find a single nail.

It was hard for me to imagine the horror that had taken place on this spot I had known for so much of my life. Instead, I imagined Dad with his feet up on the stove. I could hear the fire crackle as I fed it newspapers and smell the fresh paint. I could see Eric with Jimmy and the rest of the band in the beginning—excited by what they were doing, grappling with a new song, spilling out the doorway during breaks and, despite their sweatbands, wiping perspiration from their brows.

Mr. and Mrs. Fraser drove past on the main road. I returned their wave before turning away. My father was wrong to think that he should have heard anything the night Katie Russell was killed. I could only now hear the abrasive sound of the weather vane turning on the tractor shed because I knew it well. It was a sound I had heard so often it had become a part of my life. Who would believe that the flicker of a voice on a winter wind in the dead of night was a woman's dying breath?

WE WERE VERY LATE in getting our Christmas tree up that year. Handing us ten dollars, my father sent Eric and me to the tree lot in Pike Creek two days before Christmas. This was instead of making an event of it by pulling our sleigh into the woods and selecting one from the area Dad had reserved. Our gifts to one another were few and unsurprising as we lacked both the enthusiasm and the freedom to be creative. And when Aunt Alice vied for the dinner to be held at her house, my mother agreed without argument.

Ross and Lyle returned to Pike Creek and their families on Christmas Eve. Eric said it was probably because they discovered that they were not wanted anywhere else. Most small towns already had their fair share of punks, and in any larger place they would quickly lose credibility as being "tough," given that they really were only an act. In the real world, he assured me, there were much tougher than Ross and Lyle.

Much more infrequently now, a detective would knock on the farmhouse door. He would ask for permission to re-examine the site of the murder for a new or a specific detail. My father would ask if there had been any recent developments, any new leads, to which the detective would answer that there had been many, but unfortunately, to date there was nothing too concrete. Nevertheless, he assured Dad that they followed up on every one of them and that there were many detectives working around the clock.

My aunt and uncle drew some joy from the news that Carl landed a job as assistant caretaker of the ice arena on the last day of December. No such position had existed prior to Carl filling it, but Mr. Dikkers, who assumed the title of head caretaker now that there were two of them, was getting on, and in the winter there was just so much more to be done. Carl would be responsible for driving the Zamboni around the ice, among other things.

Megan and I wandered down to the arena one Saturday afternoon. It had been ages since we'd last skated, but we discovered it was very much like riding a bicycle. Once on the ice, it was as if nothing had changed since we were ten. The little guys pushing hockey sticks twice their height and working hard on folded ankles still cut in front of us. And Mr. Chisholm, who had once played semi-professional hockey still flew around on his own. Songs like "The Locomotion" and "Big Girls Don't Cry" played loudly over the PA system as they had when my friends and I had made human chains. It seemed that Mr. Dikkers was unaware that in the last ten years music had changed. Still, there was something comforting in hearing the old songs, kids hollering back and forth, and the echo of shoulders slamming into the end boards. Particularly at that moment in time.

A horn blew, warning us it was time to clean the ice.

Megan and I sat on the bleachers, eating sponge toffee while we watched Carl maneuver the clumsy machine around the rink. As he made each circuit, he glanced forward and back again, watching that he overlapped his previous path just the right amount and ever so precisely. I was completely amazed.

"Wow," I said. "Look at Carl. I've never seen him be so careful."

Megan peeled the cellophane away from her sponge toffee. She looked after Carl.

"I mean, have you? He's actually paying attention. He hasn't crashed or taken a chunk out of the sideboards or wiped anybody out."

Megan bit into the toffee. She didn't answer, but her eyes followed her brother in an interested, although somewhat skeptical, way.

Once Carl had parked the vehicle, he returned to the ice, where he stood with his hands on his hips, surveying his work. He grew indignant at the sight of a candy wrapper already blemishing the shiny surface and he marched over to a group of boys who stood wrestling next to the gate, impatient to get back on the ice. It didn't take long for Carl to discover that the boy responsible for tossing the wrapper was Arthur Nash. Arthur was only twelve, but he was every bit as scrappy and defiant as his older brother. So when Carl ordered him to retrieve the wrapper and deposit it in the trash, he snottily refused. It was only because Carl finally took him by the collar, and because Carl was such a forbidding giant, that Arthur finally did what he was told.

We were out of practice. We decided that our ankles were far too weak to continue and removed our skates. After tying the laces together, we draped them over our shoulders and headed toward the door. A surprising accusation made us spin around.

"Hey, freak! Why'd you kill Katie Russell?!"

It was Arthur, now at a safe distance up the bleachers.

"My brother said you did it. Everybody knows it. You're stupid enough to do it too, and you live right next door!"

Arthur continued to taunt Carl, goading his friends along, who agreed with him. Carl said nothing, but stood in the center of the polished ice looking confused. Afraid to respond in the presence of his boss, he glanced helplessly in the direction of Mr. Dikkers, who was sweeping out the penalty box.

"You did it and you should fry for it!"

"Hey!" Mr. Dikkers hollered across the arena, "That'll be enough of that! Now if you kids can't be civil, go on and get out of here!"

"Creep," Ross's brother grumbled. Laying his hockey stick across a bleacher, he fired another wrapper onto the ice and sat down to pull off his skates.

Megan made a point of passing him on our way out the door. "You'd better watch your mouth, you lying little twit, or I'll be the first to stuff a puck in it to shut you up."

It was the first time I had heard Carl accused of killing Katie Russell, and it was the first time I had heard Megan come to her brother's defense in many years.

"Do you know that they're saying Carl did it?" I asked Eric later that night.

Eric looked up from the table where he was studying and frowned. "Yeah, I've heard. Don't listen to them. They're full of it."

I was aware he had a test in the morning. Still, I lingered a little longer. "But do you think Carl could have done it? I mean, you know how easily he can be talked into things."

Eric set his pencil aside, leaned forward and looked directly at me. "What do you think?"

Not being absolutely sure, and perhaps a little flustered by the impatience in the question, I shrugged.

"Come on, Emma. Carl's just stupid, he's not a criminal. You know him—think about it. Nash is only trying to shift the blame."

"Yeah, I guess."

"Oh, and whatever you do, don't tell Uncle Pat or Aunt Alice. They don't need to know."

But Uncle Pat already had a very good idea of what was being said about Carl. He was in the habit of picking up the *Pike Creek Banner* every second Wednesday afternoon. The paper was published by Mr. and Mrs. Crossley. The couple also owned the print shop and the adjoining stationery store. Uncle Pat was standing in line, waiting for Mrs. Gillespie to pay for her stamps, when she took it upon herself to turn and offer him some advice. It might be wise, she suggested, if he and Aunt Alice were to keep close tabs on Carl for a while.

Uncle Pat glanced up from the front page of the paper. Not sure if he had heard her correctly or, in fact, if she had been speaking to him or Mrs. Crossley, who was behind the cash register, he replied, "I'm sorry, Margaret. I was reading." He then asked her to repeat what she had said.

"I'm only saying that, well, considering the atmosphere in town and the crazy imaginations of some people, it wouldn't hurt for you to keep a watch on Carl. You might even encourage him to abide by the curfew like the rest of the younger children are required to do."

"But Carl is eighteen," Uncle Pat reminded her. "He isn't one of the younger children."

"That's true. But isn't it also true that years are not always the best measure of a child's maturity? Pat, we all admire you for what you have been able to do with Carl, but you yourself would have to admit that Carl is a perfect example of this. In any case, it might be better to err on the side of caution—although I would rather not have to put it so bluntly."

"Margaret, do you ever put anything any other way?"

My uncle was hurt and astonished. He looked to Mrs. Crossley behind the cash register for support, but she only lowered her eyes. Uncle Pat lay his money on the counter and left without waiting for change.

I was reading in the sunroom when I overheard Uncle Pat relate to Dad what had happened in town.

"Geezus, John," he sighed when he had finished. "And just when that kid finally seems to be getting on alright. What am I going to tell Alice? That the whole town is after her son's hide?"

I could picture him passing his large and leathery hand across his forehead as he occasionally did when the stress of Carl proved too much.

"You don't need to say anything," Dad answered. "Just try and ride it out for a few days. Something is bound to happen—there has got to be a breakthrough. I'll bet the detectives make an arrest within the next week, in which case all this will be forgotten and Alice doesn't have to know."

Uncle Pat was silent a moment before voicing his greatest concern. "I just hope Sam Dikkers doesn't catch wind of this."

For Mr. Dikkers, it was the eggs smattering the east side of the arena when he arrived for work earlier than usual one morning that confirmed the rumors developing around Carl were widespread. Despite the cold, he hauled the extension ladder down from where it was stored in the drop-in center and washed the wall before Uncle Pat dropped Carl off at the arena that day. He continued to direct Carl on how to clean the ice, stock the shelves in the concession booth—although little moved that week—and clean the lockers in the change rooms.

Aunt Alice was hurt and confused by the accusing looks she was receiving in town. "What is the matter with people?" she asked my mother. "Turning their backs on us. Have they forgotten that we are one of them? Are they so frightened their brains have gone numb?"

My mother tried to calm her, but it is always difficult to sound convincing when you are not sure of something yourself. Standing before the sink and with my back to them where they sat at the kitchen table, I wiped the few remaining dishes. It was upsetting for me to see my aunt so distraught. I expected weakness from my mother; after all, she was not far removed from her privileged and somewhat temperamental roots. But my aunt had always faced up to adversity, tackling setbacks as though they were merely details to be dealt with, as inevitable as the first snowfall or the garden that needed planting in the spring.

Megan withstood allegations against her brother stoically, defending him in a way that was difficult for me to understand. Particularly as she had done her best to ignore his existence over the previous five years.

"Where was your brother that night?" Mandy Green asked when we stopped to chat on the steps of the public library. "Not that I believe he had anything to do with it, but you know what people are saying, and just out of curiosity."

"He was at home," Megan answered. "Reading. Magazines in his room. He's not much for books, but Carl does like to read a lot of magazines."

Carl himself could only deny his involvement. He insisted that he had not even talked to Katie Russell since the first grade, when she was moved ahead and he had to repeat the year. It scared him that so many people were trying to pin the murder on him, and without changing a word of his story, he repeated that on November 9 he had been with Ross and Lyle in the Dairy Bar until about seven o'clock. He had then driven Uncle Pat's pick-up truck home. He had remained in the farmhouse all evening and was not even near the Hippie House at any time.

Ross and Lyle began to harass Carl publicly, denying that he had been with them at all. Carl had no one to back him up. Not Katie, who, according to Carl, had been the only other customer in the Dairy Bar while on her dinner break from the nursing home that night. Mr. Gillespie tried hard to remember—yes, he remembered Katie, he knew her routine—but the three boys were in and out so often that he could not be certain that they were there together.

One evening, Ross Nash took a swing at Carl on the sidewalk outside Maury's clothing store. Perhaps he felt that with the sense of uneasiness all around he was more likely to be applauded than condemned for doing it, and so he did not choose a more secluded spot. Lyle was quick to help Ross out, landing a few punches of his own.

Eric was talking with Jimmy and Maury in his store when it happened. He told me what was said. Carl was in rough shape—doubled over from the few punches he had already taken in the stomach and sporting a split lip—before they heard the noise outside the store and broke it up.

Aiming a platform shoe, Maury caught Ross across the left side of the head. "Get lost, you goons!" He must have caught him quite hard, because for a week following the hit, his left ear glowed as he drove past us down the street.

"Let's have a look." Maury bent down on the sidewalk.

Maury and Eric helped Carl up from where he squatted close to the concrete, clutching his stomach. Eric sidestepped the blood dripping from Carl's nose. Studying Carl's face in the lamplight, Maury could see that his nose was quickly inflating. He sent Jimmy to the gas station down the street for a bag of ice. With Eric's help, he then steered Carl into the store, where they sat him on a chair.

"You ought to pick yourself some nicer friends," Maury suggested. Pulling a rag from behind the counter, he pinched Carl's nose so hard that he began to squirm in the chair. "Those guys—they're a couple of losers. They've got nothing better to do than drive up and down the street and pollute the air. When was the last time either of them had a job?"

Carl attempted to shrug, but he was prevented from doing so by Maury's firm grip.

"You've got a job. A good job. All you've got to do is hang on to it and you'll make something out of yourself. Not like them. Driving up and down looking for fights. They're going to still be doing that twenty years from now except they'll be gray and not even the kindergarten kids will be afraid of them. You get what I'm saying?"

Jimmy returned with the bag of ice. After slamming it hard against the counter, Maury removed a handful, which he wrapped in another rag and held to Carl's nose.

"Hold this."

Carl took the ice and tentatively applied it to his nose.

"Now I want you to listen to me. You should stick with what you're doing. One day Old Man Dikkers will retire and they'll be looking for someone to take over his job at the arena. You'll already know what you're doing and you can apply. Trust me, if you play your cards right, one of these days, you'll wind up as boss of that place."

A smile crept over Carl's disfigured face. Eric said he guessed it was the suggestion that Carl could actually be the boss of something—the idea, the possibility had never occurred to him before. In Carl's experience, if things were going well for him, it generally only meant he wouldn't fail.

Maury dabbed at Carl's split lip. He then gave him something for the pain so that Carl was grinning widely by the time Eric dropped him off at Uncle Pat's farm.

5

DURING THE FIRST WEEK of January, unseasonably warm temperatures turned the whole world into a sloppy mess. Tires threw soft pancakes of slush onto windshields so it was necessary for drivers to use their wipers despite the fact that not a snowflake fell from the sky. Water ran in the gutters beneath slumping snowbanks, and for days the sun remained hidden behind layers of cloud. Daylight seemed to shift only between shades of ash and slate.

Megan and I walked down the hill into town after school. Slush squirted from beneath the boots we had ordered from Eatons at the end of the summer, and the suede jacket I had longed for flapped open in the warm wind. It was missing two buttons, which I had not bothered to replace. With the flower sellers' costumes and Nancy's dress, I'd had greater things to sew. There was no great sense of accomplishment in simply sewing a button on where one had once been.

The road turned ahead of us before sloping down to the arena, where Carl scraped snow from the parking lot. The sound of metal against concrete could be heard long before we made the turn.

"I refuse to die like Katie," Megan told me as we shuffled down the hill.

We had not been talking about Katie, yet the statement didn't surprise me. The topic of Katie's murder was never far from our thoughts, and despite what we were talking about at any given moment, it was never out of context. For three weeks it had slipped in and out of our conversations as easily as the time of day.

"Well, I'm sure Katie would have refused to die like that too if she were given the choice."

"No, that's not what I mean. I mean I refuse to die having never done anything. Having experienced nothing. Don't you see, Emma? That's the real tragedy of dying so young. Katie never got to move away from here and have a good time."

I had not yet thought of it as philosophically as Megan obviously had. Until that moment I had thought only of the horrific act itself and the violent moment of her death. I'd thought it sad and frightening that a person could just cease to exist. I'd wondered what her family would do with her abandoned room, her closet full of clothes, the pictures and all that Katie treasured in her life.

But I had not once considered her death and attempted to relate it to my own life. At least no more than the fact that I had become afraid to walk alone at night.

"But how do you know she never did anything? You didn't know her."

"She still lived in Pike Creek, didn't she?"

"Yeah," I had to admit.

"Besides, Hetty told me she'd never done anything. Tanya told her Katie was really straight. She didn't drink or smoke or go to parties. She didn't hang out with anyone cool. She mostly only worked. God, she was eighteen and she'd never even had a serious boyfriend."

This depressed me quite a bit because I had never had a serious boyfriend. Come to think of it, Megan was older than me and she had never had a serious boyfriend. Not one that actually called you up and asked you for a date.

"Tanya said that Katie hardly ever went out because she was saving all her money to go to university. She was planning to go into nursing along with Tanya next year. So on Friday nights, if she wasn't working, she usually just sat at home and watched a movie on TV."

Since the drop-in center had closed and winter had come, Megan and I usually sat at home on Friday nights and watched a movie on TV.

"And on Saturdays she always took her grandmother grocery shopping. The only time she splurged was once in a while when she bought a pizza for her and Tanya. Oh, she also sewed her own clothes. Pretty dull life, huh?"

This was becoming quite distressing. The more I learned about Katie, the more I realized that, although she was older than we were, our lives were very similar in many ways.

"I mean, don't you think that if we were living on our own we'd be partying it up every night?"

"Yeah, I guess," I said.

I continued to think about our conversation for the rest of the afternoon. I had just assumed there had to be something not quite on the up-and-up with Katie. Something a little kinky that must have gone wildly out of control. I had been certain that the detectives already had discovered what it was and that it was only a matter of time before it was made public. After all, a person was murdered for a reason. Were they not?

I phoned Megan to rule out the possibilities—absolutely. "So let me get this right, if Katie didn't drink, and she wasn't addicted to anything—if Katie didn't have any vices, she couldn't have been the victim of a drug deal gone bad."

"Nope." Megan popped the gum she was chewing in my ear.

"And you said she never had a serious boyfriend. Soo—it couldn't have happened that she was involved in some kind of love triangle or anything like that. I mean, like she was murdered by a boyfriend who found her in bed with another guy and flew into a jealous rage?"

"Not a chance."

"And she didn't spend any money. So it couldn't have been some loan shark who was collecting on a debt."

"See? That's what I've been saying. Dull as dishwater. And that's what we'll be like if we don't get out of this place."

That night I sifted through the newspaper stories I had collected about Katie. Over the next few days I quizzed Hetty and spoke to Tanya myself. I tried to find the crack, even if it was only a hairline. Was it in her upbringing? Were there secrets in her family—her mother wasn't really her mother, but her grandmother, and she was really the daughter of her sister who'd given birth to her when she was only fourteen? Was there a time when she had disappeared for a month? Perhaps Mrs. Gillespie wasn't so far off—maybe Katie had escaped from a cult and now they were preventing their secrets from being told. Or had someone simply flattered her, and not being used to it, she had willingly climbed into the car and gone with him on November 9?

I turned up nothing of the sort.

Katie was born in Pike Creek on March 29, 1952. She was the second daughter of Marie and Earl Russell. Her parents were her real parents, and her father managed the Massey Ferguson dealership in town. Her mother worked at home, and her aunt ran the local craft store where Ruby sold her pottery and macramé. Katie had an older sister, Lorna, and a younger brother, Donny, who I'd already met as Bill Sikes.

Lorna was born with cerebral palsy, and although she required constant care, if anything, this seemed to have kept the family close. Katie spent hours exercising her sister's limbs every day. People who knew her thought perhaps it was because of Lorna that she wanted to become a nurse.

The family was well-off, not rich by any means, but they did own two cars, which was not usual for families on their block. But neither Katie or her brother acted superior to their neighbors or friends in any way. In fact, Tanya told me, Katie was generous almost to a fault. Tanya was hesitant to admire even a sweater Katie might be wearing because she had been known to offer it to her right off her back. It was just the way she was.

Katie had been a Girl Guide and then a Ranger. She had belonged to the 4-H club and in her last two years of high school she'd had a part-time job at the seniors' home, where she started out by sweeping floors and wiping dinner trays. But after awhile she began staying past her shift to read aloud to residents who had lost their sight. Or hold the hand of someone who was in a lot of pain.

Katie's family sold their Pike Creek home and moved to her grandfather's farm outside Grand Valley after he passed away. That's when she had moved into the apartment with Tanya to be close to work. She was committed to earning enough money to add to what her parents had saved for her so she could go to university in Toronto the following year. It didn't matter, she told Tanya, if in the short term she had to deny herself a few things.

It was a sad fact that there were a hundred reasons why I should have been murdered before I could twist anything that I learned about Katie's life into something deserving of what happened to her. I did not turn up one person who had exchanged even a harsh word with Katie. From all appearances, she had no kinky, secret side.

IT IS A VERY DIFFICULT thing to sort through the possessions of someone who has died. There is a feeling that you are trespassing; not that you have any choice, but that is really what you are doing. Against your belief that privacy is a sacred thing and is to be respected, you are forced to intrude on the most intimate thoughts and behaviors of a life.

My mother told me this when I was ten years old. She had just returned from Toronto, where she'd helped my grandmother clean out my great-aunt's home following her death. Shortly after walking in the door, she'd collapsed into her brocade chair and begun to cry. It frightened me. Realizing this, in one of her infrequent shows of physical affection she'd had me sit next to her, held me close and explained.

She told me that as you sort through these belongings—the mementos, the letters, even the books and their various subjects—you may uncover secrets that make you realize that you did not know that person as well as you thought. It makes you wish you had known, or at least thought to ask, so that you could have made an effort to reach out to them differently. "Or," my mother quietly added, looking off in the direction of—I wasn't sure what, "perhaps it's just as well that it remained hidden."

At the time, I sensed her need to talk. But I did not really understand what she was telling me. I have since learned that what she said is true.

I was at the castle the day Mrs. Russell discovered a packet of letters and a secret I'm sure she wished she had never found.

I had spent the morning perfecting the pattern for Nancy's costume. After first sewing it in muslin, I had fit it to the dress form by making tucks and darts in the fabric where needed. This was how Ruby had suggested it should be done. Late in the afternoon I had taken the completed muslin dress over to the castle for Ruby's inspection. Hetty and Tanya were out with Mr. DeSousa, clearing the last of Tanya's belongings from the apartment she had shared with Katie. Mr. and Mrs. Russell were also at the apartment; they had only the bedroom furniture and a bookshelf of Katie's left to move. It had been a long and weary task with many episodes of tears slowing progress.

After approving my work, Ruby picked up a seam ripper and carefully began to open the seams. I would now use the muslin pieces to trace the final pattern onto tissue paper. I began to spread the tissue paper on the floor. While I was doing this, Hetty, Tanya and Mr. DeSousa arrived home. Sobbing uncontrollably, and still wearing her coat, Tanya headed straight up the stairs. Hetty and Mr. DeSousa joined us in the living room, where Hetty stood over me. Ruby looked after Tanya, then questioningly up at her husband as the sound of a door slamming reached our ears.

Mr. DeSousa stood with his back to the fireplace. He was a tall man with fine, expressive hands and fair skin weathered by nothing more harsh than boardroom lights. He was also very kind, quick to laugh, and under normal circumstances he would entertain Hetty and me with stories of his trips. But now his expression was solemn, as if whatever he had to say was not something we would particularly want to hear.

"Marie Russell found some letters." He was not looking at any of us, but at the stilled work in Ruby's hands.

"Oh?" said Ruby.

Mr. DeSousa looked briefly at me, but perhaps deciding that Hetty would not let the author of the letters remain a secret for long—that is if she hadn't told me already through some mysterious series of gestures, eye movements and general teenage telepathy—he told us what they concerned.

"The letters were from Lewis Gillespie. It appears that he and Katie were having an affair."

Naturally, I thought I must have heard him incorrectly. Or perhaps he had confused something between the hearing and the telling of what he had just said. Unless, of course, it was a joke. But how unlike Mr. DeSousa to make up something in such bad taste. Whatever the confusion, it was simply beyond belief, for not only was Mr. Gillespie half bald, but he also sported a gold tooth and he was more than twice Katie's age!

I glanced at Hetty, who screwed up her face. "Have you ever heard of anything so sick?"

"You mean it's true?"

"Uh-huh. Tanya's been freaking out since she heard."

"Oh my, I'd better go speak to her." Ruby folded the muslin piece she was working on and placed it in a neat pile on the arm of the chair. "Have you turned the letters over to the police?"

Mr. DeSousa confirmed that despite Mrs. Russell's protests, he had left the packet of letters with Constable Wagner at the station on the way home. Mrs. Russell was concerned that if their existence were known, they might harm Katie's reputation. It had taken some convincing on Mr. DeSousa's part to persuade her that they might contain information crucial to the investigation. He was visibly worn from his efforts, and he was only thankful that she had finally seen it his way.

Ruby's steps rang out as she climbed the stone staircase. Hetty and I looked back to her father.

"I'm sorry," he said, shrugging slightly, tossing his hands in the air. It was as though he felt the need to apologize for Mr. Gillespie's behavior on behalf of all middle-aged men. He turned toward the kitchen.

Hetty and I wasted no time in reaching the privacy of her bedroom to discuss this incredible news. Once the door was closed, we quickly decided that this new piece of information far outranked all other discoveries of the past year. It was more sensational than the news that Mrs. Young, Megan's former history teacher, had been hospitalized after becoming addicted to diet pills. It was so wild it outdid the discovery that Mandy Green's older sister had not quit school and moved to Toronto because she was spotted in line at a movie theater and offered a modeling job, but because she was pregnant and had gone to live with her aunt until the baby came.

At that time in our lives, we knew only certain facts related to the word "affair." Most of these facts we had gleaned from movies, sitcoms and trashy romance novels. The facts were: An affair was almost always spoken of in the negative by adults who were not directly involved. One or both parties in the affair were married, so that carrying out the affair involved a lot of sneaking around and covering tracks. Satisfying an uncontrollable physical attraction to one another was at the core of every affair. Love never seemed to be a part of it, unless of course the word "love" preceded the word "affair," as in "love affair," in which case it took on an entirely different meaning. But when it was simply "an affair," we knew that the emotional attachment was absent, and sex and finding a time and place to engage in it were of much greater concern.

Since "an affair" was how Hetty's father had referred to the relationship between Mr. Gillespie and Katie, obviously this brought our understanding of the term seriously into question. This was because a physical attraction to Mr. Gillespie on Katie's part was simply inconceivable to us.

Once we had decided this was the most sensational news of the year, Hetty sat down on the bed while I drew up the desk chair across from her. She didn't say anything for a moment, but the way her lip curled in an expression of disgust I guessed she was thinking hard about what an affair with Mr. Gillespie would involve. I was right.

"But he has so much hair sticking out of his nose," she remarked, as though I had challenged what she was thinking. As though I had suggested that it really wasn't all that strange.

"Yeah. And when it's hot and he's been cooking all day, he gets all sweaty and greasy on top of his head."

"Maybe he was giving her money," she suggested, certain there had to be another reason. "I mean, she really wanted to go to school next year."

"Maybe. It would make more sense than if she did it because she actually thought he was good-looking or sophisticated or something."

Sitting cross-legged with her arms around her knees, Hetty tilted forward on the edge of her bed. "But then that would make her a prostitute."

She was right. And my research showed this was virtually impossible. With any stretch of the imagination, it was not within reach of her character. "Then that couldn't be it. Katie wasn't like that," I said.

Hetty looked up. "No, she wasn't. And that's what everybody would think. But say he somehow talked her into it. Say he convinced her that she would have enough money to leave Pike Creek in six months instead of being stuck in this one-horse town for a whole year. Eventually, she realized how wrong it was and she threatened to expose him."

"So he killed her?"

"Well, yeah. Because in this town he'd be ruined if the truth were known."

"Nah." I shook my head. "It's too far-fetched. I've been going to the Dairy Bar since I can remember, and it wouldn't happen. Mr. Gillespie isn't such a bad guy. He gets grumpy sometimes when kids start throwing fries around, but I can't see him murdering anyone."

Hetty frowned. But she didn't disagree.

We were convinced there had to be some hidden reason Katie would have had an affair with Mr. Gillespie. It was unthinkable that she could have found anything attractive about the man.

I bounced it off Eric, who was in his bedroom, organizing his forty-fives, when I got home. His lack of interest surprised me.

"Well, don't you think it's just about the grossest thing you've ever heard?"

"Not really."

"But he's an old man—at least forty—maybe fifty. He's probably even got false teeth. He's got hair growing from his nose and two chins."

"Ever seen Mrs. Gillespie? She's got about four."

He had a point.

"Yeah, I guess. But do you suppose he could have killed her?"

Eric pulled "Layla" from its sleeve. He set it on the record player and blew dust from the needle. "Why?"

MR. GILLESPIE HAD NO CHOICE but to come to his own defense, and within a few days all of Pike Creek knew the details of the affair. It had begun six months earlier, Hetty told Megan and me with some authority. Hetty had learned the details from her dad earlier in the morning at breakfast as he'd attempted to explain the situation to Tanya.

Flush with secret knowledge, Hetty had rushed Megan and me out to the smoking area during the first break in classes. With only a matter of minutes to fill us in, she hastily began.

"Gillespie said it wasn't a sleazy affair," she told us, rolling her eyes like it would be easier to believe the moon was made of cheese. "Dad said she came on to him when he was closing the Dairy Bar one night."

Megan made a face. "Wait a minute. She came on to him? Your dad said it like that?"

"Well, no, he didn't say it like that. He said 'the first time she'd confessed her feelings,' which boils down to coming on to him, right?"

Megan and I looked at each other and shrugged.

Hetty rushed on. "Anyway, so he was flattered and what's he going to do? He's this old guy and, let's face it, married to Mrs. Gillespie, the original hag of the Hockley Valley. Katie wasn't exactly Cybill Shepherd, but compared to his wife she must have seemed like a real babe. So anyway, she starts flirting with him, and because it's probably been months, maybe even years, since he's got any action from Mrs. Gillespie, he gets all hot and worked up and, well, there's no turning back."

Megan and I were both gaping at her, somewhat confused. As it turned out, we were thinking the same thing. "Your *dad* told you all this?"

"Well, yeah, but like I said, not exactly like that."

The warning bell sounded, summoning us to our next class. We never did hear how Mr. DeSousa's version really went. But we did eventually hear what was the more likely story from Aunt Alice, after Uncle Pat had spoken to Mr. Gillespie himself.

Mr. Gillespie often kept the restaurant open longer on nights when Katie worked the night shift. They were alone in the restaurant when Katie confessed her feelings to him on one of these late nights. Mr. Gillespie was flattered and admitted that he'd always felt an attraction to her. Then, when she'd unexpectedly embraced him, it had awakened something inside of him, something he thought had left him long ago.

Anyway, Pike Creek folks could call it whatever they liked, but it had been nothing less than love, and Mr. Gillespie was glad that it was now out in the open. He had suffered in silence long enough, having to sneak around like he was some kind of a criminal and keep his true feelings hidden from a wife who had allowed him no affection in years and a town that would never understand. And then Katie's violent death—well, the weight of it all had almost been too much, and no one could possibly know how sick he had been.

Mr. Gillespie's confession further convinced Megan that we had to get out of Pike Creek as soon as possible.

"Poor Katie. Every decent guy her age had moved away. She obviously got desperate. See what I've been saying, Emma? We've got to get out of here or before you know it we'll be stuck here too."

"Yeah." I said, "I guess. But I'm glad we know about it. Not that Katie having an affair with old Mr. Gillespie isn't totally weird. But knowing about it is kind of a relief. I mean—" and I realized this observation was more to myself "—I think we've found Katie's secret side."

"Maybe so, but that doesn't make it any less pathetic," Megan told me, "and if we stick around something similarly pathetic will happen to us. Oh man, when you think about it, the whole thing is just sad."

Tanya refused to believe there had been an affair at all. She lived with Katie. How could it have been going on without her knowledge? Hetty was in the kitchen when Tanya was interviewed by the police.

"The thing is, we talked about guys all the time. We talked about looks and how we liked to be treated. Katie liked guys to be clean-cut, not nerdy or anything, but like the Beatles, not the Rolling Stones. Nicely dressed, styled hair, they didn't have to be stunning, but they did have to take some pride in themselves. Look, all I'm saying is that Mr. Gillespie was not Katie's type. I don't know whose type he is, except maybe Mrs. Gillespie's, but he wasn't Katie's, that's for sure."

Tanya could offer no explanation for the existence of the letters, but she insisted Katie had never mentioned his name. "The only thing Katie said was, once, she asked me what I thought about going out with older guys. I asked her how much older she was talking about. 'Much older,' she said.

"I told her I didn't see any problem. But of course I assumed she meant Maury Kaplan. He's hardly clean-cut, but he's always so friendly and lots of fun to talk to. I knew she always sort of liked him."

Mr. Gillespie was cleared of any suspicion implicating him in Katie's death. On the night of November 9 he had closed the Dairy Bar at the usual time—ten o'clock—and was home by ten thirty. His wife and two neighbors confirmed this was true. Still, the Dairy Bar remained closed for a week following his confession. Mr. Gillespie moved his belongings from his home and made the empty apartment above the restaurant habitable. It had been used only as his office until then.

My mother and I passed Mrs. Gillespie outside the drugstore in Pike Creek shortly after news of the affair became known. She had been one of the worst offenders for stopping Mom on the street and grilling her with questions about the murder. What were the detectives working on? Had they made any headway? Why would the murderer have picked your farm? How could you have not heard anything that night? She was the reason Mom had almost lost it many times. Now she passed us with barely a nod.

"What's she so snooty about? We didn't have anything to do with it."

"She's not mad," Mom replied. "She's embarrassed. She's a proud person, Emma. This is very difficult for her."

"She's a busybody."

Mom smiled a little. "She's that too."

It wasn't often we held the same opinion and I smiled at my mother for agreeing with me.

During the week the Dairy Bar was closed, Megan and I began to miss dropping by for chips and gravy after school. There was nowhere else to go. The only other place to get decent junk food was the Dairy Queen, and it was way out on the highway on the outskirts of town. By the time the restaurant reopened, Megan and I were well into withdrawal. It wasn't just the chips and gravy. It was a warm place to hang out with our friends for an hour before going home after school. It was just too cold to hang around the outdoor bleachers or the smoking area unless we dressed like geeks and wore woolen toques and mittens, which we were not about to do. So when Mr. Gillespie opened the doors again, we were the first to slide into a booth. Only friends of the Russells and Mrs. Gillespie no longer came into the restaurant. We could see them through the picture window as they walked past the building with their eyes set straight ahead and their chins firm.

To a few of his customers, Mr. Gillespie became a sort of celebrity.

"Who would have guessed Lewis had it in him?" Mr. Fraser's farmhand guffawed. He elbowed the man seated next to him at the counter.

They both laughed in an annoying way.

If Mr. Gillespie noticed, he kept to his work. Very little seemed to distract him. He moved mechanically through the motions of slicing pickles, filling ketchup bottles and flipping hamburgers. Often, I noticed, people had to repeat his name to get him to look up. And when Doug McCrae made fun of Mandy Green's stringy shag haircut and fries flew across the table, Mr. Gillespie didn't react.

"Maybe they really were in love," I said to Megan.

Mandy thumped Doug across the back of the head.

"Who?"

"Katie and Mr. Gillespie."

Megan shrugged. It was already old news and we'd absorbed it. "I guess. We'll probably never really know."

6

ABOUT THIS TIME, the dreams I had been having since the discovery of Katie's body took on a face. Not a real face, but some melding of their scattered segments. Until then the dreams were simply disruptive. I would wake up during the night anxious, but the reason why had already dissolved. I was left with the feeling that I'd been involved in an unpleasant situation, a minor accident or a problem that remained unresolved.

I now woke up from my dreams terrified. I felt fear long before I was conscious enough to open my eyes, and by the time I did, my chest was damp with sweat. I also did not forget these dreams.

Always, I was on the farm. In one I was doing my chores, feeding the chickens. In another I had gone into the workshop to call my father for dinner, but he was not there. There was never anyone else at home except me. I would be carrying out a regular routine when I suddenly felt that something (I couldn't even be certain it was human) had entered the room. I could not see it, but its presence was unmistakable. A shadow. I could feel it move about. At all times I knew exactly where it was in the room.

As the thing stalked me, I mentally prepared to escape. I sprang from its reach the second it lunged at me. And I kept on running. I had never run from anything the way it was necessary to run in these dreams. Behind me I could hear it breathing and feel its soundless footsteps. I took shortcuts, in the barn and through the fields, but whatever pursued me seemed to know them as well as I did. There was no place I could ditch it, where it would not follow. I would hide, but it was like an owl in the night and could pick me out wherever I went. I never got away. Cornered, with no way out, I woke up sweating and with my heart racing against my chest.

One night I awoke from one such dream where I was in the cellar, cringing behind the tall heavy cabinet my father had built to incubate duck eggs. The moving form had just stepped from the last wooden tread into the small concrete room. It knew I was behind the incubator. There were no windows in the old damp cellar. There was no alternate escape. The steps to the kitchen were the only way out. Trapped and terrified again, I woke up.

My bedroom was dark and still. I could only make out an outline of the ornaments on my dresser, and the large pink roses on the wallpaper were inky blots. The rest of the house was silent, and only the light over the stove in the kitchen trickled up the stairs. But from outside, below my window, I could hear voices. It was the sound of men talking on radios, the back-and-forth mumble of conversation, like on the night Katie's body was found. I tried to recall the day's events—what had happened that they would be there? There was no reason for it. I strained to catch a syllable of what was being said because they were speaking in very low voices. I could not decipher a word. When I realized they were working without the benefit of light, I became frightened. Perhaps these were the gas thieves Dad had set out booby traps for in the summer. Leaving my bed, I walked in bare feet down the cold hardwood hallway and opened Eric's door.

"Eric."

"What?" his groggy voice answered.

It never took much to wake him up.

I stood next to his bed, shivering in my nightgown, and told him what I had heard. Without saying anything, Eric threw back his covers. He was wearing only pajama bottoms. He pushed a length of hair from his eyes and stumbled sleepily out the door. He was back within minutes. Jumping into bed again, he pulled the covers beneath his chin.

"There are no men talking. Go back to bed."

"Yes, there are. You didn't listen long enough. They have radios. I heard them talking on car radios just like the police did the day Katie was found."

"I listened. You were dreaming. There are no radios. Now go away. I want to go to sleep."

How could he not have heard them? They were right outside my window. "Eric, they're there."

He sat up again. "Okay, what were they saying?"

"I don't know. I couldn't understand them. Something serious. They were discussing something."

Once again, Eric got out of bed. He dragged me by the arm and pulled me with him back to my room, where we stood just inside the door.

"See? Nothing. No voices. No radio. Now get into bed."

He was right. There were no voices. There was no radio. But there had been. "No."

"Emma—"

"If you leave they'll come back."

"They won't come back because there was never anyone there."

"Not now, but—"

And suddenly realizing what had occurred, a chill raced down my spine. "They were discussing me," I whispered. My knees went weak.

Eric frowned. "What do you mean? Why would they be discussing you? Look, there is nobody there to discuss anything. I'm telling you, you were dreaming."

"They found me. They were discussing my murder. I was dreaming, but I was awake. I keep dreaming about getting chased by something horrible. I get the same dream at least three or four times a week. I can't sleep here tonight. Not after the voices." The sweat clinging to my chest had cooled and I began to shiver.

I half expected Eric to shove me into bed, but instead he took pity on me. As it turned out, he'd had one or two bad dreams of his own.

"All right, grab your quilt."

Hauling my quilt behind me, I followed him to his room.

"You can sleep in the chair for tonight."

I tried to get as comfortable as I could in the armchair by the window. When I was very tired I moved to the floor.

COCO CHANEL, the fashion designer, died in January of that year. I was a little surprised when Mrs. Suringa told me. I guess I had just assumed that she had died many years before. Coco was responsible for bobbed hair, making suntans fashionable, the little black dress and her own brand of perfume. She was also the designer who got rid of that ancient mode of torture, the corset, which is why, I think, I was so surprised she could have still been alive. How could anyone still be alive who actually wore a corset? Women had been going braless for several years.

On an afternoon late in January I sat at my favorite Bernina machine in the sewing room. The company of *Oliver!* was rehearsing in the theater across the hall. Mrs. Suringa was hustling actors back and forth between the stage and the sewing room, where I was hemming cuffs, replacing buttons, adding trim to costumes and generally doing whatever last-minute alterations she deemed needed to be done.

I didn't think it was tedious work. It was actually the best part, detailing the costumes when the fitting and basics were already done. I especially liked doing it because Mrs. Suringa often sought my opinion.

She had recently brought in a secondhand store find: a brown satin dress with a simple round neckline. She suggested it needed something to date it to the nineteenth century. "A choker. With a gold brooch or cameo perhaps? Emma, what do you think?"

By then I had spent many lunch hours in the sewing room and was familiar with every spool of thread, every remnant and every unusual button in that room.

"There's a piece of black lace in the remnant box. I could make a standing collar and gathered cuffs at the wrist."

Mrs. Suringa nodded. "Very Victorian. There's some suitable interfacing on the bottom shelf to the left of the door."

She left me to my work and went back to the stage.

I found the lace in the remnant box and the interfacing where Mrs. Suringa had said it would be. I lay the fabric on the cutting table and trimmed the ends as I straightened the grain. I was smoothing it flat when I sensed a presence in the doorway behind me. I turned. It was Donny Russell dressed as Bill Sikes in a long black coat, leaning against the door.

"Hi," he said, moving into the room.

Donny was a year older than me. He wore his dark hair layered and it fell to his shoulders beneath the top hat he wore. The hat gave him the appearance of being much taller than he was, and I thought he looked a little intimidating, a little evil, dressed all in black. Although that, of course, was the intended look. I wondered how it could possibly be improved.

"Great costume," I said. "You look, well, like a real creep."

He touched his hat and smiled.

He reminded me of somebody. "I know, you look like Roat in *Wait Until Dark*. Cool but creepy. Did you see that movie?"

"Yeah, I did. But I'm not like Roat. I may be cool, but I'm not usually a creep." He swept the hat from his head.

"Yes," I said, "I know."

"Hey, look." Donny pulled at his waistband. "Good job taking my measurements. My pants haven't fallen down yet."

I laughed a little. "Well, let's hope that they don't."

"No, I don't suppose I'd make a very convincing bad guy with them dragging around my knees."

I laughed again. "Did Mrs. Suringa send you in here? You look great. I mean, I wouldn't change the length of the coat if that's what she was thinking."

"No, it isn't. Actually, I wanted to talk to you about something else."

My stomach tightened as I thought of the only thing that connected us outside of this play.

"Alright." And to avoid his eyes, I began fussing with the lace on the table before me. I inadvertently knocked the small dish of straight pins on the floor. With a tinny sound, they scattered in all directions. I bent down to pick them up.

Donny bent down to help me. "Emma?"

I looked up. It was the first time he had said my name. I didn't even know he knew it.

"I've been wondering if I can come by your farm. I want to see where it happened."

I looked at him a moment as I continued gathering the pins. "Are you sure?"

"Yes."

Leaving the rest of the pins, I stood up. "Just you?"

Donny also stood up. "Just me."

"Okay. When would you like to come out?" But I had no sooner said it than I suddenly remembered that the Hippie House was no longer there. It was a horrible feeling, like now that he had made the agonizing decision to come out and see it, I couldn't help him.

"Oh my god," I said. "The Hippie House is gone. It was torn down. There's only the woods and the creek where it used to be."

"Never mind about that. After I get home from school I can drive out in my grandfather's truck. What time does your bus drop you off?"

"Three forty-five."

"Can I come just after that? I can see it before it gets dark."

DAD WAS ADDING SUET to the wire-mesh bird feeder stapled to the fir tree outside the sunroom window when Donny drove up the lane in his grandfather's old truck. I had warned him Donny was coming. We had agreed that we would walk Donny down to the site of the Hippie House together, then get a feel for what he wanted us to do from there.

As always, Halley was glad to have visitors, and when Donny emerged from the truck she showed her enthusiasm in her usual messy way. During the excitement of a greeting, she would dance and whine and pant heavily. To rid her jowls of the excessive slobber Clumbers are known for, without warning she would give her head a shake. Halley's target range was phenomenal. I had wiped dog spit from the chandelier in the dining room and been nailed on the cheek from ten feet away.

So it was not unusual that shortly after Donny arrived I was wiping dog spit from the sleeve of his coat. Thankfully, Donny thought it was funny, and with Halley unaware of the trouble she'd caused, she led the way up the hill and past the barn.

The sun was very low, just barely above the tree line on the opposite side of the field as we walked down the hill. The surface of the snow glittered in the last rays of sun, and it appeared crisp, but it was not like that beneath. With each step, Halley plunged through the surface as she set out to blaze a new path.

Dad talked to Donny about his plane and the pitfalls of using a pasture for a runway. Gesturing with both arms, he explained which of his fields he used for crops, when they were left fallow, and where the cattle grazed.

Dollops of snow flew from wet branches down the necks of our jackets as we walked along the road through the woods after passing the duck house. Fresh rabbit tracks ran next to the lane, crossing not once, but twice, just before we reached the creek. The concrete sluiceway we could walk across in summer was slick with ice and it would be extremely dangerous to attempt to walk on it now. My father stopped. Standing next to Donny, he quietly indicated the spot where the Hippie House had been. I stood behind them, off to the side.

It was not much to look at. It had snowed several times since the murder and there was no longer even an outline on the ground. Over the last few days, however, the top layers had melted and a number of footprints had surfaced. This suggested that the area had been the scene of something chaotic not too long ago. Donny stared at the space for some time while a thick lump formed in my throat and tears began to burn my eyes.

I knew from my brother's example that boys rarely spilt tears in public. For that reason I really didn't know what to expect. Maybe he would cry quietly or swear angrily at the unfairness of it all. I certainly didn't expect him to ask straightforward questions.

"What did it look like?"

Dad appeared a little puzzled. I think he was unsure of what he was being asked to describe and perhaps he was even a little alarmed. "I'm sorry. What—"

"The Hippie House—what did it look like?"

"Oh." My father's voice betrayed relief. "It was only one room, twelve by sixteen feet. I built it from a small stand of spruce that was struggling in this spot when I first took over the farm. I originally used it as a workshop before I built a bigger one closer to the house. I built workbenches against the east and south walls. There was a window facing this direction and another at the back facing the road. The exterior wood was weathered and the door was from the farmhouse, from the original root cellar. Now the doorknob, that was an antique…"

"Jimmy Bolton painted a bunch of big paisleys on the walls and a peace sign on the front door."

They both turned.

"You know, like big blue amoebas with eyelash fringes."

I shrugged. Dad was making it sound so dull and dowdy. In the end, it was not like that at all.

Donny smiled a little. "Paisley?"

"Yeah, it was paisley on the inside walls. The trim was bright too. Purple and red. It was a party house. The walls were covered in posters and song sets. Here, in the front window, Eric took down the curtain I made and hung a Canadian flag. But he left the curtain in the back. It was nice in the summer because of the blackberry bushes and goldenrod that grew up all around the foundation. I know it's a weed, but it looked really good against the weathered gray wood."

Halley had been tracking a grouse and now she flushed it from the brush in a flurry of motion. She pounced into a snowbank where she sank to her chest.

Dad made a motion toward the empty space. "I bought an old wood-burning stove and moved it into the center of the room. Even without insulation it was warm and cozy even on the coldest winter days."

"It was clean too," I said. "Eric and I got rid of all the garbage and swept it out at the end of summer."

I knew it would be a bit of an exaggeration, but I was about to tell him you could have eaten off the floor when Dad caught my attention. He held up a hand.

I now saw, as he did, that Donny was not listening to either of us anymore. He had turned back to the space where the

Hippie House had stood, and it occurred to me how ridiculous we were beginning to sound. Like two realtors trying to push a handyman's special on a reluctant client.

My father lay a hand on Donny's shoulder. "If you would like, son, we'll leave you alone now."

Donny nodded.

"We'll meet you back at the house. Will you be alright down here on your own?"

Briefly lifting a hand, Donny waved us on.

"I couldn't do that," I said as we climbed up the hill past the duck house. "I wouldn't want to do that. I wonder why Donny does."

"He needs to know it's real," my father said. "He needs to know it's real and that his sister's not forgotten in this circus of finding out who's responsible for her death."

That is all we said on the way back to the farmhouse. Halley heeled close to Dad when he signaled for her to quit snuffling around the duck house and to keep ahead as she was supposed to do. She lumbered up the hill. At the top, she turned, glancing hopefully at Dad before heading for the airplane hangar.

"Not today, Hale."

When we got back to the farmhouse I wasn't quite sure what to do. I thought I should probably have something to offer Donny when he returned. Not knowing what he would feel like, I set a few choices of pop on the kitchen table. But it was a somber occasion, so I decided he might prefer tea. I plugged in the kettle and got out the teapot. Mom had baked cookies, and there was banana bread and pound cake, which I sliced and arranged on a plate.

My mother stood in the doorway with her arms folded, watching me fuss without saying a word.

It was more than an hour before I spotted Donny's dark figure moving down the hill between the barn and the workshop. He didn't come to the farmhouse, but he walked straight to his grandfather's truck, where I heard the engine start up. Twenty minutes later it was still running and Donny had not moved. From the second-story guest room I could see his outline against the steering wheel in the faint glow cast by the yard light. Eric wandered in, wondering why I was standing in the dark. Seeing Donny sitting in the truck, he swore quietly before walking out again. I found Dad in the kitchen.

"Should I go talk to him?"

Dad shook his head. "Give him another ten minutes. If he's still there, I'll go."

Five minutes later I looked out and the truck was gone.

7

THE LONG WEEKS BETWEEN Christmas holidays and the end of February were a real struggle that year. Somehow the gray skies appeared grayer, the walk down the lane dragged on longer, and March and the promise of spring seemed much more distant than they ever had in the past.

Oliver! was performed at the high school at the beginning of February. Donny did a fantastic job as Bill Sikes, stepping into the part, hot-tempered and murderous, and out again as easily as the flowergirls stepped in and out of their skirts with their elastic waists. The only glitch came when Oliver stepped on Nancy's trailing dress hem as she was about to leap across the stage during a choreographed scene. The rip could be heard at the back of the theater. Mrs. Suringa and I were called on to do a very quick patch job as Fagin launched into a solo. The bustle didn't sit quite right during the final act—it was substantially off-center—but then Nancy didn't last much longer anyway.

I had nothing exciting to sew now, and I became fidgety. As we did the dishes one night, Eric suggested I sew a tarp for the MG he was going to buy.

"There's got to be tons of sewing to it. It will keep you busy for weeks."

Suds rolled off the dinner plate I set in the dish drainer. How naïve he was. "Do you know how boring that would be? It would just be running through seam after seam. It would be about as challenging as if you built an orange crate out of your balsa wood."

"Why would I do that?"

I rolled my eyes. "Besides, where are you going to get the money to buy this MG?"

Eric wiped the plate. "We're starting up the band again. Miles has already got us a paying gig in Shelburne. We're going to blow all those fiddle players right out of the water. Hey, that's what you can make me. I'll need a new shirt to wear at the gig."

"When I said I didn't have anything to sew, I wasn't asking you to put in an order."

There was a knock at the door off the back kitchen. Before Eric answered it, he quickly skimmed suds from the water and tucked them down the neck of my shirt.

"Eric!"

The screen door slammed, the heavier door closed and Malcolm followed Eric into the kitchen. He had driven out to the farm to pick Eric up for a band practice. He nodded at me, then sat down at the kitchen table to wait.

I hadn't seen Malcolm very much in the last two months, or perhaps I hadn't paid much attention, but it struck me that he was looking rather mangy. He'd grown a full beard, and his black hair was now halfway down his back. This wouldn't have been so bad—it actually could have been quite cool—if it looked like it had been washed sometime in the past week. Maybe it was his jacket. A pocket flapped where the denim was ripped, and it was so grimy he looked like he'd rubbed up against a dirty bus to relieve an itch.

It wasn't just me. Moments later my father passed through the kitchen on his way to the workshop. I caught him doing a double-take when he saw Malcolm sitting at the table. He then said something that was most unusual for my father. "Oh, Malcolm. It's you. I didn't recognize you under all that hair."

Dad was normally very good at not commenting on appearances. I could not recall him ever arguing with Eric, as many fathers did with their sons, about the length of his hair. So his comment made Eric look up.

Malcolm lifted a hand. "Hey, Mr. Jenkins."

Dad sounded almost apologetic as he quickly tried to undo any damage. "How are you? Are your mom and dad back from Florida yet?"

"Yeah, they got back Sunday."

"Uh-huh. And did they have a good time?"

"Yeah, I guess."

Dad nodded. "Good, good. Well, say hi to them." He now seemed in a sudden hurry to leave the room.

Malcolm fiddled with the barometer attached to the inside of the window while Eric stood impatiently, waiting for me to scrub a pot so that he could finish drying the dishes before going out. He figured I should finish for him. Normally I wouldn't have minded, but I could still feel the slimy dishwater slinking down my back. I suppose I was pouting when I told him no.

"Come on, Emma. I'd do it for you."

"No, you wouldn't."

"Yeah, I would."

"Shhh!" Malcolm said.

Eric and I turned. We were unsure if he was telling us to stop arguing or if it was something else.

I should explain that our farmhouse was built in 1886. The date was engraved in the stone arch above the front door. The solid building had appealed to Dad, but there were problems resulting from not only the age of the house, but also its rural location that, despite my mother's meticulous housecleaning, could never be resolved.

In the heat of summer, battalions of houseflies buzzed in the sunny dormers. As they died off, their bodies fell among the jade plants, cluttering the windowsills. To my disgust, vacuuming the thick piles of shiny husks was added each summer to my list of chores.

Bats regularly made their way into the house. For this reason my father kept a tennis racket next to his bed. It was a foolhardy bat that risked a midnight flight above his head because Dad possessed the well-developed arm of a seasoned fisherman. His swing was nearly always fatal. Even when barely awake, he could pick a bat from the air with one well-aimed thwack. I would hear the small thud as it hit the floor, Dad's footsteps and the toilet flush in the bathroom down the hall.

But it was the mice that caused the greatest problems in the house.

So when Eric and I turned at Malcolm's exclamation, we were not surprised to see him pointing to a mouse. It was sniffing around the floor by a leg of the table. Of course it was not a pleasant sight to see a mouse in our kitchen, but since it was not highly unusual, it did not cause a great amount of alarm.

Eric's automatic reaction was to reach for the minnow net my mother kept on a hook at one end of the cabinets for just this purpose. Armed with the net, he walked with soft footsteps toward the bold little creature, preparing to scoop him up. Malcolm stopped him.

"Leave it," he demanded, shooting an arm before Eric.

My brother had been at the point of lunging forward. He was a little put off at being stopped so close to catching his prey. "Why?"

"Because—"

But Malcolm didn't finish what he was about to say. He appeared suddenly confused and, instead, looked away. He shook his head a little before pressing his fingertips to his forehead as though he might physically be able to manipulate his mind into concentrating on what was happening in the room.

"Because what?" Eric prompted.

Finally, Malcolm continued, "It will—I mean, it could upset the balance of things."

"The balance of things?" Eric repeated. He looked at Malcolm and then over to me as if I might be able to better explain what Malcolm had just said.

I raised my eyebrows and shrugged.

The mouse began to skitter across the open floor. Eric moved forward with the net again.

Malcolm insisted, "No."

"What's with you, Malcolm?" asked my brother, now quite frustrated at this second interruption. "What are you talking about—the balance of things? It's a lousy mouse running through the kitchen where it's not supposed to be."

"You don't know that. I mean, you don't know that it's not supposed to be here. Running through your kitchen may be what it was assigned to do. And if you catch it—if you prevent it from fulfilling its purpose, then you could screw the whole thing up. Who knows what could happen? You could be killing some innocent kid in some place like Katmandu. You could be starting a tsunami in Japan."

If Malcolm had not looked so serious, Eric and I might have laughed. But it was apparent in his eyes that he did truly believe what he'd just said.

"A tsunami?" Eric seemed to have forgotten about the mouse and was now looking at Malcolm like he was the intruder. The minnow net dangled next to his side. Glancing at the doorway in case Mom was within earshot, he lowered his voice. "I've got

a news flash for you, Malcolm. Mice aren't assigned to do anything. They go where they can get food."

"Oh no, that's not true. They have a purpose. All of them. Like
you and me, they're assigned to do certain things."

"Oh yeah? And who hands out these assignments?"

"The um," Malcolm leaned closer to Eric and whispered, "You
know, the ones behind this whole thing."

"Malcolm, you idiot! Are you on something? I don't believe it,
you're ripped and you drove out here like that?"

"No, no. I'm not. It's just that mouse, he's got to do what he's
supposed to do. You wouldn't be doing any of us any favors if
you threw him off course."

Wide-eyed, Eric looked over to me again. The mouse was
following its nose along the line of cabinets in the direction of
Halley's dish.

"Hey," I said, snatching the minnow net from Eric's hand.
"Look, why don't you guys just get going. I'll finish up here.
There's not much left. You can pay me back some other time."

"Yeah," Eric answered in a subdued way. "Alright." And
wearing an expression of complete bewilderment, he draped the
dish towel over the handle of the stove. "Let's go."

Malcolm watched me swing the net while he waited for Eric
to grab his coat from the closet in the hall.

"You're not going to do anything with that are you?"

"Me?" I stopped swinging it. "Oh, no, I was just going to hang
it up for Eric."

He continued to watch me. When I realized how truly agitated
it seemed to make him, I hung the net on the hook at the end of
the cabinet again. "See?"

"Good. It's best just to let the little guy go about his business.
That way nothing can go wrong."

I nodded like the Katmandu and the tsunami thing made
perfect sense.

Eric returned and the two of them headed toward the door. Eric held out a hand, blocking Malcolm just before they reached it. "Malcolm, give me your keys. I want to try out this torque you're always bragging about."

I retrieved the minnow net from the cabinet as soon as they had left. I'd had my share of practice catching mice, and it was only a matter of seconds before I had it imprisoned in the web. Carrying the squirmy little animal through the back kitchen, I let it loose outside the back door just as Eric pulled away in Malcolm's car.

The following day, as Eric collected his textbooks from where he'd been working on his homework at the dining room table, I asked him about Malcolm's bizarre behavior. He didn't seem to want to talk about it and brushed it off as quickly as he could.

"He was just being a goof," he told me. "It's nothing. He gets like that sometimes. He says ridiculous stuff just to see if he can get us to believe it."

"Oh," I said. I thought about this and frowned. "What's the fun in that? I mean, what if sometime he wants you to believe what he's saying? It's like crying wolf, don't you think? How do you know if what he's saying is true and he's not just goofing around?"

Eric shrugged. "It's getting more and more difficult."

He then changed the subject, asking me if I had seen his calculator.

"Yes," I said. "It's in your hand."

DURING THE WINTER MONTHS, my father spent most of his days in the workshop, where he labored on various woodworking projects. Over the years he'd supplied the county parks with barbecue shelters, picnic tables and playground equipment. He'd provided purple martins with towering apartment houses, and many of southern Ontario's Canada geese had my father to thank for their nesting platforms. He volunteered for most of these projects, and I'm sure the various clubs and organizations he built them for thought he was a very generous man. But I knew his reasons were somewhat selfish. My father was passionate about tools and wood, and it gave him a reason to be in the workshop surrounded by both.

It was in the workshop that he discussed crops and weather with my uncle, and in the summer it was where he entertained friends who dropped by Ruddy Duck Farm to fish. This was not necessarily because my mother preferred it, but because the men preferred it. As my father explained, his friends were comfortable tipping back on folding lawn chairs with a beer in hand and their boots shuffling wood chips. It was a relaxing way to finish a day spent outdoors, particularly compared to sitting on brocade furniture with their socked feet embedded in the living room rug. In a rustic way, the workshop, with its smell of freshly cut wood and new stain, was a homey place to be.

In the winter, Dad kept a fire burning in the stove to heat the room. When we were young, Eric and I and my cousins would sit on stumps of wood around the stove and thaw our hands after sleigh rides. We didn't own a horse, but Dad would hook an old sleigh to the tractor and pull us through the fields.

It seemed my father must have owned every tool manufactured. This included two walls of neatly organized sockets and wrenches, screwdrivers, clamps and a table saw, which was the dominant feature in the room. Over the weeks, soft piles of sawdust accumulated around its base. Often, when I had nothing else to do, I would offer to sweep the floor just so I could be in the warmth of the room. While he worked, my father whistled. He did this compulsively and continuously. I was never able to distinguish one song from the other; they were just endless tunes that would be cut short by the scream of an electric tool or would start and stop abruptly depending on the amount of concentration needed for a particular job. But it really didn't matter what he was whistling. It was a cheerful sound that told me he was close at hand and all was right on the farm.

He had a vantage point from the workshop. The building sat on a rise and through any of the north-facing windows he could see past the farmhouse to the main road. From there he was able to spot an unfamiliar vehicle even before it turned into the lane.

Following Katie's murder, when it became important that no one but my father be left alone on the farm, I did not notice it as an inconvenience. He was at home most of the time anyway. Mom would simply accompany Dad on his errands, or he would not go out until Eric and I were home from school. The only time I was aware of this new routine interfering with my father's life was when he had to forgo his annual ice-fishing trip. It was his custom to fly "north" with some buddies from Toronto for a week every February. But that year his fishing gear remained in the barn, and not until I overheard Mom insist that he go anyway did I notice that he hadn't pulled it out.

Mr. Fraser had brought over half a dozen frying chickens earlier in the morning. I was helping my parents pack them into the large freezer Dad had built across one wall of the back kitchen. In a normal year, by the end of February the freezer would also hold the fish he caught on his trip.

"Not this year, Clare," he told my mother as they discussed the annual trip. "I'm not about to leave you alone. Not under the circumstances."

"But I'll be just fine. Eric's here, and during the day I've got Pat right next door." Mom was trying for nonchalant, but she was unconvincing. She called on me for assistance. "Emma, we can manage if your dad goes on his fishing trip, don't you think?"

I'm not sure why, but the first thought that leapt into my mind was waking up in the middle of the night after one of my terrifying dreams. There was some comfort in hearing my father flush a bat down the toilet in those moments.

I shrugged.

Dad smiled and placed his hands on Mom's arms. "Alright, how about this—next year I'll make up for missing this year by going twice?"

I quickly nodded. The perfect solution. This was enough to satisfy my mother, and the conversation was dropped.

My cousin's family was in the same position. As a farmer, Uncle Pat was almost always at home. If he had errands to run, there was Carl, who, despite all else, did cut an imposing figure. Any potential murderer was likely to think twice before tangling with him. And the Frasers had always hired farmhands. While Mr. Fraser was delivering chickens or organizing his investments, Mrs. Fraser was also never alone.

It was not so easy for Hetty's family. Mr. DeSousa remained at home for two months following the discovery of Katie's body, but by February he could not avoid traveling any longer. It was a large part of what his job entailed. Comfortable with our own arrangement, it did not occur to me how difficult it was for Ruby, Hetty and her sister to be alone.

A few days after Mr. DeSousa left for Montreal, my mother asked if they were alright.

"I guess so," I replied.

"Emma, you be sure and tell Ruby that if she needs your father or Uncle Pat—if she needs a man to come over for any reason—either of them would be happy to and she should not hesitate to ask."

I blinked at her. It was such a vague and wide open thing to tell Ruby.

"Never mind. I'll phone her myself."

I was waiting for Megan outside school one day when I stopped Hetty on the way to catch her bus. I asked her if she wanted to come with us to the Dairy Bar. She said she would like to but she had already made other plans.

"I promised Mom I'd be home right after school. We've got to practice."

I knew she didn't take music or dance lessons. I shrugged. "Practice what?"

"We have to practice in case Katie's murderer is still around."

"Oh," I said, thinking it a strange reason, but more concerned with catching Megan as she came out the door.

"Yeah, Mom has got a system all worked out. We just need to go through it a few times to make sure it will work."

Megan appeared, Hetty's bus arrived and I didn't have a chance to ask anything more. By the next day I'd forgotten all about it.

A few days later I found Ruby's pinking shears in my sewing basket. I felt terrible. She had loaned them to me when mine, in need of sharpening, had chewed an uneven finish in a seam of Nancy's dress. I'd forgotten to give them back. I'd had them at least a month and wanted to return them immediately. I talked Eric into driving me over to the castle.

It was nearing nine o'clock by the time we reached the DeSousas' house. The night was very black; it had been overcast all day and snowing off and on. Eric was worried about getting Mom's car stuck in the driveway. It had not been shoveled since Mr. DeSousa had left a week before. Pulling to the side of the main road, he put the car in park and waited for me to get out.

"Make it quick," he warned me. "I don't want to sit here all night."

"You're nuts. I'm not walking down that lane by myself. I could get jumped by someone in those trees and dragged off and you wouldn't even see it."

"There's no one in those trees. It'll take you five minutes."

"No."

Rolling his eyes, Eric pulled the hood of his parka over his head, opened the driver's door and got out. I got out as well and, leaving the car idling, we trudged up the lane. I was glad he was with me. The snow had drifted in the lane beneath the fir trees, making it difficult to walk. Eric made it easier by walking ahead of me so that I was able to step in his footprints and avoid snow leaking into my boots. Once we were past the trees we had no difficulty seeing where we were going. The castle was ablaze with light and it appeared that every light in the entire house was on. Reaching the front door, Eric slipped on the icy surface where the eavestrough dripped on the concrete, and rather than knocking gently, he unintentionally slammed the brass horsehead against the plate. We waited several minutes but there was no answer.

"Knock again."

This time it was Eric's intention to hammer loudly. We were cold and it was getting late. Another few seconds passed.

"Someone said come in," Eric told me.

"I didn't hear it."

But then I had a close-fitting hat on. Eric had a looser hood and was likely able to hear better than I.

He listened again. "I heard them. They said come in."

"Go ahead then."

He pressed the thumb latch and walked in the door. All I recall of the next few moments was Eric's startled scream, "Don't shoot!" the pinking shears crashing to the floor, women screaming and a blinding flash of light. I crept in behind my brother. He was lying flat on his stomach, with one cheek against the cold marble in the middle of the front hall. A bright light beat down on both of us and, shielding my eyes, I looked up.

"It's Emma!" cried Hetty's voice.

The light suddenly went out. I blinked, momentarily blinded. When I was able to look up again, I saw Ruby on the staircase.

She stood on the landing behind a gun mounted on a tripod. It was aimed directly at the front door. Tanya crouched behind a spotlight in the hallway and Hetty was at the bottom of the stairs, shouldering a wide broom. She reminded me of a young but defiant soldier.

"Oh, Emma!" Ruby left what turned out to be a BB gun and ran to help Eric get up. "We thought you were—well, somebody else. I'm so sorry, Eric."

By then Eric had raised himself on his elbows, determined it was safe and crawled to his feet. He pulled off his hood and shook his hair. "Man, Mrs. DeSousa, you scared me half to death."

I had to admire my brother. He was shaking. His cheeks were drained, no longer bright from the cold, yet he managed to remain reasonably calm. I could just about guarantee that if I had done what they had done to him, I would have been throttled until I was nearly dead.

"Oh, dear. I do apologize. We didn't want to answer the door when we didn't see a car, and then the door just began to open. It's just the three of us. We have to be ready for anything you know."

Eric studied the gun, the spotlight on its rolling trolley, and Hetty armed with her broom. The tripod and spotlight set-up was something he might have devised to prevent me from invading his room. He ran a hand through his messy hair and cracked a wry smile. Bending down to pick up the pinking shears, he handed them to Ruby. "I hope they didn't damage the floor. Emma wanted to return these."

Ruby assured him there was no damage to the floor.

"We've been rehearsing every night," Hetty told us, clapping her hands together. "This was just perfect. It was like a dress rehearsal. Like the real thing."

Eric nodded. "Glad I could be of help. But next time I think I'll phone first."

"Yes, well, maybe next time," Ruby said. "At least until the killer is caught and we're not so jumpy anymore."

8

THERE WAS A RED corduroy jumpsuit with flared pants and a full front zipper in the window of Maury's store that Megan just had to have. It was, for sure, the coolest, sexiest piece of clothing we had ever seen. Aunt Alice did not think it was a very prudent purchase. It was far too frivolous in her mind, hardly a classic that you could depend on for several years of service. Just how many seasons could you get from a red jumpsuit with flared pants anyway?

"But it's my money," Megan told her. "I earned it and I can buy what I want."

"Yes, I know." My aunt sighed as she pulled to the curb in front of Maury's store. "All I'm trying to do is teach my children to handle their money carefully. If it's really what you want, go ahead and buy it if you think it's wise."

Hetty and I thanked Aunt Alice for the ride. We followed several feet behind Megan, who had already slammed the door and was clomping ahead into the store.

"Geez," Megan moaned. "My mother would dress me in potato sacks if she could get her way. They'd cost next to nothing, they'd be easy to slip into and they'd last for centuries."

The jumpsuit looked terrific on Megan. She stood before the full-length mirror hung on a wall of the change room Maury had created in a corner of the store with a curtain of fabric and beads. Megan filled the jumpsuit in all the places the darts and gathers allowed. I looked at her reflection in the mirror, and with a small jealous pang it struck me that my taller skinny cousin had turned into a woman. Less than a year and a half younger, I suddenly felt a decade behind.

"Well?"

"You look almost like Raquel Welch. But here."

Hetty pulled the ring attached to the front zipper down to reveal a little more cleavage. More than even Megan had dared to show.

"Hmm. You don't think that's too much?"

"No way. If we had even half of what you have, me and Emma would do the same thing." Hetty looked to me for agreement.

"Right, even half," I said.

Maury was moving between the racks of clothing carrying a roll of labels, marking down old stock. For a number of weeks, he and his business had come under scrutiny. I had heard this through my brother, who had learned that detectives had made more than one trip through his store. Eric's sources said that Maury was always accommodating, answering their sometimes ambiguous questions politely. On this particular Saturday morning as Megan tried on the jumpsuit, Constable Wagner, accompanied by two detectives, again swept into the store. After a cursory glance around, they began to question Maury. This time there was nothing ambiguous in what they asked. They wanted a list of his customers.

"A list?" Maury set the role of labels on the front counter. Disappearing for a moment, he returned from the back room with a couple of chairs. He held forth a hand and invited the officers to sit down. "Have a seat, gentlemen. Can I interest anyone in coffee?"

Constable Wagner shook his head. The detectives remained where they were.

"A list. Well, at one time or another I guess I've sold something to pretty well every young person in this town. And a few not so young. I could pull out copies of last month's receipts, but that's quite a stack you'd have to go through. Can't you get a list of kids through the high school?"

"You know that's not what we mean."

The younger of the two detectives took Maury up on his offer and sat down. He scanned the row of suede jackets, the shiny paisley shirts and the chunky-heeled shoes. He leaned forward. "Mr. Kaplan, we want a list of every pot-toking, hash-head, acid-head, speed freak, coke-snorting, pop-eyed junkie you supply."

I could see Maury's face through the beads. Until the final few words he hadn't flinched. It was the speed freak, coke-snorting, pop-eyed junkie references that got him mad.

"Hey, wait a minute. There are some things I don't sell."

Which was very true. There were no junkies in Pike Creek, and if Maury was responsible for anything, he could take credit for this fact. Maury Kaplan had been the first to make many aspects of underground culture accessible. This meant, for my generation, he'd brought cool to Pike Creek. But with or without him it would have arrived at some point, so it could hardly be said he was singularly responsible. What he was responsible for, for all of us who admired him, was fostering a sort of self-respect.

The men were silent for a moment before the subject was abruptly changed. "Tell us, Mr. Kaplan, what brought you to Pike Creek and how long have you owned this store?"

"I thought I already told you guys that stuff."

It didn't seem to matter that he had already told his story; it was apparent they wanted to hear it again.

I knew the story well myself.

Before coming to Pike Creek, Maury had owned a music store in his native Detroit. He sold records—rhythm and blues made up most of his stock. Six months before President Nixon sent troops into Cambodia and the National Guard shot four students at Kent State University, Maury received his draft notice. He and his partner immediately made the decision to sell. Maury moved north to Canada. He'd first spent a bit of time on the West Coast, where he had met people in the same situation and become active in the anti-war crusade.

"But most of all, I wanted to keep a low profile. I didn't come to this country to cause trouble. All I ever wanted to do was to blend in." He put a question to the detectives. "With the FBI on your tail and the possibility of spending the next twenty-five years in prison, wouldn't you?"

The officers left his question unanswered. Constable Wagner told him to go on.

He was driving to Wasaga Beach one Sunday when he stopped in Pike Creek. He liked the open spaces, the rolling hills and the town's proximity to larger cities. The Dairy Bar was jammed with local kids the day he passed through, and after touring around he saw an opportunity to open a hip and trendy store. With all the young people, it was something the small town seemed to lack. Maury invested what money he had left from selling his previous business. He had been operating the store just over a year.

"And your former partner? Your other friends?"

The detective was referring to Maury's American buddies who had taken up residence in other parts of the province and dropped in on him once in awhile.

Patiently, he told them where each of his friends ended up and how they were employed. One had a teaching job in a high school, one was a journalist, and his former partner was in Montreal working on a master's degree in fine arts. Joey Schuster, who was a childhood buddy and grew up in the same area of Birmingham, was now working as an electrician in Mississauga. And not one, he adamantly insisted, was a murderer, which of course was why they were struggling to build lives north of the border rather than be sent to Vietnam.

"And your wife?" the detective who was still standing asked.

"Ex-wife," Maury corrected.

"Where is she?"

Maury tugged at his beard. He shrugged. "You know, I haven't a clue." He then went on to describe his marriage as a brief and crazy thing that happened in '68. He laughed as he told the story. He'd met his wife on a Friday evening at an outdoor rock concert. Saturday morning as they stood in the food line they were planning their wedding; they would exchange daisy chains and they would quote from *The Little Prince*.

On Sunday, with buttercups laced through their hair, they were married by a lawyer who happened to be standing behind them in line. Two weeks later, lying in bed after waking early in the morning, Maury realized the lines he'd read from *The Little Prince* made no sense. At least not in the context of their marriage. Thankfully, his wife did not need to be convinced how ludicrous the whole thing was. They parted amiably and went their separate ways.

"Look," Maury finished, "what is all of this about? Am I a suspect in the murder?"

The detectives glanced at one another. Finally, the one sitting down stood up. "No, you're not. But another girl has gone missing. She was last seen outside of Caledon two days ago. We're checking all angles. Thanks for your time."

They left without getting their list.

THE MISSING GIRL WAS seventeen-year-old Fiona Young. She was last seen riding her bicycle along the highway ten miles west of

Pike Creek near Caledon as she returned home from the stable where she had spent the afternoon riding and grooming her horse. The bicycle was found in a farmer's field near a water trough. Fiona's purse lay nearby, where it had been crushed by cattle as they came to drink from the trough. But it was not crushed so much that detectives missed the small envelope of powder in her change purse. It had once been a tablet of LSD. This was no doubt the reason detectives first targeted Maury as they searched for a connection between the two disappearances and the two towns.

It was probably understandable that investigators would think her abduction could somehow be related to the drug, but Fiona's best friend was quoted in the *Pike Creek Banner* as saying that it wasn't connected in any way. She and Fiona had been given the drugs by a mutual friend at a dance the previous weekend. Fiona had been too uncertain to take it. She had not known what to do with it, and so there it was for her parents to wonder about anyway.

Hetty believed Fiona's friend's story, although Megan didn't. "She's covering. What else is she going to say?"

"You mean the way you tell your mom you smell like smoke because you've been standing in the smoking area at school? Like your mom believes it."

Megan ignored her.

"Besides, why would she cover it if it could lead to the murderer? That hardly makes any sense."

"They don't even know if she's been murdered," I reminded them. "There's no body, remember?"

"Emma," said Hetty, "there isn't a body yet, but I think we all know how this is going to end."

Hetty was right and I had no reply.

That evening the three of us sat in Megan's living room, where we watched Mr. and Mrs. Young appear on TV. They were appealing for someone—anyone who might have seen Fiona—to step forward. This was followed by a film clip of searchers fanning out over the fields surrounding their home.

A week later, Fiona had still not been found despite search efforts centering on the fields, the roadsides and particularly on the farmers' outbuildings in the area.

One afternoon I spotted my father returning from the direction of the duck house. I knew he had been down there earlier in the day and I wondered why he had gone down a second time. There was a small sense of relief in his voice when he spoke to me next, and it occurred to me that he had not been to the duck house at all. He had been checking out the area where the Hippie House had once stood.

Like Katie, Fiona Young had just disappeared. But unlike when Katie disappeared, there was little talk of her running away. We obviously didn't know her, but nobody talked of hidden personality quirks or questionable activities, despite the drug found in her purse. Instead we braced for another body to be found.

9

A T THE END OF MARCH there seemed to be no happy news in the world. On March 29, Charles Manson and three of his "family" were sentenced to death for the murders of actress Sharon Tate and several others. On the same day, Lieutenant William Calley was found guilty of the massacre of twenty Vietnamese civilians at My Lai. The pictures of children starving in Biafra broke our hearts, and Bangladeshi civilians, under attack by Pakistani troops, streamed by the thousands toward the Indian border.

And three weeks after she disappeared, Fiona Young's body was found.

She was found in a drainpipe by Boy Scouts on a scavenger hunt. It was a large drainpipe with room enough for a child to stand up. It connected the road ditches at the end of a lane leading to a rural community hall about two miles from where Fiona's purse had been found. A chill spread through me when I read about it. What a horrible place to be left until somebody found you. Especially at that time of year with the snow melting and the water running through it, with all the muck and animal waste and winter debris winding its way to the sewer. I only hoped she wasn't lying face down in it, in which case her eyes and mouth would be filled with mud—a suffocating and almost unbearable image for me to entertain.

I wondered how the twelve-year-old boys who discovered Fiona's body were coping. Boy Scouts, like Eric had once been. In a race against other members of their scout pack they'd set out to search the park, fields and ditches for perhaps a duck feather or a rusty nail. Maybe it was a pine cone they were after, or a stone of a specific diameter, when they stumbled into the drainpipe. Did they trip over her? Or did they stop and stare, unable to speak as Eric had been unable to speak after discovering Katie, wondering if they could believe their eyes?

Fiona had been strangled in much the same way as Katie, although the newspaper article didn't say what with. Her hands had been bound behind her back before she was killed—the work of a wimpy, spineless coward, Megan and I agreed. Her murder caused a sudden influx of detectives into Pike Creek once again. My father said they were likely looking for similarities. It could not have been their hair color; Katie's hair was dark and straight, and Fiona's was curly and blond. It also could not have been their size because Katie was petite and Fiona was big boned. They must have been looking for something less apparent, perhaps something cryptic that connected the two girls. It could have been the friends they had, but more likely, Eric told me, it was something taken or left behind.

On a Sunday afternoon, Detective Mather showed up at Ruddy Duck Farm. He took another walk around the area of the Hippie House, through the woods and up and down the ditches on both sides of the road. He wandered down the lane between the barn and the workshop, leaned against his car, lit a cigarette, and smoked and thought. After a while, Dad invited him into the house for a cup of tea. At first he declined, but finally he tore his gaze from the treetops that rose from the woods where the

Hippie House had once stood, stamped out his cigarette and followed Dad into the house.

I remembered him from a few months earlier when he had
questioned my brother. We had been so thankful when he'd
arrived at the farm and taken control, particularly at a time
when my father was not able to tell us things would be alright
and assure us that this was a normal blip in life. I recalled Detective Mather being forthright in his questions, concerned and
confident. I remembered his shadow, how when he'd stood up
and put on his coat it had filled most of the wall. He'd left us
believing that Katie's murderer would be found in a matter of
days. But on this day in April it was apparent the long weeks of
work and frustration were beginning to erode that confidence. I
could see this in the way he leaned forward hopefully when he
asked a question. And in the dark shadows that had developed
beneath his eyes.

"These guys are our worst nightmare," he told my father. "They
just get the urge or they blow a fuse and we can't predict them.
What happens is they get bolder each time."

He was telling us they were not even close to catching the
murderer. He was telling us it would happen again, and maybe
again after that. It would happen until whoever did it was so
certain he was invincible that he made a mistake big enough to
get caught.

"Oh my gosh," my mother lamented once he had left. "I can't
believe this. We're living a nightmare. Emma, you're going to stay
in this house until this crazy person is behind bars. Or electrocuted
or hung—whatever they do, it will be too good for him!"

"But Mom what about school?"

Dad intervened on my behalf. "Clare, you know that's not
practical."

Of course I went to school, but again, I was not to leave the
house without a bodyguard. And because Halley was so friendly,

she didn't count. The rules that had relaxed a little over the five months since Katie's death were reestablished. It was the same in every house; no girl or woman would walk alone. No girl or woman would drive down a country road to visit her neighbor, at least not without a couple of large dogs.

Once the news of Fiona's murder reached Mr. DeSousa, he returned home and stayed for two weeks. When he left for Vancouver, Ruby's brother came to stay at the castle. Buddy Garland—or Uncle Bud as he had us call him—was living in a motel at the time. He had recently separated from his wife. Ruby explained to Hetty and me that the separation was the result of some communication issues that the couple needed to resolve. Whatever the reason, the stress of the separation had proved too much for Bud and he had also taken a leave of absence from work. He was able to move in immediately. This put Mr. DeSousa's mind at ease. He knew how capable his family was, but somewhere out there was a monster, and he did not want to leave them on their own.

The snow was now melting in the open fields and the ice was creeping back from the edge of the pond. The cattle were almost done calving, and twice that week, large flocks of geese had passed overhead. The long winter was drawing to an end. It was time to shed our winter boots and for the buoyancy to return to our step. But it didn't happen that year. There were too many restraints on our movements. We were too frightened to stray from what had become routine. The mood in town was subdued and the conversations that had just begun to drift away from murder returned to it.

Yet a stranger who wandered into Pike Creek might think it was a vibrant little town. The population had boomed with all the plainclothes policemen standing on street corners, straining for any scrap of information, waiting for hours hoping the killer might sit down at their table and brag a little about what he'd done. One of the most likely places for this to happen, aside from the Dairy Bar, was the local pool hall.

Blane's Pool Hall was on the main street of Pike Creek, tucked in between the Army Surplus Store and General Seed. I had never been inside it. I was underage, of course, but aside from that, there was nothing appealing about it. The windows were greasy and yellow with smoke, and if the door was left open the smell of stale beer and sweaty men wafted into the street.

The pool hall was the only drinking establishment serving a large rural area, and judging by the number of bodies visible through the window, there was no shortage of thirsty farmers around. Sportsmen would drop in on their way north, or bikers on their way to the beach or a rally. There was also the parade of surveyors and highway road crews who needed a place to unwind.

The younger men who frequented the pool hall, the James Dean wanna-bes, often stood on the sidewalk outside the door. Leaning with one foot up against the brick wall, they would comb their hair, loudly comment on the pedestrian traffic and whistle at passing girls. Cars, money and women dominated their conversations. But for all their talk, the Rosses and Lyles of Pike Creek never went anywhere.

On occasion a fight would break out on the sidewalk. Mr. Blane was a heavy, gray-haired man who had owned the pool hall for more than thirty years. In that time he'd seen many tempers lost, and he knew the motivations and weaknesses that ended in swinging fists. He was also a busy man. He had a business to run and as he was no longer young, his patience was leaving him. From experience, Ross and his boys had learned the limits of his tolerance. They also knew they would have no place to go if banished from the pool hall. Mr. Blane had only to step out onto the sidewalk to break up their fights.

I didn't understand the attraction of hanging around the pool hall. It seemed like such an idle thing to do. But then I didn't understand much about the group of guys who hung around on the sidewalk except that most of them had dropped out of school.

I knew my brother and his friends were very different sorts of people. "Long-haired hippie freaks" the pool hall regulars called after Eric and Jimmy when they passed them on the sidewalk. Eric and Jimmy in turn called them "greasy-haired punks." A lot of it was in the image. But there was an avid interest in knives, brass knuckles and all things leaning toward physical violence that really separated Ross and his friends from the boys I knew. Switchblades looked good in a boot, and chains could be used for more than just propelling bicycles. It seemed to be an image based on muscle, threats and retaliation, and it had always frightened me.

Eric had already told me that in bigger places there were tougher punks than our own homegrown Ross and Lyle. Getting drunk and smashing up playground equipment was kid stuff. There were guys with serious issues. Hoods you wouldn't want to turn your back on, who stayed alive at some unlucky sucker's expense.

The detectives confirmed what my brother said was true. I knew they had spent a few minutes interviewing the pool hall regulars after Katie's murder, but now they virtually ignored them. Which made me wonder—if Ross and Lyle were the most dangerous Pike Creek had to offer, yet they were of no interest to the detectives, what warped sort of animal were they looking for?

DESPITE HAVING TO PLAN our every move and the constant presence of the police, we tried to continue on with our lives. But fear does nasty things to people. At its most rudimentary it's a life-preserving response. In nature there are two options: to flee or to fight back. We could not flee from Pike Creek, and even if we could, we did not know who or what we were running from.

Feeling powerless to fight back, the entire town was left in a heightened state of terror.

After news of a second murder, doctors heard more than the normal number of complaints; unexplained illnesses—headaches and stomach aches—and absences from school rose. People developed phobias to things that didn't exist. Megan said that every time she walked somewhere she heard footsteps behind her. She was getting a stiff neck from turning suddenly to check it out. Hetty was now in the habit of closing every blind in the castle as soon as dusk hit. It had become a ritual because the thought that someone was peering in on them just creeped her out.

Those already predisposed to a general fear of life were paralyzed completely. Doug McCrae's older sister was a timid person and had been a good friend of Katie's. After Fiona's death, she and her month-old baby moved back in with Doug's family. Her husband worked out of town for days at a time and she was too frightened to leave the house and do the normal things a person does. She had trouble dragging herself out of bed, so she lay around day after day, lamenting the fact that her baby had been born into a world filled with violence and dread.

I became jealous of Eric, who went about his business freely. He drove himself to band practice. They were practicing in Jimmy's garage in town now. And he walked where he wanted to go after school. Eric and his friends continued to drive down to Brampton to see movies that wouldn't make it to Pike Creek for months, if at all. After returning one night he stopped by my room to tell me about a new restaurant they had gone to after the movie.

"For less than a dollar you can get a hamburger, fries and a pop. And—"

Envy and cabin fever and I don't know what else suddenly overwhelmed me. Not to mention I stabbed myself with a needle at the exact same time. "You are so damn lucky you weren't born a girl!" I bellowed before he'd had a chance to finish his sentence.

Standing in the doorway, he went silent for a moment. I sucked my finger while he looked at me like I was a spoiled kid who had spoken out of turn. He finished what he'd been telling me. "Like I was saying. You can get all that and you still get change."

I felt stupid. And without even knowing how close I'd been to falling apart, I started to whimper. "It's not fair. I haven't been to a movie without you or Dad or Uncle Pat holding my hand in a month. I'm going to live and die in this place. I'm never going to get to go anywhere good again."

"Want to know something?"

"Not really."

"Yesterday I was walking through the parking lot at the IGA and I saw Mrs. Gillespie had her arms full of groceries. So like the nice guy that I am, I stopped and asked if I could open her car door."

"So? What's that got to do with anything?"

"You know what she said? She told me she could do it herself. Mrs. Gillespie," he repeated in amazement. "The old bag who would normally yell at me and I'd hear about it from Dad if I didn't offer to help. And you know what else? If I hold a door for a girl at school, you'd think it was an insult. Malcolm picked up a book for Angie Lucas—she dropped it in the hall the other day—and she didn't even say thanks. I saw it. She gave him a look like he'd stolen it from her, grabbed it and walked the other way. There's one creep out there and all of a sudden we're all guilty. It's a great big drag for us too."

"Us," meant the entire male population. It had not even occurred to me how it affected them.

I didn't tell Eric, but in a way I could relate to Mrs. Gillespie being suspicious. Anyone could be the killer, and anything could point to the murders if you were creative enough. Particularly when nothing was for sure.

Like the glove Uncle Pat found a few days later in his field.

It had always strained my imagination to think of Mom and my Uncle Pat growing up in the same household. This was because my mother was always so fastidious and conscious of proper etiquette. That's not to say that my uncle didn't have manners, or that he wasn't particular in his own way, but he loved being a farmer and working outside. I thought he looked as regal as any king, perched on his Massey Ferguson, sculpting Zen-like patterns in the brown soil every spring. Uncle Pat knew every inch of his land: the low swampy parts, the rocks and stumps he had to steer around and what crops grew best where. He never looked so happy as when he was mucking around the barnyard in his big rubber boots, ensuring that his cattle were healthy and well-fed. I always thought the winter months, when he was confined indoors, must have been particularly difficult for him.

At the first sign of spring we would see Uncle Pat tramping across his fields, checking what the winter had left behind. It was on a day like this, when the crocuses were just beginning to show and the awakening grass sweetened the air, that he set out across what had been a potato field the previous year. He wasn't too sure he would grow potatoes again. Last year's crop had been fine, but several farmers in neighboring counties had been hit with blight and he didn't know that he would take the chance.

The soil was particularly hilly, hoed up for potatoes and now still partially frozen so there were many large clumps. He had to watch where he was walking so that he didn't stumble, lose his balance and go over on an ankle. If it wasn't for the fact that he was so intent on watching his step, he might never have seen the glove. It was a man's glove lying in a small gully between mounds of soil. It was sodden and badly stained. He turned it over with his foot and was about to pick it up when he noticed a long slash across the width of the palm. He called Detective Mather instead.

Uncle Pat stood guard over the glove. He would not let Megan or Carl onto the field while he waited for the police to arrive. I stood next to my cousins, leaning against the fence. My uncle was a solitary figure standing a quarter of a mile away in the wide expanse of muddy brown field.

"Why won't he let you go out there?" I asked.

"I don't know. I guess he thinks I'd freak out if I saw it, or maybe that Carl would wreck it somehow."

I didn't actually see the glove. I got tired of standing there waiting for the detectives and I went back to the house for lunch. According to Megan, a small clutch of officers descended on it and it was whisked away in a plastic bag. She was only able to catch a glimpse of it as it went by. But what surprised her was that it did not seem all that big. She said she didn't know why, but as she stood at the edge of the field watching her dad stand over it, she thought it must have been huge. Like something a lion tamer would wear, or someone who trained guard dogs. Nevertheless, despite its being so small, it still gave her the creeps. She worried that the killer might remember he'd forgotten a piece of his property and that he might want to get it back. My uncle tried to reassure her that this probably wouldn't happen, that it was actually a good thing the glove was found. It might very well be the piece of evidence the police needed to solve the crime.

We could only guess how the glove ended up in the middle of the potato field. The most likely theory was that it had been picked up and dropped by the snowmobile when Carl was out jumping snowdrifts. Police officers began searching for its mate. If the killer dropped one glove, it was quite possible that he had dropped both.

Megan didn't put it into words, but I knew she also felt a little like we had when Katie's body was found on our property. Violated. Soiled, cheated and angry.

"What did it look like?" Hetty asked.

Megan shrugged. "Like a normal winter glove. Like the kind a normal person would wear."

"What was it made of?"

"Leather, I guess."

"What color was it?"

"Black."

"Ah-hah," Hetty and I both said.

"What do you mean, ah-hah? That's a very normal color for a glove. Anyway, at least I think it was black. I only saw it quickly through the plastic and it was all muddy and stained."

"Have they found the other one yet?"

No, despite a thorough search of the woods, fields and ditches the second glove had not been found. I became convinced that I would be the one to find it, that I'd open my closet door and it would fall from the shelf into my face. That I would fold my hands beneath my pillow at night and find it lying there. One night I woke up suddenly from a dream. In the dream a bloody glove had been flapping over my head. Listening to the night sounds, I realized the toilet had just been flushed. I heard my father's footsteps in the hall and the scrape of the tennis racket as he lay it back down on the hardwood next to his bed.

We began to wonder what else the killer had left behind. What ghosts of Katie's murder still lurked in the shadows of our farm?

I'm not sure if we were more relieved or disappointed when tests on the glove came back and Detective Mather dropped by to deliver the results. The glove was stained with animal blood. Then, when Mr. Fraser came forward after reading a description of it in the *Pike Creek Banner*, the mystery was solved. He had been so busy with calving, as well as looking into the prospect of mining gold in Costa Rica, that he'd fallen behind on his reading and had just learned of Uncle Pat's find. He'd immediately recognized the three-snap adjustable strap and the slash in the palm. He'd torn it when repairing the barbed wire fencing. When he thought about it, the last time he remembered wearing the glove was a month earlier. He'd been in the back field, which ran parallel to my uncle's property—it was there, behind a stand of alder, that he'd buried a stillborn calf.

10

MEGAN'S SIXTEENTH BIRTHDAY fell smack in the middle of these feelings of unease and suspicion. Megan felt she was ripped off and that nobody cared. The truth was, it would have been difficult to get too excited about anything short of the police making an arrest. Her birthday also fell in the middle of exam week, which meant that a party couldn't be too distracting. And the day itself was not a good one for her mom and dad. They both had meetings they couldn't miss. Uncle Pat was voting on something important for the school board, and Aunt Alice had to chair the ladies auxiliary that night. Megan couldn't believe they wouldn't skip their meetings to celebrate her birthday on the actual day. Aunt Alice explained that if she expected to be extended the privileges that came with growing up, she would have to accept the drawbacks. At sixteen, she should be old enough to understand that a birthday is just another day. Things had to be accomplished like on all the others. The family would celebrate the following day when nothing was planned.

"So that's it. Nobody cares about me anymore. Their meetings are more important than I am."

"I don't think that's what your mom was getting at. It's just more convenient for her to make a cake and have your birthday tomorrow night."

"What would be more convenient for them is if I'd never been born. This is just lousy. I'm sixteen. Your sixteenth birthday is supposed to be all sugary and pink with guys fawning all over you because they've suddenly realized you're not a kid anymore. Not only do my parents not care, but I'm living in a place where if a guy looks at you, you run the other way."

Considering the general doomsday atmosphere surrounding her sixteenth birthday, I didn't blame her for feeling ripped off.

I arranged a sort of party for her on the day she turned sixteen. We would meet a couple of her friends from school at the Dairy Bar, where we would give her our gifts. With my aunt and uncle busy, we needed a ride into Pike Creek. Dad had loaned his van to Eric for a band practice, so Uncle Bud volunteered for the job. He didn't mind, he'd sighed. He'd just wait around town until we'd finished eating. He assured Mom and Ruby that with all the frightening things that had happened around Pike Creek he'd keep a close eye on us girls.

I got a strange phone call from Hetty just before she and Uncle Bud left the castle to pick me up. "If he cries, Emma, try to pretend you don't notice. Just start talking about the weather or something else."

"Uncle Bud? Why would he cry?"

"It could be any reason. It could be because he discovered a button is missing from his shirt or because his socks don't match. But just ignore it, he'll stop." She hesitated. "Well, at least for a little while."

Uncle Bud was a rumpled man with a stubble of beard, bright watery eyes, and shoulders that slumped in conspicuous defeat. Hetty said he had a great sense of humor when he wasn't crying, and he'd always brought her the most wonderful gifts.

For instance, she had been one of the first kids to have an Easy-Bake Oven. Uncle Bud was a cook and he'd given her one when they'd first come out.

But on Megan's birthday, Uncle Bud had been separated from his wife for exactly twenty-three days. I learned this within thirty seconds of slipping into the backseat of his station wagon next to Megan. His wife's hair, he informed me immediately after Hetty introduced us, was as curly and thick as my own.

I was about to make a joke. To offer his wife my sympathy because I thought my hair was such a curse. But I thought better of it because we had not even started down the lane and Uncle Bud was suddenly weeping. His arms were wrapped around the steering wheel and his head was down. Hetty looked at us in the back and rolled her eyes.

She let several seconds elapse before she said, "Uncle Bud, we should get going now. Megan's friends are going to wonder where we are."

Uncle Bud attempted to pull himself together. "Yes, yes, you're right." He took a deep breath as he let his foot off the brake. "I'm sorry, girls. It's best if you don't talk about my wife. You know we're separated. It's been twenty-three days."

We didn't tell him that it was not us who had brought up his wife.

Of course he talked about his wife the entire trip into Pike Creek. This was intermittent between the buckets of tears he cried. He wasn't absolutely sure why she had asked him to leave the house. He thought they had a good life. They lived in a good neighborhood with their three teenage boys. He thought he had been a good provider. What was this thing about her getting a job? Hadn't he bought Helen the crushed velvet furniture she had wanted? The dishwasher she could roll over to the tap, and when the dishes were done, push back against the wall? And two weeks before she'd asked him to leave they'd finally collected a twelve-place setting of Corel dinnerware. Fifty cents a plate. They had bought it at the grocery store, one piece at a time.

He broke into tears again. It was the dishes. It seemed that every time he opened the cupboard when he was staying in the motel, it had reminded him there were four plates, four cups, four saucers and four bowls.

We invited him to have dinner with us, but Uncle Bud wanted to remain in the car. In his own words, he told us that he had not come to crash our party and that we should just go ahead and have a good time. We were not to give him a second thought.

"Okay," Hetty agreed more quickly than I thought she should have. "If you insist."

From the table in the restaurant we could see him shift between two positions. He would either be staring straight ahead, all mopey-faced with his lower lip extended and eyes drooping, or his head would be down while his shoulders shook with grief. There were five of us at our table: Megan, Hetty and me and Megan's friends Holly and Rose.

"It's pathetic," Hetty told us. "He can't even go ten minutes without breaking into tears."

"I think it's rather sad," Rose decided. "To be rendered help-less by love. To be reduced to a quivering jellyfish. It's romantic, don't you think?"

We all looked out at Uncle Bud again. He was in shoulder-shaking mode. I thought Hetty was a little harsh, but I also didn't see a lot of romance in the sight of a puffy-eyed, forty-five-year-old man crying in a station wagon all alone.

"Maybe we should ask him to join us," Holly suggested.

Hetty quickly said no. She'd eaten every meal in the last few days with Uncle Bud bawling across the table from her. She needed a break.

Before our dinner came, Megan opened her gifts. I gave her the pair of plum-colored elephant pants I had seen her looking at in Maury's store. Holly and Hetty gave her the same album, Grand Funk Railroad. She said that was okay, she'd save the extra for someone else's birthday. Rose gave her three differently colored crocheted bun holders for when her hair was in a granny knot. We all looked out at Uncle Bud again. He was just pulling a large handkerchief from his pocket. He took off his glasses and wiped his eyes. He blew his nose hard and for a moment it looked as though he might have stopped crying.

"Maybe that's it," Megan said.

"Oh no," Hetty assured her.

And within a few seconds, Uncle Bud began crying again.

"This is ridiculous." Megan started to get up from the table. "I can't stand him sitting out there crying while I'm trying to have a birthday in here. I'm going to ask him to come in."

Hetty quickly stood up to block her from leaving. Megan sat down again. Mr. Gillespie brought our chicken in a basket. We began to eat, forgetting all about Uncle Bud for the next little while. We didn't think about him until he was guided roughly through the door with a detective flanking him on either side. He looked absolutely mortified.

"Do you young ladies know this man?" one of them asked.

"Uncle Bud!" Hetty jumped up from her seat. "Yes, that's Uncle Bud," she said to the officer who had asked the question. "He drove us here. He's watching out for us tonight."

The detectives appeared surprised.

"I told you," Uncle Bud muttered, pulling his arm free from one of the officers' grip.

The other officer let go of his arm and they both stepped aside.

"Our apologies, sir," the same one who had spoken said. "But considering what's gone on in the last few months, it's best if you try not to look like you're sitting in a car, spying on young girls."

Poor Uncle Bud. It only added insult to injury. Hetty relented and we asked him to sit down. We piled all the chicken and potato salad we hadn't eaten yet onto a plate and passed it down his way. While he ate, Megan showed him the Grand Funk albums, the plum-colored elephant pants and the crocheted bun nets from Rose.

FINALLY, IN THE THIRD WEEK of April, we had something to look forward to. A school dance. Too many things had already been cancelled and our social lives had become stifled and very small. The dance was supposed to have followed a Miles for Million walk-a-thon. Student council had planned the walk to raise money in aid of the starving children in Third World countries. But after Fiona's body was found, parents and teachers cancelled the walk to Shelburne. It was the idea of a large part of the high school population spread fifteen miles along the rural highway that panicked them. The dance, however, would be allowed to go ahead.

This was a chance for Megan to finally wear her jumpsuit. It was a chance to just hang around and be together. We always had live bands at school dances, and The Rectifiers were booked to play that night.

Before the band had played even a note, the dark gym was bulging with people wanting more than anything to have a good time. Eric was on stage adjusting his amplifier and testing the microphone. Jimmy was tuning his guitar. Miles was standing in front of the stage talking with friends. Malcolm didn't seem to be around.

I knew Eric was beginning to seriously worry about Malcolm. Over the last couple of months he'd become progressively less dependable. He didn't show up when he said he would, and although he hadn't dropped out of school, if he didn't go a little more often he wasn't going to graduate in June. His behavior suggested that he was doing a lot of drugs, heavy stuff, acid and mescaline. But what was most disturbing to his friends was the fact that he was doing them by himself. Nobody knew where he was getting them. If they did, they would have found a way to cut him off.

Eric didn't usually tell me much about his personal life, or at least the parts he thought it best I didn't know. But he was truly concerned about Malcolm. I may have learned some of what I did because in trying to make sense of Malcolm's behavior, Eric was thinking out loud.

A month before the dance, Malcolm's friends were convinced he'd completely flipped out when he holed up in a storage closet beneath a stairwell at school. Until a janitor discovered the heap of butts behind the door, it had been a favorite spot to have a smoke when it was too cold to go outside.

It was the teachers, Malcolm had told Eric and Jimmy when they finally tracked him to the closet. Mr. Wellington, the drama teacher, and Mrs. Irwin, who taught him math. He'd seen them discussing him at a distance in the smoking area during lunch hour. Mr. Wellington had raised a hand as if to scratch his forehead—a signal that they were onto him—and then had suddenly left. Malcolm knew it was only to get reinforcements. He couldn't leave the school in case Mr. Wellington already had it surrounded. He planned to wait it out in the closet while he considered his escape.

Eric had to get Miles out of class to talk some sense into Malcolm and take him home.

But Miles didn't know what to do himself anymore. Things weren't any less strange at home. Malcolm had stopped eating with the family at the table, preferring to eat in his room alone. He'd been going out at strange hours—often not leaving until after midnight and sometimes not coming home until six in the morning. Miles had no idea where he went or what he was doing.

A few nights before Malcolm hid in the storage closet, Miles had heard his brother in his bedroom arguing so loudly he thought his father must have gone in and confronted him. Miles opened the door. Malcolm was standing on his bed, red in the face and furiously shaking a fist. He was accusing the poster of Alice Cooper on his wall of stealing a twenty-dollar bill.

Half an hour after the band was to begin, Malcolm still hadn't shown up. People on the floor began to get restless. Miles left for a while, probably to make a few phone calls and see if he could track down his brother. He obviously wasn't successful because he returned to the stage, shrugged when Eric and Jimmy questioned him, and sat down at his drums. Jimmy filled in the vocals when the three band members started without Malcolm, who normally sang and played rhythm guitar.

The dance was a tame affair. Everyone was on their best behavior; we were so thankful to do something other than sit at home. Megan was dancing, and Hetty and I were standing watching the band when I felt a tap on my shoulder. It was Donny Russell.

I had missed talking to Donny since *Oliver!* was over. I had seen him, but it was always from a distance. We were never close enough to talk. I often wondered how he was doing and what he thought of Fiona being murdered. I had wondered if it made him feel any better, which sounds callous, but I thought that then he would know his family wasn't alone or that Katie wasn't alone in the horrible thing that had happened to her.

After he tapped me on the shoulder, it took me a few seconds to recognize him. He'd had his hair cut very short, which was a bit of a shock because it was not the fashion at the time. Except perhaps among prison inmates and military men.

"Hey," he said.

"Hey." I couldn't help it—it was impossible not to comment. I tapped my head. "Your hair. I almost didn't recognize you."

"Yeah." He pulled a hand across the bristles. "Something different."

I was curious. "Why'd you do it?"

He shook his head like he couldn't hear me. Taking my hand, he led me through the crowd into the hallway. The music faded behind us and human voices took on a much larger sound.

"What did you say?"

"I just wondered why you cut it."

Donny shrugged. "It just seemed like the right thing to do at the time."

There was something puzzling in his smile, and I wondered if it had been his choice to cut it so short or if it had just seemed the right thing to do in a fit of anger or grief.

"Listen, I thought maybe you'd like to go to the cafeteria and get something to eat."

I said that I would.

Donny and I didn't talk about Katie or Fiona that night, but we did spend the rest of the dance together. When The Rectifiers quit and Eric and his friends were packing up their equipment, he walked me out to the parking lot where Hetty and Megan were already waiting in the station wagon with Uncle Bud.

ERIC GOT A CALL FROM MILES early the next morning. We were all in the kitchen eating breakfast when he answered the phone. After saying hello, he immediately asked what was up with Malcolm. This was followed by a long period of silence as he listened to the answer. His face drooped visibly and although he opened his mouth to speak, the words never left his lips.

"There's no way" was his only comment after listening for several minutes. "There's no way. It's impossible," he repeatedly disagreed.

Finally he hung up. His gaze wandered over to where Mom, Dad and I sat eating our cereal. He continued to look at us like we didn't exist.

"What is it?" my father asked.

"Malcolm. He's in the hospital. There's a police guard standing outside his door. He's been arrested."

"For what?!" Mom summed up our surprise.

Eric paused to take a breath. "For killing Katie Russell."

We stared at him in amazement, although I don't think anyone was quite as amazed at the news as my brother was.

"It's impossible," he repeated again. He seemed to be straining every muscle in his body to remain in control.

Dad attempted to console him, trying to convince Eric that it was obviously a mistake and they would get to the bottom of it. A hoax. It could be that someone's joke got out of hand. Such things certainly happened.

Eric shook his head in a way that told us this was not the case. He began to pace back and forth as he tried to hold himself together. I remember thinking how our large kitchen suddenly did not seem nearly large enough to accommodate his nervous steps.

It was Maury who had spotted Malcolm wandering down the middle of the street just before nine o'clock the night before. He was about to close the store when he heard car horns blaring. He glanced out the window to see a figure weaving down the center line of the road. A small wave of traffic had backed up. Recognizing it was Malcolm and that he was wearing jeans but no shirt, Maury grabbed his jacket and hurried outside. He hailed Malcolm from the side of the road but was ignored. Maury ran into the street, draped the jacket around Malcolm's shoulders, steered him around the cars, and guided him into the store. He tried to get him to sit down, to warm up and calm down. But he wouldn't sit down. He was shaking, confused and disoriented. Maury assumed that Malcolm was strung out on something.

Maury attempted to talk him back to reality. He told him he'd seen the dance posted and asked Malcolm why he wasn't at the school. Malcolm didn't answer but only muttered to himself.

From what Maury could understand, he said that everyone knew he'd done it now. He didn't think they'd figure it out but they did. To be honest, he had to give them credit. He didn't think they were that smart, but he now heard them talking about it everywhere he went. Especially at school. The teachers. Mr. Wellington had figured it out. And the girls in the hall. They would warn each other and walk the other way as soon as they saw him coming.

Maury asked what he was talking about. What were the girls at school warning each other about?

In answer to Maury's questions, Malcolm stopped talking. He turned suddenly, looking at Maury with surprise, as if until then he'd been unaware of his presence in the room. He told him he must be the only one in town who didn't know. They didn't go near him because he was a murderer. He killed Katie Russell. Hadn't Maury heard? He'd strangled her with a guitar string at Jenkins' farm.

When Eric finished telling us this amazing story, he dropped into a chair and ran a hand through his hair. We sat in disbelief, trying to digest what he had told us.

"This is such a drag!" Eric was on his feet again. "I can't believe it! My own friend. Why would he do it? It's so sick!"

Perhaps because Eric was so upset, I was able to keep my own emotions under control. But I do remember thinking it was very difficult to believe. It was just too bizarre that a friend of my brother could do something so violent and continue to live among us like he'd done nothing at all.

"But I saw her. Malcolm wouldn't do that. Malcolm—he couldn't do that. I know him. He hardly ever even gets mad."

"Alright, son." Dad had an arm around Eric. "Get your coat. I'll take you into town and we'll see what's going on."

Eric spent the day with Jimmy at his house in Pike Creek, where they waited for word from Miles, who was at the hospital with his parents. By late afternoon, according to the doctor who admitted him, Malcolm's condition had not improved. He was becoming increasingly disoriented. It wasn't something he had meant to happen, Malcolm had told Miles, his parents and Detective Mather earlier in the day. The murder that is. He didn't plan it. It's just that he happened to see Katie when he was driving home.

When Detective Mather asked him where he was driving home from on November 9, Malcolm answered, "From Jimmy's. We'd been working out some chords. You know, for some songs."

"What were you driving?"

"I was driving my van."

When Mr. Fritz pointed out that Malcolm didn't own a van, Malcolm didn't reply. Instead he continued with his story. It was shortly after ten o'clock, maybe closer to ten thirty, when he stopped and picked Katie up. It was dark, of course, and she was on her way home from work.

"Do you remember why you stopped?" asked Detective Mather.

"No, I don't."

"But she got in the van willingly?"

"Yeah, she did."

"She didn't struggle?"

"No, she didn't struggle. I didn't have to drag her in or anything like that. I didn't even get out of the van."

"She just opened the door freely and got in?"

"Yeah. We talked for a minute and that's what she did. Ask Mr. Gillespie."

"Mr. Gillespie was there?"

"Well, yeah. He was standing across the street. By the arena next to the streetlamp. He watched her get in and he stood there watching us drive away."

"You saw him watching you?"

"Yeah."

"In the rear viewmirror as you drove away?"

"Yeah, I guess."

Miles told Eric that Malcolm's story rapidly disintegrated after that. He had no recollection of his conversation with Katie or why he drove out to the Hippie House. He described where they had parked and the path they had walked along to reach it, but he spoke as if it had happened in the summer. He recalled the night sounds of Fiddlehead Creek and the wild chirping of crickets and bullfrogs that had drifted to their ears.

According to Miles, Malcolm then stopped talking entirely. After he described their walk to the Hippie House, his eyes remained fixed on the floor. Detective Mather attempted to prompt him into speaking again. "Malcolm, when did you rip the curtain off the window facing the road?"

Malcolm looked up at the detective and then over to Miles. "Why would I do that?"

"Well, it was a black night. You would have needed the light of the moon to see what you were doing."

"No," Malcolm answered, "I didn't need a light. I didn't need any kind of light. I knew that place like the back of my hand."

Miles told Eric that his brother then withdrew completely. Despite the detective's questioning, he could not, or would not, tell them what prompted the killing or when or how it had occurred.

11

Two days after he was hospitalized, Malcolm was moved from Pike Creek to Toronto, where he underwent a psychiatric evaluation. He was still confused, paranoid and withdrawn. This was despite having been in the hospital where he had no access to street drugs. Some of his friends figured he was suffering one long flashback or that he had taken hallucinogens one too many times and it was now the permanent state of his brain.

Eric didn't know what to think, but he was quick to come to Malcolm's defense. It upset him that many people had already convicted Malcolm. Yes, Malcolm had said that he killed Katie, but so far none of the circumstantial evidence added up. He said he picked her up at ten thirty, yet both his mother and younger sister recalled he was home by eleven o'clock that night. They did not remember him looking the least bit disheveled, like he'd been involved in a struggle or anything like that. And he was in a good mood they insisted. The three of them had watched a movie together and he had laughed at all the right parts.

There was also the question of the van. No one in the Fritz family owned anything that even remotely fit the vehicle's description.

And Malcolm could still not recall details of the actual killing. Detective Mather had questioned him several more times.

"There are certain things," he told Eric, Miles and me at the farm, "that we don't tell the public. These are details about the crime or the crime scene that only the killer would know. Problems he might have run into. How he dealt with them. Under questioning, these details might come out. Malcolm has not alluded to any of them. What he tells us he could have read in any newspaper."

"You don't think he did it?" Miles anxiously asked.

"We still haven't ruled it out, but no, not from what he's told me. And so far we have no physical evidence to suggest that it was him."

"What about Mr. Gillespie? He saw Malcolm drive away with Katie. Did you ask him if what Malcolm said was true?"

The detective nodded. He had spent many hours talking to Mr. Gillespie, everybody knew this. The Dairy Bar had been closed on a day when it was normally open and Mr. Gillespie's car had been parked outside the police station.

"Did he say he saw them?"

"He said he saw the van stop and Katie get in."

"But did he say the driver was Malcolm?"

"Yes," Detective Mather answered. "Yes, he said he was pretty sure it was."

"How could he tell?" asked a frustrated Miles, who sat next to me on the chesterfield. He got to his feet. "How did he know it was Malcolm when it was black out, and why would he suddenly say he saw him when he hadn't said anything before?"

"Miles," the detective said in a calming way, "Mr. Gillespie gave us four possible colors for the van. He listed a number of possible makes. He's not the most reliable source I've come across."

Miles slumped down on the chesterfield again. "Did he say why he was there?"

"Yes. He had met Katie after work and he was walking her home. At least as far as he dared. They were afraid of being seen together. Just before the arena, where the street was well lit, they said goodbye. She had passed the arena and was halfway down the next block when he saw the van pull over."

My brother then asked the question people were asking all over town. "But Miles is right. Why didn't he say anything? Everybody thought old Mrs. Bolton at the nursing home was the last person to see Katie alive. Why didn't Mr. Gillespie set them straight and tell them it was him?"

Detective Mather clasped his hands together. Holding them as if in prayer with his thumbs pressed to his lips, he thought for a minute.

"He was concerned that if people knew, they would think even less of him than they already did. He felt he was already having enough trouble holding his head up after his relationship with Katie became common knowledge. He didn't think it was important enough to bring up."

"How could he have not thought it important?!" Eric exclaimed.

"Because Katie got in the van willingly. He said he just assumed she was getting a ride from a friend. He believed the murder took place after she left whoever was in the van. He didn't think enough of the incident to mention it."

Detective Mather was not making excuses for Mr. Gillespie. He was only telling us what he had been told himself. But his retelling made it clear that he obviously did not think Mr. Gillespie's story was all that credible or that his reasons for keeping what he knew a secret were all that sound.

I arrived home around five o'clock one afternoon. Megan and I had hung around the Dairy Bar before getting a ride home with Carl. Hearing me in the kitchen, my mother called me into the living room where she and my father sat reading. Eric was lying on the chesterfield, trying to teach Halley to retrieve the TV guide. He'd managed to get her to bring it to him, but she refused to let it go. Finally, after bribing her with a potato chip, he was able to pull the soggy magazine from her mouth.

Mom glanced up when I appeared in the doorway. She lay the book she was reading in her lap. She had discovered a new author, Margaret Laurence. No, she did not write mysteries, she'd told me in answer to my question the previous day. I was prompted to ask by the illustration on the cover of *The Fire-Dwellers*. Unaware she'd given up on murder mysteries, I'd been surprised at the painting of a melancholy woman rather than some well-dressed dead body lying in a lavish hall. She'd gone on to explain that it was Laurence's characters she found so absorbing. She just related to them, that was all.

Mom removed her reading glasses. She sat them on her head at the base of her highly teased hair. She did not want me or Megan to go to the Dairy Bar after school anymore. Mr. Gillespie was unstable. "First we learn of his illicit affair, and now we find out that he saw Katie drive off in a van. Regardless of whether it was Malcolm who was driving or not, there's something wrong with the man."

Dad folded the *Pike Creek Banner* and asked me to sit down. He was a little more forgiving than my mother. He tried to explain Mr. Gillespie's behavior. This was mostly, I think, because he seemed to feel he owed us an explanation for everything that went on in our world. But even we knew there were some things that couldn't be explained away. He began by saying that Mr. Gillespie was not thinking straight and therefore he couldn't be held wholly responsible for what he said or did.

"But why is he not thinking straight?" I asked.

"Why?"

"Yeah, why would he be sane and then suddenly go crazy just like that?"

"Well—I guess the reason he went crazy was, well, because his wife is a nag and his marriage had gone bad."

Eric laughed.

Mom gave Dad a look—like he had a lot of nerve blaming his crazy behavior on his wife or his marriage.

And since it was the only explanation he appeared to be able to think of, and it wasn't a very convincing one at that, Dad gave up. "Perhaps your mother is right. You'd better just stay away from the restaurant until this whole thing is cleared up."

Many people felt the same way. While we waited for word of Malcolm's official arrest, Mr. Gillespie lost what little business he had left at the Dairy Bar. This was not much of a crowd, anyway. It had not been a pleasant place to eat in the preceding few weeks. The quality of food had become unpredictable and Mr. Gillespie seemed to have lost the will to clean. The same coffee spills and stuck food lingered on the countertop and booths for days at a time.

He closed down completely and indefinitely when Mr. Russell, shaking with rage and shouting obscenities, stormed into the restaurant one morning shortly after Malcolm's story became known.

Mr. Gillespie tried in vain to calm him down. After all, he told him, they were in this together. Didn't he know that he had loved Katie too?

This comparison—the sheer nerve of Mr. Gillespie to even suggest that they had shared a similar affection for Katie—got Mr. Russell spitting mad. He grabbed a chair and, swinging it above his head, advanced on Mr. Gillespie. Lucky for Mr. Gillespie, both Maury and one of the undercover police officers happened to be picking up coffee at the same time. They managed to disarm Mr. Russell of the chair and wrestle him to the floor, where the police officer handcuffed him.

Mr. Russell was at fault, but considering all he'd been through, the image of him nose to nose with week-old ketchup splatters and squashed fries seemed unfairly undignified.

As a result, Mr. Russell was legally required to stay a minimum distance away from Mr. Gillespie, who, after the assault, willingly confined himself to his apartment above the Dairy Bar. Walking in town we would often see his face behind the lace curtain. He rarely moved but stared pensively through the window onto the street.

"It's spooky," Megan told me as we walked to the library. "The way he's always just sitting there like that."

I agreed that it was very spooky. We changed our route, walking two blocks out of our way so we didn't have to walk by him anymore.

THE AMERICAN ELM TREES that grew along the lane next to the lower pond became infected with Dutch elm disease that spring. Many branches did not bud at all, and those that did drooped, and the leaves that unfurled quickly turned brown. This was a terrible heartache for my father, who adored the forty-foot trees. Not all the branches were sickly, but it was progressing. To stop the disease from spreading to other farms he had no choice but to cut them down.

The scream of the chain saw woke me early one morning. It was not normally a sound I minded hearing from a distance—it only meant that Dad was building or perhaps altering something, creating or repairing. Some part of Ruddy Duck Farm was always being constructed or maintained. But that morning the sound was painful. I did not want to get up and I lay with the pillow over my head. Finally the sound bore deep enough that I realized my father would never leave us on our own to do something as agonizing as this must be for him.

By the time I was dressed and outside, Eric was already helping to cut branches into firewood. There would be far more than we needed to replenish our woodpile. Mr. Fraser was going to take a couple of loads, and Uncle Bud would be by later in the week for the very large pieces of branches and trunks that could burn in the castle's big open fireplace all day.

My job was to load the pieces into the trailer. It had been determined in my absence that I couldn't handle a saw.

Mom was also outside. Dressed to ward off the dirt, dung and dust particles in a ridiculous kerchief, heavy overcoat and rubber boots, she looked more like she'd come outside to transport dangerous goods. It was a little early for her to be turning over the rose garden. I guessed that her reason for being outside was the same as mine: to be near Dad in case it became necessary to offer support.

Both Eric and my father worked quietly, burdened by their separate thoughts. Now and again I noticed Eric frown. I knew he was thinking of Malcolm. He was running through all he knew and trying to make sense of the last few days. Since Malcolm's confession he had become more and more withdrawn, and I'd noticed he also stayed closer to home.

Funny how he could be so focused on what he was thinking yet still manage to harass me. He had already told me to make sure I didn't leave the bark and smaller branches behind because they made good kindling. I'd thanked him for the tip. But now he was telling me how much more efficient my work would be if I carried four logs in my arms in a bundle rather than swinging two at a time.

He was just lucky I felt sorry for him about Malcolm. Otherwise I would have had a lot more to say. "You know," I said, "you're beginning to sound more like Mom every day."

"I heard that," Mom shouted across the lane.

How could she have heard it? The sound of the chain saw was cutting in and out, and her head was all bound up in that kerchief. She looked as airtight as an astronaut.

Halley thought our work was great fun, cutting down trees and chopping them up. It was even more fun digging in the freshly turned earth, prodding her nose into smells that had been buried for months. My mother turned her back for only a minute. When she turned around, our formerly white dog was brown from head to tail. Mom chased her out of the garden.

Halley came barreling across the lane toward the land bridge that would take her to the opposite side of the pond. She was desperate to get over there—the geese were out after their long winter in the barn and that's where they were nesting. Halley would have loved nothing more than to plow through the long grass and underbrush and flush them out. I headed her off by throwing a small branch. She galloped to the edge of the pond where it landed, but instead of retrieving the branch she was distracted by a smell. She pawed and tugged at something stuck in the mud. I didn't pay much attention until her persistence made me look back. My heart jumped as I suddenly remembered the glove my uncle had found. What if Halley uncovered a real piece of evidence? The thought of stumbling over something foul and bloody was never out of my mind as I walked the fields and lanes of our farm.

"Halley!"

Dad and Eric looked up. I had not meant to sound so panicked.

"Halley," I repeated. "Come here, girl."

Wagging her tail, she struggled to haul what looked like a long piece of wood toward me. It was not until she was a few feet away that I recognized it as a swollen paddle, another victim of Carl's reckless game, which had spent the winter beneath the ice.

A car turned off the main road into the lane. Detective Mather's Chevrolet. When he reached us, he pulled to the shoulder and parked. After getting out of the car, he walked over to the toppled tree where we had gathered. He studied the chain saw in Dad's hand, the raw stump, and finally the long arch of trees lining the lane. I couldn't help thinking how he was analyzing the crime scene: the violent mode of murder, the gruesome state of the victim who had never stood a chance, and all the potential victims he had to save.

Dad explained why the elm trees had to come down.

"What a shame," he said.

"Yes," said Dad. "It certainly is."

"An awful shame," the detective repeated as we wondered why he was there. He coughed, then sniffed a little. He appeared to be getting a cold. No doubt his resistance to all the little bugs and bacteria humans are susceptible to was down, what with greater evils plaguing his mind. Mom immediately dragged a wad of Kleenex from the pocket of her overcoat. Trust Mom. Never leave the house without a pound of Kleenex, you never know what you might have to mop up. Detective Mather thanked her, sniffed again and wiped his nose. "I have news I thought Eric would want to hear."

Eric lay his saw aside and drew closer to where the detective stood. I dropped my armful of wood in the trailer and listened too.

Malcolm would be going home soon. They could not hold him for Katie's murder; they did not believe he had anything to do with it and he wouldn't be charged. He was, however, very ill. The doctors had diagnosed him with schizophrenia. This explained his bizarre and often paranoid behavior. He had not been taking an inordinate amount of drugs at all.

This news was a huge relief to us. Not that we had been convinced Malcolm had done it, but that he had been cleared. Eric was particularly glad to hear it, although it was not good news that Malcolm was so sick.

"But why did he say he did it?" Eric's voice had a rough edge to it, not unlike the chain saw. It struck me that he was beginning to wear out too.

"We believe he saw the van," Detective Mather answered. "He saw Katie get into it. This coincides with what Lewis Gillespie has also confirmed. What we don't know is why, or exactly where Malcolm was standing at the time she was picked up. We suspect he was walking home from Jimmy's house. His description of the van is not very good and it leads us to believe he only saw it from the back. Perhaps he was half a block away. Regardless of where he was, he didn't think anything of seeing her get into the van until the body was found. When he remembered, it frightened him. You have to understand that with his illness his thinking was disjointed. With talk of a murderer, and knowing what he had seen, the doctors feel he probably began to believe he was more involved than he really was. He projected himself as the driver of the van. After a while he believed that if he himself picked Katie up, he must have killed her as well."

Mom leaned her shovel against a tree and pulled off her gardening gloves. "Oh, poor Malcolm. What an awful thing for him to go through. I hope they can help him."

Detective Mather agreed that it had been difficult for Malcolm. The doctors had told his family that Malcolm had no doubt been suffering with the illness for some time. On his own, he had managed to develop ways to cope with the routine of his daily life. His recollections of the night Katie was murdered, however, probably stressed his coping ability much further than he could handle and sent him wildly out of control. But there were medications and they were now monitoring Malcolm, trying to get him stabilized. Eric was relieved to hear this.

"If this is true," he asked, "why did Mr. Gillespie say he saw Malcolm driving the van?"

To this question, Detective Mather shrugged. "He's retracted that statement. He now says he couldn't be sure it was Malcolm after all."

"Man, Mr. Gillespie is nuts."

Neither the detective or Dad disagreed.

"But Katie was not a risk taker. It had to be someone she knew," my mother persisted. "Otherwise she would not have got in the van."

Detective Mather nodded. "It's beginning to look that way." He then turned to me. "Emma, are you frightened?"

I didn't answer his question, although in light of the fact that he would even ask it, the answer would have been a resounding yes. Instead I told him what I thought about what he had just told us. "I know he didn't do it, but I think Mr. Gillespie is trying to hide something."

"What makes you think that?"

"Because he keeps changing his story to suit the situation. People who do that are usually trying to cover something."

Detective Mather told me it was funny, but he'd been thinking the very same thing.

After the detective left and Eric was piling wood in my arms, I asked him if he knew anybody who owned a dark van.

"Dad. Mr. Wright, the basketball coach. Frasers have one they carry chicken pens in. Maury. Mr. Blane. Pretty well anybody who has a business where they have to haul stuff around."

"You didn't say anybody who could have killed her."

"I don't remember that being part of your question."

"Do you know anybody who owns a dark van that could have killed Katie?"

"No." He piled a fourth piece of wood in my arms.

"But you are glad it wasn't Malcolm aren't you?"

"Yeah, of course I'm glad it wasn't Malcolm."

"So how come you're not smiling?"

"Look, I never did believe it was Malcolm. I've known him nearly all my life. But there were a lot of other guys who hung around the Hippie House last summer. Some of them I didn't know at all."

I knew this was a possibility that weighed heavily on Eric's mind. I thought about it as I sat at my sewing machine that afternoon.

Sunlight filled my room as a new crop of houseflies, already congregating in my dormer window, competed loudly with the machine. I was sewing a short-waisted baby blue corduroy jacket for spring, and it was going well. I enjoyed working with cotton; it always did what you told it to do, and when you ironed the darts and seams they stayed in place.

An advantage of my sewing going well was that I could forget about what I was doing as I was doing it. This allowed me to concentrate on the things that actually needed thinking about in my life. It's funny how your brain works, one thought touching off another, sometimes one you haven't thought about in years.

It began with my memories of who had been through the Hippie House, and the puzzle of why Katie would have opened the door and climbed into the van. Mom was right; Katie wasn't a risk taker. The idea that she would just drive off with some stranger, late at night, when she was on her way home, made no sense at all. There were certain things all girls just naturally knew.

The thought took me back many years to two little girls, one approximately a year and a half older than the other one. As I topstitched a pocket on the jacket, I saw these two little girls carrying their Barbie doll lunch boxes on their way home from school. The smaller girl, about six, wore a well-worn lime green coat with big navy buttons that was a size too big for her. She loved it despite this because it had once belonged to her cousin, who she admired very much.

It was fall; the maple leaves were crisp beneath their saddle shoes and their hands were turning red without gloves. The older girl stopped and rubbed the younger girl's hands between her own when she complained they were cold. She gave her a Chiclet from her pocket and told her it wouldn't be long.

"Your mom's picking us up in front of the post office, Emma. It's only one more block. Come on."

The little girl followed her cousin, but "another block" could mean just about any distance when you're that small. All she knew was that she was cold and tired of walking. The two girls came to a crosswalk, where they stopped to let a car turn. The car turned the corner slowly while they waited, but instead of continuing down the street it rolled to a stop. The driver, a man, leaned over the seat and rolled down the window on the side where the two girls were standing. At first he didn't say anything, he just looked at them; his eyes ran down their hair, their skirts and their shoes. The older girl didn't say anything but grabbed the hand of the smaller girl and held it like she would never let it go.

"Do you girls want a ride home?" the man in the car asked.

He seemed a nice enough man. The younger girl thought he must be poor. His car was old and dirty, and his face was rough, covered in whiskers. She was also aware that all the fathers she knew worked at that time of day, so she decided the man must not have a job. If he was poor, she didn't want to hurt his feelings and say no. Besides, it was so cold, and it would be nice to have a ride to the post office. In one way she was hoping her cousin would say yes. But at the same time, even at her young age, something made her wonder why a man she didn't even know would want to give her a ride home. This thought was magnified by the fact that her cousin was gripping her hand hard.

Her cousin didn't answer the man. Instead she darted around behind the trunk of the car, pulling the little girl with her. She ran across the street and down the sidewalk toward the post office without stopping, tugging the little girl so she almost fell. The little girl ran with her. She could feel the panic and she now knew there was something very wrong.

She was glad when she spotted her mother's car parked ahead on the side of the road. When they reached it, the older girl stopped. She let the little one climb in first and sit next to her mother. Once she was in, the older girl sat next to her and closed the door. There were no seat belts to buckle. They pulled away from the curb. The younger girl was happy to be warm and close to her mother. She had already forgotten about the man in the car, and when her mother asked, she chatted about her teacher and what she had done at school. The older girl was quiet and let her chatter. She looked out the window and never mentioned the man who had offered to drive them home.

When I told this story to Megan in 1971, she smiled a little and told me what she had been thinking as the man sat there looking at us. In the split second before she decided to run, she'd had to make some decisions fast. She was going to hit him again and again with her lunch box while she told me to run. She was going to slam his hand in the door if he tried to reach out and grab us. If he had managed to get us into the car somehow, she was going to distract him and just lean on the horn so the whole world would come running. All this had gone through her mind while I was thinking that he must be poor.

I smiled as I thought of eight-year-old Megan whacking her lunch box over the man's head. How ineffective it would have been.

This, of course, was before either of us really knew what a man would want with two little girls. But even then, as young as we were, we could tell something was wrong. People act in certain ways and you learn to read the signs.

Katie had to have been surprised and overpowered the night she was killed. But not by the person who was driving the van. Because if that person was her killer, she would never have willingly got into the vehicle. She would have just known, as Megan and I did when we were very young.

12

O N A SATURDAY MORNING in late April, I sat behind Eric and my father in the Maul Rocket. Eric had been working on building flying hours, and Dad let him take control for a while. His takeoff was a little shaky, but he smoothed out once we were soaring over the newly plowed fields. It was wonderful being up in the air again, high enough so I could see the world all at once. Somehow things seemed to come together and did not appear so scattered and complicated as they did when I was on the ground.

From the air I could see Uncle Pat on his tractor—and cattle sprinkled like poppy seeds over the greening fields. We passed over the sloped clay-tile roof of the castle with its turret and the stand of aspen where Ruby kept her kiln. Once Eric had reached cruising altitude we followed the winding gray strand of the Grand River.

The roar of the engine made it difficult for me to hear what was being said in the cockpit, but my father's voice was calm as he gave my brother directions. For the moment the challenge of learning something new absorbed Eric, and he appeared more content than I had seen him in some time.

For nearly an hour I felt free of all anxiety. It was not until we were landing that I was reminded of how, over the winter, our lives had changed. Where Fiddlehead Creek weaved through the dark fringe of woods and the roof of the Hippie House had once been visible, there was now only a break in the trees and a small square of yellow grass.

Still, there were some good things happening in our lives. For one, Carl was given more responsibility at the arena now that spring had arrived. Mr. Dikkers had bad knees and wanted to cut back on the number of hours he worked. He asked Carl to take over some of what he'd done. He would never have asked him to do this if Carl's work ethic hadn't improved. But Carl was, in general, more conscientious and trustworthy since Maury had helped him focus on a career. This was a huge relief for Megan, because with Carl useful and employed, the stress level in their house had taken a dive.

Uncle Bud carried on in his role as cook and housekeeper of the castle. He appeared to even flourish in it. We smiled behind his back at the apron he wore and the smudge of melted chocolate across his cheek when he served his latest dessert.

And in the first week of May, Donny Russell asked me out on my first real date. That is, it was not something prearranged by my friends. No, when Donny stopped by my locker and asked me to go with him to the spring dance at the community hall, I realized that the awkward arrangements where I would meet a boy in the company of our friends with the ultimate objective of holding hands were long behind me now. This was the real thing. This was serious stuff and could lead to all the things I'd read and heard a relationship entailed: stolen kisses in empty hallways and long embraces before saying goodnight.

Megan came over to the house to iron my hair before Donny picked me up. She also offered to lend me her red jumpsuit, but it fit poorly. I had nothing to fill it the way she did. Instead of flattering my thin figure, it looked prison-issued on me. I wore jeans and the baby blue corduroy jacket I had made instead.

Donny drove his grandfather's truck out to Ruddy Duck Farm to pick me up. It was beginning to grow dark when we left for the dance and it was raining lightly. Fat raindrops dimpled the pond, and without quite enough moisture to dampen the sound, the old windshield wipers ground against the glass. My mother's rose garden was beginning to come to life and I caught the scent of emerging growth through the window I had opened a crack.

"Too bad about the elms," Donny commented in a way that said he really meant it. "It was a bit of a shock to see that row of stumps when I turned up the lane."

"It was tough for my dad."

"I'm sure it was." He looked at me. "But I do like your farm much better in the spring."

"So do I."

It was the only reference he made to Ruddy Duck or Katie or knowing me for any other reason than having met me at school—until we ran into Ross Nash.

We only stayed at the dance for about an hour. The band was unfamiliar; it was a very large one with a horn section. The Rectifiers had not played together since Malcolm was sick. They didn't want to replace him, and Eric, Miles and Jimmy had been spending much of their extra time trying to help Malcolm catch up on his schoolwork.

Donny didn't feel much like dancing, so we decided to go for a drive instead. We ended up at the Dairy Queen on the edge of town. With detectives hanging around their regular spot outside the pool hall and with the Dairy Bar closed, I guess it shouldn't have come as a surprise that Ross Nash and Lyle St. Vincent were there.

Donny bought us sundaes. We ate in a booth by the window where we could watch the traffic on the highway fly in and out of Pike Creek. Cars sped past the Dairy Queen, the Texaco station, the Pike Creek Motel and on down Highway 10 to Shelburne. Donny talked about the changes his father had made since they'd moved out to his grandfather's farm. He liked living there—he liked to putter with mechanical things and he now had plenty of space. It was his mother who was having a difficult time. His older sister required a lot of assistance and his mother had depended on Katie, who had been happy to share the work. Donny was trying to make it easier for her, but he couldn't do a lot of the things Katie had done. Donny pulled a pack of cigarettes from his shirt pocket.

"Want one?"

I shook my head, no. But then I changed my mind. "Yes, thanks."

It wasn't like I'd never smoked before. I just hadn't taken it up as diligently as some of my friends. I wasn't very good at it, and it was also not a trait I admired in my mother. But I was beginning to really like Donny, and if it endeared me to him, I was not above having a smoke. I helped myself to a cigarette.

Donny held the lighter to the end while I inhaled. The smoke tickled my throat and I let out a little cough. He flicked the lighter again, but when I tried to inhale a second time I began spluttering like a spout full of air.

"Here," he said. Taking the cigarette from my hand, he puffed twice and got it going for me. But by then I was grabbing for my Coke. I waved it away.

He laughed. "That's probably a good decision. They seem to be finding more and more reasons why they're not good for you anyway."

He kept the cigarette for himself.

"So what do you do with yourself when you're not sewing?"

"Well—"

I had to think about this. Because sewing was pretty much all I did when I wasn't in school. Unless I was doing my chores, and I really didn't think it would interest him to hear about cleaning duck pens or collecting chicken eggs. No, if I had to sum it up, I led a very dull life. The thought depressed me. "I don't know. I guess I do stuff with my friends."

Donny laughed. "Oh yeah? What kind of stuff?"

But before I had a chance to answer, I noticed Ross Nash sauntering toward us. He stopped next to our table, leaned one shoulder against the post separating our booth from the one next to it, and flashed his nicotine-stained teeth. "Well, what do we have here? The Jenkins and Russell kids. I see you inherited the old man's truck."

He was referring to Donny's grandfather's Dodge.

"Not really," said Donny. "I mean, I didn't inherit it. I just drive it. My dad's got his own. We've got more vehicles than we need."

"What year is it?"

"Fifty-eight."

Ross nodded. "Does your dad want to sell?"

"I don't know. Maybe sometime. But not right now."

"Hey, can I bum a smoke?"

"Yeah, sure." Donny dug into his pocket again. He offered Ross the pack of Exports.

Ross helped himself, struck a match and leaned back against the post again as if he had no intention of ever moving on. He blew a gust of smoke over our heads. "So, what's up?"

Donny and I looked at one another. Donny shrugged. "What do you mean? We're having a bite to eat."

"Oh, I thought you were maybe putting your heads together and trying to solve your sister's murder."

"No," Donny's eyes darkened, "that's not what we were doing. You've got your cigarette, Ross."

"Hey, don't be so touchy. It only makes sense."

"What are you talking about?"

"Well, you'd both know things. You know, you put all that information together and you might come up with something."

"Yeah, well the subject hadn't come up."

Ross took another drag and tapped the ashes on the floor. The length of chain connecting the wallet in his pocket to a belt loop scraped against the metal table edge. "Well if you want my two cents, I'm leaning toward Gillespie, although he's supposed to have some kind of alibi. But I saw the way his tongue hung out when he looked at your sister. You couldn't miss it. He tripped over it when she came in the Dairy Bar. I wouldn't put it past him that he jumped her, there was a struggle and he was afraid he'd get caught. And then what would Old Lady Gillespie do if she knew? She'd make his life a living hell, that's what."

I really wished he would shut up. Donny was concentrating hard on snuffing out his cigarette, and I didn't know him well enough to know how he would react.

"Anyway, that's my take on the thing."

"Yeah, well, thanks for that." Donny stood up. "Let's go, Emma. I've got to get the truck back. It's getting late."

"But it's only nine o'clock."

"Yeah, well, I have to work in the morning, early."

Oh how I wanted to strangle Ross Nash! He'd just destroyed my perfectly good first date.

Donny was relatively quiet on the drive back to Ruddy Duck. He spoke a little about the cross-fencing he was doing with his dad. It was no longer raining; it was just a heavy, damp night now. The tires against the pavement churned up the rain we'd had earlier. Donny drove slowly up the lane, past the row of stumps, and parked in front of the garage. He hopped from the truck, came around to the passenger's side and held the door for me.

"Thanks, Emma," he said as I jumped to the ground. He closed the door behind me. He stood close to me, pressing me a little against the door. "I'm sorry for pulling out like that. I guess I still have a hard time when people start on the topic of my sister."

"You don't have to explain."

He leaned forward and pressed his lips to mine. I wasn't quite sure what to do, but he tasted so good. I tried to respond the way it felt I should. His arms tightened around me, but then they suddenly went slack. He backed up a bit.

"Look, I'm sorry."

"About what?" I hadn't meant to sound panicked. But I could still feel the pressure of his lips against mine and I wanted it back again.

"It's no good."

No good? What did he mean, no good? Was I that awful? Maybe it was my hair. I knew ironing it was useless; one drop of humidity and it was all thick and frizzy again.

"I mean, it's not you. Well, yes, it is. It's you and this place. I like you a lot, but I can't seem to separate you from what's happened."

I felt like I was about to cry. I heard my voice break, "I understand."

But I didn't understand. Well, I did, but I didn't want to. I wanted to shake him and tell him to try—to try real hard to separate me from the farm.

"Maybe when it's all over it will be different. But right now I don't seem to be able to concentrate on much else. It's in my head all the time."

Of course it was in his head all the time. With nothing solved, how could it not have been constantly in his head? Still, I wished that he could have spared a little room for me.

"Will you call me if that happens? I mean, if, when it is over and it is different—will you let me know if you're able to concentrate on other stuff again?"

He nodded.

I had never felt so abandoned as I stood and watched Donny drive away that night.

"That's so tragic," Hetty commented the next day when I told her about my evening. "I mean, it's romantic and tragic at the same time. Poor Donny. Poor you. You must just feel, well— empty inside."

This made me feel a little better. Like I was the hapless victim of a doomed love affair in a romance novel. It was not failure on my part, but fate that had torn our lips apart.

Still, I had been dumped after one date. I felt ugly and rejected, although Donny continued to smile and wave at me at school. For many days following the end of our relationship I clung tightly to self-pity. I felt justified in calling it a relationship considering it ended with what could well have become a very passionate kiss.

"Maybe you should write a song about it" was Megan's advice.

This only prompted me to slump further into the stack of pillows on my bed. Megan sat in my sewing chair, filing her nails. It suddenly struck me as a ridiculous thing to be doing. Frivolous. Something you would only do if you had no other cares in the world. I knew I certainly would never have time to be fussing over my nails again. I could only foresee chopping them off out of necessity. I now had far greater worries requiring my time. "Why would I do that? I can't sing."

"You don't have to be able to sing. It would just be therapeutic. Write it as a poem then. Or, I know, a quilt. Sew a quilt in honor of your lost love."

"That's a stupid idea."

Megan stopped filing. Instead, she used the nail file to punctuate her next words. "No, it's not a stupid idea. The idea is to channel your negative energy. You'd be channeling it into creating something rather than letting it just sit there, eating away at you and making you miserable."

"You'd be miserable too if you'd been through what I've been through. If you'd been told you're the ugliest person in the world."

"He never said anything like that."

"He didn't have to. But it's pretty obvious that's really why he dumped me."

"Emma, he didn't dump you. You can't get dumped if you've only gone out once. And besides, he told you the reason. I think it's legitimate. You know, if you keep this up you're going to end up exactly like Mr. Gillespie."

This comparison made me sit up fast because I'd seen Mr. Gillespie and I knew exactly what Megan was talking about. We'd passed him in Pike Creek when we'd been shopping with Aunt Alice a few days earlier. And what Megan said—to end up like Mr. Gillespie—was truly a frightening thought.

It had been difficult to believe that the crumpled, unshaven shadow of a man stumbling down the sidewalk had been one of Pike Creek's upstanding businessmen only months before. Despite Aunt Alice urging us on, Megan and I had stopped and stared after him, because, except for the odd glimpse of his sullen, moon face behind the lace curtain above the Dairy Bar, we had not seen him in a month. The transformation was incredible.

He had aged fifteen years in that month. His clothes were tired and stained, and even his scruffy beard could not cover the rosy blotches on his face. The man who had sat at meetings with our fathers, presiding over the administration of Pike Creek, emerged from the liquor store and, without any sign of recognition, passed my aunt on the street. We watched as he progressed down the sidewalk, slowly and unsteadily, with great concentration on each step.

"He's not a well man" was Aunt Alice's understated comment as she touched our shoulders to turn us around.

"No kidding," Megan said. "He looks like hell."

My aunt frowned but she did not chastise Megan for her language. Probably because she could not have summed up his appearance more accurately herself.

"Can't somebody do something to help him?"

"There are people looking in on him now and again. He'll get better. When this is all over. Right now he's carrying a huge burden around."

Aunt Alice could not have known the size of the burden Mr. Gillespie was carrying at the time. Nobody did until a week later, when I had almost fully recovered from being jilted by Donny, but Mr. Gillespie had sunk even deeper into despair.

We heard the story from my aunt, who heard it from Mr. Dikkers himself when she picked Carl up from the arena a few days after Mr. Gillespie was hospitalized.

Late on a Tuesday afternoon, Mr. Dikkers, who was one of the people looking in on Mr. Gillespie, arrived at the Dairy Bar with a bag of groceries in one arm. He started to climb the wooden staircase, an old fire exit that led directly from the ground to the apartment above the restaurant. A wonderful fragrance in the air made him stop partway up. It was the delicate scent of lilacs wafting from the bushes at the side of the building. He turned his nose toward the bushes, pulled in a deep breath and continued up the stairs.

Once he had reached the rickety landing, he stopped and studied the door. He wasn't sure where to knock. The door was splattered with broken eggs that had dripped down the wood forming gummy rivulets. One chunk of rubbery yolk still had a piece of the shell attached.

Mr. Dikkers found a clean spot, rapped twice and waited for Mr. Gillespie to answer. The scent of lilacs, he realized, was now smothered by an overpowering smell of gas. This caused him some alarm. Setting the groceries on the step, he opened the unlocked door. The dark, airless apartment belched fumes in his face and he immediately began to splutter and choke. Covering his mouth and nose with a handkerchief, he raced into the kitchen, shut off the stove and closed the oven door.

Mr. Gillespie lay semi-conscious on the sagging chesterfield. Mr. Dikkers was able to haul him off and drag him outside onto the landing at the top of the stairs. He called his name loudly while smacking his blotchy cheeks. He had him breathe deeply until he was able to sit up. When Mr. Dikkers was certain that Mr. Gillespie was conscious enough that he wouldn't tumble down the stairs, he returned to the apartment where he flung open all the windows and propped open the door.

"Was it an accident?" Megan interrupted Aunt Alice after she had told us this much of the story.

Aunt Alice stared into the bowl of cookie batter she was stirring. I knew my aunt to be an empathetic sort of person, but there was no characteristic she admired more than truthfulness. As she was about to tell us, Mr. Gillespie had not been truthful in the details of his relationship with Katie. This trapped my aunt somewhere between sympathy for what had happened to Mr. Gillespie and wanting to wring his storytelling neck. But despite Aunt Alice's own misgivings, she would want us to remain respectful of adults. It was a tenuous set of circumstances for her to juggle, and her explanation would require a delicate approach.

In answer to Megan's question, she shook her head. "No, it wasn't an accident."

"I didn't think so," Megan sniffed.

Aunt Alice then went on to tell us that following the near-fatal incident, Mr. Gillespie had been hospitalized for several days. In the hospital he was visited by both doctors and the police. It was during this time that he finally confessed to what had really happened between him and Katie. He could not sink any lower. Whatever he said could make no difference anymore, and it was time the truth was known.

"At least he claims he's telling the real story this time," my aunt muttered, unable to restrain herself. She was now glaring into the bowl with what I knew to be her "what's the matter with some people?" frown. She vigorously beat another cup of flour into the batter. "Anyway, I suppose it might be true that he was in love with Katie."

Megan and I looked at each other. Megan scrunched up her nose. It was again the whole idea of love and an intimate relationship between Mr. Gillespie and Katie that grossed us out.

Aunt Alice pretended not to notice.

"He wasn't sure when he fell in love with her," she continued, "but he'd always enjoyed her company in the restaurant because she was such a friendly girl. One evening, just before closing, he sat down next to her and told her what he was feeling. She was flattered, she told him, and although she also enjoyed his company, he was married, and in a year she would be leaving to go to school. A relationship between them would be totally impractical."

Megan grimaced. "Did she mention the fact that he was bald, old enough to be her father and his gold tooth was a major turn-off? Man, how could she be so polite? If it was me, I would have plowed him."

"Yes, well, that was a difference between you and Katie. Anyway," my aunt went on, doing her best to ignore Megan, "obviously Mr. Gillespie would have been very disappointed by her answer if he'd expected that she felt the same way about him. He was still hopeful though, and so last summer he began to write the letters Mrs. Russell found. Katie hid the letters in a book without showing anyone. Mr. Gillespie didn't want her to stop coming into the Dairy Bar altogether, so he continued to pretend the letters didn't exist. But he secretly wished that they would win her over. The night she was murdered she had asked him to stop writing the letters. She told him that if he was going to continue to write them, she would no longer be able to go into the restaurant."

"Ah-hah!" Megan cried. "Now this is making way more sense. I never did get how she could go for Gillespie."

Aunt Alice set the bowl on the table, placed her hands on her hips and frowned. "Megan, if you keep interrupting me I'm not going to get through Mr. Dikkers' story."

"But he had a motive. It's so obvious. It was a reverse black-mail kind of thing."

"No, it's not obvious. Nothing's obvious. I know it's hard for you to understand, but he really thought he was in love with Katie. He couldn't imagine not being able to see her anymore. It wasn't a motive. All that happened was he became frightened that he had scared her away."

"Come on, Mom. Why do you keep making excuses for the guy? Admit it. You think he was just a lecherous old man too."

Aunt Alice and I gaped at her. I was very impressed. Lecherous. It was an incredibly cool word to just be able to throw out there like that. It was a small matter that I could only guess at its meaning. But I knew I must have been close by my aunt's reaction.

"Megan! Wherever did you learn a word like that?" Aunt Alice suddenly removed her apron announcing that she had other things to do.

I was forced to appeal to Eric, who had heard the story from Maury, who had heard it from Constable Wagner. He filled us in on the rest.

Mr. Gillespie had closed the Dairy Bar ten minutes early the evening Katie had asked him to stop writing the letters. At ten minutes to ten to be exact. Katie was off work at ten o'clock. He walked briskly down the sidewalk the two blocks to the nursing home. It was unseasonably cold and threatening to snow, so he wore the hood of his duffle coat up to protect his ears. He'd had frostbite once when he was a child, and they were still particularly sensitive to the cold. Standing out of the glare of the streetlight, he waited outside the nursing home for Katie to come out. When she appeared, he let her walk half a block before catching up. She wore earmuffs and didn't hear him approach until he was almost by her side. This was approximately a block before the arena.

Katie was surprised to see him. She wished he hadn't come. She thought she had made it clear that there could be nothing between them. She was sorry to have to tell him straight out, but he was forcing her; he was far too old for her, and even if she had time for a relationship, she would want it with someone more her age. Did he understand this?

Yes, he did. But why? What difference did age make when he cared for her and could offer her as much affection as any young man?

Katie burst into tears at that point. She turned and started to walk quickly ahead of him. Mr. Gillespie followed, attempting to comfort her as he tried to fall in step. She broke into a run. He again tried to keep pace with her. He followed her for several more feet before giving up. He must have been somewhere in front of the arena, he couldn't remember the exact spot. But he stood watching Katie as she hurried forward for another block. She turned once. She stopped running when she realized he no longer followed her. A van—the van he had already described to police passed him. It pulled to the side of the road. Katie glanced back at Mr. Gillespie, still standing by the arena, stepped from the curb and opened the passenger door. She climbed into the van and it drove away.

He had no recollection of who the driver was or even what he looked like to be honest. He was focused only on Katie. He also did not recall seeing the Fritz boy that night. He must have been walking down an intersecting street as the police had already suggested. Mr. Gillespie had then walked home. His wife had previously confirmed that he arrived at the house just after ten thirty.

That was what had happened and he now had nothing left to tell. If he hadn't followed her, if he had not pushed her to the point where she felt she had to escape from him, she would no doubt be alive today. Mr. Gillespie believed that he was as responsible for Katie's death as the killer himself.

After hearing the story, people were split between agreeing that Mr. Gillespie was responsible and the belief that he was a brave and a tormented man. My mother was somewhere in the middle.

"Yes, he was wrong in the way he handled himself," she told me. "But in this case the punishment doesn't fit the crime. He will have to live with this for the rest of his life."

I had never thought of guilt as punishment.

"Oh yes," she said. "We have to at least credit Mr. Gillespie for having a conscience. Something I guarantee the man who killed her doesn't have."

I thought about this. I thought about the circumstances that led Mr. Gillespie to be imprisoned by guilt. I realized that my mother was right. Even after confessing, Mr. Gillespie would never be a free man.

13

IT WAS NOT LIKE Hetty to be in a surly mood. If Megan spent too much time introspecting on some aspect of her world and got herself in a slump, I could always count on Hetty to be positive. So during the second week of June, when she commented that Rose's new haircut made her look like a fat-face, that the gap between Mandy Green's front teeth was wide enough to drive a bus through, and that Mrs. Irwin's purple pantsuit made her look like an overripe eggplant—all in the space of one morning—I knew something was drastically wrong. Then when she didn't return my call after school for the third day in a row, I felt I'd better drop by the castle and find out the cause. After all, perhaps it was me.

"Was it something I said?" I stood in the front hall of the castle. Through the arched doorway I could see Tanya stretched on the chesterfield. The drapes were drawn and the blaring TV threw shadows around the room. "'Cause if it was that comment about your freckles, I didn't mean there was anything wrong with them."

I glanced through to the living room at Tanya again. Even though it was nearly five o'clock, she was still wearing pajamas. I looked back at Hetty who was squinting at me, confused.

"What are you talking about? Tanya! Could you turn that thing down? I can hardly hear Emma."

"About why you're mad at me. Was it the freckles thing? You've been in such a lousy mood."

Hetty frowned. "No. It wasn't the freckles thing. I mean, there was no freckles thing. And I'm not mad at you. Come up to my room. I'll tell you who's been getting on my nerves."

"It's her," Hetty told me once we were in the privacy of her unusually messy room.

"Who?"

Hetty moved some plates off a chair, told me to sit down and flopped on her bed. "Tanya. I can't stand living in the same house as her anymore."

Hetty made a vague attempt to sound sympathetic as she went on to explain what had been happening with her sister—much of which I already knew—but clearly, she had little sympathy left.

In the weeks following the discovery of Katie's body, Tanya had little time to reflect on her friend's murder. She was too absorbed in remembering and talking about Katie as she was called upon to answer detectives' questions and talk to reporters. She'd spoken with people who stopped her on the street, as well as with patients at the seniors' home who wanted to reminisce.

Perhaps it was because of this—because Katie was still so much on her mind and in her conversations—that to Tanya it felt like she was only temporarily away.

Mrs. Russell had depended on her to look after many details of the funeral. It was left to Tanya to select the outfit Katie was dressed in; she ordered Katie's favorite flowers and she decided which of Katie's friends should be asked to speak. It was up to Tanya to choose the music.

"You'd think she was organizing a party," I remembered Hetty telling me at the castle. Tanya was chatting on the phone in the kitchen, finalizing details. "I mean, she sounds so cheerful about it. Shouldn't she be really depressed? It's kind of weird, don't you think?"

Ruby's answer had been simple. "It hasn't hit her yet."

Aunt Alice had explained that it was in Tanya's nature to handle Katie's death the way she did. It was what she did every day; she was used to taking control, ignoring her own needs and putting her energy into easing the lives of those in her care. "Still," she'd added, with obvious concern, "I don't think there's been time for it to really sink in yet."

Tanya had helped Katie's mother sort through her belongings. She'd made decisions that Mrs. Russell just couldn't bring herself to make. She'd helped go through Katie's old room at home, packing the clothes she'd long grown out of but that still hung in her closet from when she was a little girl.

Tanya cried in her bedroom behind the closed door, particularly when the letters from Mr. Gillespie were found and before the story behind them was clear. But outside of the house she'd answered questions and made decisions as if, in Katie's absence, she was simply looking after the personal business of a friend.

For some time, Hetty and I wondered when Katie's death would sink in. As both Ruby and Aunt Alice had predicted would happen, we wondered when Tanya would crash.

It happened at the end of May. Tanya suddenly quit her job at the seniors' home. The thought of living on her own in town again had been too frightening, and by May the drive between the castle and Pike Creek had become impossibly long, particularly after she finished a night shift and was the only car traveling the rural roads. There were just too many places she could be ambushed by a potential murderer, and nobody would see it happen. Why, even the walk from the back door of the building to her car under a black sky in the wee hours of the morning seemed like a foolish risk.

She'd had a dream about that walk—in the weeks before she quit her job she'd had it nearly every night. In her dream she had finished her evening shift. She had just left the seniors' home through the rear door and was walking toward her car. Katie appeared, dressed in a blue skirt and white blouse. She smiled and waved, signaling for Tanya to follow her. Tanya started to, but she always sat up in a sweat, shocked awake at the vision in her dream of Katie's matted hair and blood-soaked back when she turned around.

Uncle Bud reconciled with his wife and left the castle in the first week of June. It was after he was gone that Tanya took to languishing on the chesterfield, watching soap operas and smoking pot when Ruby went out. She couldn't seem to get motivated to do anything. "What's the point?" she asked Hetty. Anything she did would only be to waste time. We were all going to be dead in the future anyway.

Megan and I decided that Tanya had definitely crashed. She slipped further into depression. With nothing else to do she had plenty of time to ruminate about Katie's death.

Mr. and Mrs. DeSousa tried to be understanding. They didn't push her. They took her to the doctor and suggested things she might do to help improve her spirits. They didn't force her to do anything she didn't feel capable of doing.

"Which boils down to she gets to lie around here like some kind of princess," Hetty summed up Tanya's day-to-day existence. She picked up an empty bag of chips, crumpled it and pitched it in the garbage next to her desk.

I now realized the unusual clutter of wrappers and dirty dishes meant she'd been spending a lot of time in her room.

"She can do anything she wants. They cater to her, and she doesn't have to lift a finger. So guess who gets to do all the joe jobs around here? She cracks up and I'm transformed into Cinderella. Maybe I should take up being depressed."

"She'll get over it." I realized I didn't sound all that convincing.

"God, I hope so. It's like living with the walking dead."

A week after this visit to the castle, Tanya was watching *Dark Shadows* when she fell asleep. The cigarette she was holding slipped from her fingers, igniting the goatskin rug. She began to dream—a strange dream about being in school again and the guy in the seat behind her flicking a lighter and igniting a gum wrapper. She wasn't sure if it was the smell or Ruby arriving home from the craft shop that woke her up.

"Tanya!" she heard Ruby call from somewhere in the distance. Tanya's eyes fluttered. Her mother stood in the doorway. Her face was distorted—her eyes wide and her mouth open—a panicked look. Tanya sat up. It was then she realized the rug was smoldering, and if something wasn't done quickly, the drapes would also soon be in flames. She choked as she made her way through the smoke into the kitchen, where Ruby was phoning the fire department.

"Outside!" ordered Ruby.

Tanya did as she was told. Ruby threw buckets of water along the edge of the rug and on the drapes. It was only a matter of minutes before the fire engines were on their way from Grand Valley. Tanya heard the sirens screaming, announcing their arrival, from where she sat on the front steps. Ruby's efforts helped control the spread of the fire, and it didn't take long for the firefighters to douse the flames. Aside from some smoke and water damage, the fire had destroyed the goatskin rug along with Ruby's patience.

That evening, while Hetty scrubbed soot and ashes from the stone floor, her parents instructed Tanya to sit down. They were well aware how difficult the past six months had been and they assured Tanya that she had their sympathy, but it was time she got off the chesterfield. If she wasn't going to go through with her plans to attend nursing school in the fall, she was to look for another job.

"As a matter of fact," Ruby told her, "I know where you can apply. I bumped into Mrs. Fraser in town yesterday. They've expanded their chicken houses again. Honestly, I don't know how that woman does all that she does. Anyway, she mentioned she was going to advertise for someone to help dress and pluck the chickens. I think you should think about it. It would be close to home."

Tanya's eyes widened. Hetty said it was like, until then, she'd been sleeping with them open and it was the suggestion of plucking chickens that startled her awake. She stared at her mother as if Ruby was the one who had lost her sanity. The following day, she asked for her job back at the seniors' home.

THE SUMMER MONTHS WERE always, in a way, cathartic. But that year more than ever we looked forward to them as a time to rejuvenate, a time to leave the terrible events of the winter in the past.

At least most of us did. The exception was Arthur Nash. His thoughts turned to mischief.

Hetty and I emerged from school one day to an unusually excited crowd. The news of another murder was the buzz among the swarm of kids waiting for buses. Where the news had came from, who had reported it and, most importantly, who was the victim were not known.

I was not swept up in the news immediately. I was deeply disappointed because my sewing teacher, Mrs. Suringa, had just told the class that she was moving back west. She was a young teacher and she'd lived in Pike Creek for only a year. She'd come with her new husband, who had been raised in the area and promised her a friendly, small-town atmosphere to raise their family. It had been nothing of the sort. If she was terrified to walk the streets alone, how could she even consider letting any children they might have go out and play? No, she'd had enough. She was packing up and moving back to Saskatchewan. Nothing this frightening ever happened in Biggar. And if Mr. Suringa wanted to come with her, the choice was up to him.

On this afternoon, from bits of conversation we overheard it sounded like the latest victim had been killed behind the Dairy Bar. There was no body at the site, someone reported. Just all the evidence of a struggle and violent death.

Hetty cocked an eyebrow. "If there's no body, what's the harm in checking it out?"

I shrugged, and we soon found ourselves part of the pack heading down the hill into town. On our way we passed others who had already been to the Dairy Bar. "It's gruesome. There's blood—it's everywhere," we were warned. By the time we'd reached the arena, I'd heard the comment just one too many times. "I don't want to go," I told Hetty.

"Come on, Emma." She took hold of my arm. "They said there's no body. You don't have to look close."

Reluctantly I continued and we walked the rest of the way to the Dairy Bar.

I found it surprising that the police had not yet arrived. Everyone else seemed to know someone had been murdered, but there was no police tape cordoning off the site or detectives on the scene. People from school wandered around the steps leading to Mr. Gillespie's apartment, scrunching up their faces and looking confused. I squinted toward the windows of the apartment, but all I could see were the reflections of trees. If Mr. Gillespie was up there, he wasn't showing his face.

Hetty and I moved closer. There were dark stains on the cement block the steps rested on and on every step leading to the landing at the top. It was as though the victim had been dragged up or down. Hetty pointed to a shoe. It was a woman's shoe teetering on a step. An ugly, old-fashioned woman's shoe, brown and with a solid heel, like something Mrs. Gillespie might wear. That was all I saw. I refused to move closer, even though some people had skipped over the bloodstains and ventured up the stairs.

Constable Wagner pulled up to the curb in his police car—finally, someone had called him. It seemed amazing that in light of such a serious crime he'd been the last one clued in. Alarmed at the number of people tampering with the site, he hollered for them to get off the stairs. He made his way over to the cement block, bent down and studied it. What he did next I thought a little odd, or at least unscientific, but he dabbed his finger in the pool of blood, rubbed it between two fingers testing for consistency and brought it to his nose. He stood up, pursed his lips and frowned. His eyes followed the stains up the stairs. He focused on the woman's shoe teetering on the step. The crowd was hushed, waiting for an announcement or direction, someone to tell us what to do.

"Arthur Nash!" Constable Wagner suddenly snapped without turning around.

From behind a lilac bush, Ross's twelve-year-old brother was either yanked or pushed. Whatever happened, he appeared quite suddenly. Even his own expression revealed that he was a little surprised at how prompt he'd been.

"Yeah?"

Constable Wagner remained where he was. "Isn't that your mother's shoe?"

Mrs. Nash was the woman killed? I wondered how Constable Wagner had figured it out so quickly. And it suddenly occurred to me that he must be a very intelligent man. But if this was so, why had he ever given up what most certainly would have been an astonishing career in criminal investigation to spend his life writing parking tickets in Pike Creek?

"Uh, I don't know."

The constable asked someone on the steps to throw the shoe down to him. Again, I thought this was odd. On TV they were always so cautious with evidence, handling it as though it were infectious, picking it up with a stick and sealing it in a bag. The boy standing closest to the shoe must have thought as I did for he appeared reluctant, but he did as the police officer asked.

Constable Wagner signaled Arthur to come closer and identify the shoe.

Arthur walked meekly toward him. I didn't blame him, because Constable Wagner looked far more formidable than compassionate. An odd reaction, considering the kid's mother was likely dead.

"Well?"

Arthur shrugged. "Yeah, I guess it is."

The constable nodded. "I thought so. I was behind her in the market yesterday."

I now noticed Arthur's expression, and it dawned on me that he appeared more embarrassed than distraught.

"Now," said the constable, "why don't you turn around and apologize for scaring these people half to death."

Arthur glanced up at Constable Wagner, whose defiant chin was set. Folding his arms across his chest, he nodded at the boy.

Arthur Nash turned toward his audience. With his eyes fastened to the ground, he murmured a barely audible, "Sorry."

"Alright," Constable Wagner continued. "Now I want you to hose down these steps. But before you do that, I want you to get in the car—you and I need to have a little talk."

ARTHUR WAS SAVED THE EMBARRASSMENT of apologizing to Mr. Gillespie because, as Eric informed me, Mr. Gillespie had already left Pike Creek.

"Where did he go?" I asked as we bumped along on the bus.

Eric sat sprawled across the seat in front of me, facing sideways, an arm draped over the back of the seat. Megan sat next to me, grinding loudly on a jawbreaker.

Eric shrugged. "Probably somewhere where nobody knows him. Maybe he's gone to open a Dairy Bar in North Dakota or some other place far away like that."

Megan pulled the jawbreaker from her mouth. "He moved in with his brother in Toronto."

I stared at her a moment. Not because I didn't believe her, but because her tongue was fluorescent blue.

"Well, it's true. Mom heard it from Mrs. Gillespie herself."

Wherever he was, he was no longer in Pike Creek, so attention turned away from Mr. Gillespie when Suzy McLaren disappeared. Suzy went missing in the third week of June, somewhere between Pike Creek and her farm near tiny Marsville.

Suzy was fourteen—the same age as me, Hetty made a point of telling me as we walked back to school from the Pike Creek Market after lunch.

"Yeah, and the same age as you were last month. So what's your point?"

"Oh nothing. It just seems to me that his victims are getting younger. Katie was eighteen. Fiona, she was sixteen. Now Suzy."

"I doubt if it means anything. It's probably who's available at the time."

"Yeah, I guess."

Suzy's disappearance set my mother off again. Although her excitable episodes had tapered off some since Fiona's death, even something as mildly unnerving as Halley barking at Mr. Fraser when he dropped off Dad's extension ladder could get her upset. She began to talk in earnest about moving back to Toronto. She knew at least four families in Pike Creek that had already put their houses up for sale. It would be infinitely safer than the farm, she maintained. The city was at least comforting in its numbers. It was not one long stretch of barren road bordered by woods where murderers could lurk, waiting to snatch young girls. Not like this—this dark and sordid world around Ruddy Duck Farm. Then a horrifying thought occurred to her. Even if they did put it up for sale, with its morbid history, who in their right mind would buy the place?

My father didn't respond. He left her ranting in the kitchen and went out to feed the trout instead.

An hour later Detective Mather drove up the lane. Mom was crashing around the kitchen, throwing carelessly wiped silverware into the utensil drawer. Through the window of the sunroom, where Megan and I were studying for exams but mostly painting our toenails metallic gold, I could see Dad standing on the spillway, tossing handfuls of Purina trout chow into the water now percolating with fish.

Detective Mather parked his car and, moments later, followed my father into the kitchen. He informed us that he had some news.

"What is it? Have they found Suzy McLaren?" My mother removed her apron and invited him to sit in the nearest chair. But she was still in a dark mood, and I noticed she didn't offer the detective so much as a glass of water. It appeared that she was beginning to blame even him for the state of the world.

"Yes," Detective Mather answered. "Suzy's been found. And she's safe. She took the bus to a cousin's house in Brampton. She had a disagreement with her mother and decided to leave home. It was an unfortunate decision under the circumstances."

Unfortunate was hardly the word. With half the province looking for her, I was sure she was going to look back on that disagreement like it was a tea party compared to what she was in for now.

"Oh, man," said Megan, "I wouldn't want to be in Suzy McLaren's riding boots."

"Don't be too hard on her." Detective Mather made an effort to smile. With little success. "If she hadn't run away, what I've come to talk to you about might never have happened. We have a description. It's not terrific, but it's more than we've had up until now."

"Where did you get it?" my mother asked.

"It was given to us by a young girl in Shelburne. She tells us that in early May she was walking to a girlfriend's house when a man grabbed her from behind. After blindfolding her, he dragged her into a vehicle where he tied her wrists. Somehow she was able to twist free and she escaped within a few blocks."

It was an amazing story and I wondered if it was true. Detective Mather answered my unasked question, as I'm sure it had been the first thought to strike him.

"We believe her story. It hasn't changed, and although she saw little of the vehicle, her description suggests it was some sort of van."

My mother was calmer now, although skeptical. "But why would she wait a whole month to say anything?"

"She was terrified," the detective explained. "She was trying to cover it up, maybe thinking that if she ignored it, it would go away. Or maybe she thought if she said anything, her abductor might retaliate. Or perhaps that she would somehow be blamed. It's not always easy to know why people do the things they do, but thankfully, after she'd heard that Suzy disappeared, she thought it was important enough and she somehow gathered the nerve to tell us."

"That poor child," my mother moaned. "Oh, this is awful. It means he's still around."

Detective Mather nodded. He then opened his briefcase and withdrew some drawings. "Eric, I would like you to take a look at these and tell me if this man resembles anyone you might have seen at the Hippie House last summer."

My brother bent over the first drawing. He frowned. I frowned too, because they were rough pencil drawings of a very generic-looking man. All I could really be sure of was that the man was white skinned, dark haired and probably more than twenty-five years old. He did not wear glasses—at least they weren't included in the sketch—and he did not have a moustache or a beard. Okay, so that ruled out one guy.

"It's not Maury."

"No, it's not," Megan agreed. "But Emma, don't you think he kind of looks like that new guy who works at the post office?"

I could sort of see it, although the eyebrows were too heavy. "No, I think it looks like Mrs. Suringa's husband more than anyone else."

Detective Mather set the first drawing aside, exposing a profile beneath. The detective once again turned to Eric.

Eric shrugged. He stood up. "I can't say. I mean, that guy looks like a ton of people, and on the other hand, he doesn't look like one person I know. I wish I could help you. I wish I could say, 'Oh, yeah, that was so-and-so,' but I can't. I can't tell you if that guy was here or not."

"Geez, Eric," Megan said. "Don't be so paranoid. So you don't recognize him. There's no crime in that."

Eric looked at her. He sat down again.

Detective Mather placed the drawings back in his briefcase. "Well, if anything comes to any of you, please give me a call. Thanks again."

My mother was suddenly on her feet. "Thank you, Detective Mather. Thanks for letting us know Suzy's alright and for, well, looking after things."

The detective gave her a weary smile.

And as if suddenly waking up after a knock on the head, she apologized, "Oh dear, what have I been thinking—you must be hungry. Let me get you something to eat."

Detective Mather shook his head as he held his palms in the air. But, of course, Mom wouldn't allow him to leave empty-handed, and despite his protests she loaded him up with pickled vegetables and sausages to cheer him up. My father accompanied him back to his car.

"Isn't it amazing that girl in Shelburne got away?" I asked Eric an hour later.

He sat at his desk where he was replacing a string on his guitar. Halley and I lay flopped across his bed. Lifting a leg in the air, I admired the sparkly gold nail polish on my toes.

Eric shrugged. "Yeah, it is. It also sounds to me like the guy's getting sloppy."

"What do you mean?"

"Exactly what Detective Mather said would happen. Remember? He said he'd get bolder each time until he made a mistake big enough to get caught. He picked her up in town and in broad daylight. And she somehow got away."

I suddenly sat up. "I'm scared."

"Yeah, I don't blame you. I would be too."

I watched Eric tighten a machine head. He tested the string by playing a couple of chords. "How come it bugged you so much that you didn't recognize the pictures Detective Mather showed us? I mean, they're so general, they could be just about any guy."

"Because I should. Look, it was obviously somebody who knew about the Hippie House. I've always been pretty sure about that. But so many people came out here. I guess—if anybody should recognize him, I should—that's why."

14

I WAS GLAD TO BE FINISHED SCHOOL. In the final week of June we spent our lunch hours in the courtyard, propped up on our elbows, soaking up the sun. It became harder and harder to leave the warmth outside and return to the fluorescent halls. The classrooms seemed stale and suffocating when the fresh air was so deliciously fragrant. Even our teachers were anxious to leave the dusty rooms. Mrs. Suringa allowed us to take our textile projects to the courtyard. Sitting on the grass we passed around fabric swatches, discussing, identifying and recording the individual characteristics and care.

Megan got a job that summer as a cashier at the drugstore in Pike Creek. At first I went to visit her a lot, we were both so excited that she was old enough to have a real job. She'd show me what was new in cosmetics, then run and look after customers while I tried all the testers. But when I got home I realized it was the first summer I didn't have her around to help occupy my time. I missed her. It was no fun drifting in the canoe, tanning, by myself. Those long hazy days of doing nothing were over for Megan, and I was too old to spend them swimming, ignoring how slimy the pond was anymore. Then Megan started going out with Duncan Friesen, who delivered prescriptions for the drugstore. I felt even more abandoned. I thought of Donny and I sighed. I wondered if he would ever be able to separate me from what happened to Katie. I doubted it. I knew I would never be able to look at him without remembering what had happened on our farm. So while Megan spoke of Duncan with starry eyes, I lamented my own past love affair. By then, in my mind, it had escalated into a love affair.

During the first two weeks of July, Hetty and I made a bit of money picking strawberries. Early in the morning, while dew still glistened on the fields, we rode our bicycles out to the gas station on the corner of Highway 9. Here, Mr. O'Callaghan would be waiting in his truck. The last to be picked up, we squeezed onto the benches in the open box next to the other berry pickers. The sun climbed higher and we shed our jackets as Mr. O'Callaghan drove down the gravel road headed toward his farm. Dust thickened our hair, and our rubber sandals left scuff marks on the rough plank floor. Mrs. O'Callaghan had set out a long table covered by a bright vinyl tablecloth on the lawn. She served plates of sandwiches or she cooked a big pot of chili for the workers at lunch. At four o'clock we were returned to the gas station where we again collected our bikes.

It was sweaty work that turned my hands pink and earned me more than one blackfly bite. But over the two weeks I made enough money to buy the most exquisite piece of periwinkle silk. Enough for a midi-skirt and waist jacket. I'd had my eye on the fabric in a store in Brampton for some time. Hetty bought a transistor radio with her money so she could listen to CHUM radio station wherever she went.

Late one sticky afternoon we walked along the highway on our way to the Dairy Queen. Hetty's radio hung from a wide leather belt around her waist. From the tinny speaker we heard that Louis Armstrong, the great trumpet player, had died.

"Never heard of him," Hetty said.

Megan kicked an empty DQ cup in the ditch. "Sure you have. You know, the guy whose eyes pop out when he plays." And while Hetty and I watched, Megan blew her cheeks up to the size of cantaloupes while her eyes looked about ready to pop out of her head.

Hetty and I laughed.

A few weeks later, as we sat on the spillway dabbling our feet in the water, watching Dad's white Chinese geese cruise lazily across the surface, the radio told us that two of the crew of Apollo 15 had gone driving on the moon.

"Hey, look at that land rover." Eric sat forward as we watched the broadcast on TV that evening. "It's like something out of a science-fiction movie. And look at those pictures of the astronauts. They're even in color. This is incredible. Can you believe it—while we're sitting here, those guys are actually up there driving around on the moon?"

Eric worked on the highway that summer as a flagman. He, Jimmy and Miles all got on as part of the crew. They made good money, and after only a few weeks of standing on the hot tarmac in the blazing July sun, they were as deeply tanned as Uncle Pat.

"Look at this," Eric said, stopping to wave a piece of paper in my doorway. "Four more paychecks and I'll be able to buy a secondhand MG."

"Oh yeah?" I said, somewhat distantly. I was not really paying attention. I was more concerned with my reflection in the mirror as I sat cross-legged on my bed. I'd had my braces removed the day before and I was still fascinated by my ability to speak without the metallic glint.

Eric noticed there was something different. "There's something weird about you."

I smiled brightly. "My braces—I got them off."

"No, that isn't it."

"Yeah, it is. You're just not used to it."

"No, it's—what's that black blob next to your mouth?"

I looked in the mirror again. I touched the mark just above the corner of my mouth. "It's not a black blob. It's a beauty mark. Megan drew it on to go with my new teeth. She said it made me look like Marilyn Monroe."

Eric frowned. "Trust me, you don't look like Marilyn Monroe. You look more like you were chewing a pen and it squirted all over your face."

MAURY WAS ONE OF THE promoters behind a rock music festival held on the first weekend in August. In the weeks leading up to the festival, whenever we wandered into his store he was on the phone, organizing permits and bands. It was a good thing. It focused his energy. Eric had told me that Maury was becoming seriously disillusioned—not only with what was happening around Pike Creek, although that certainly couldn't have helped, but also with the waning anti-war efforts. With the escalating brutality and force used when there was a protest or march. We'd all seen the news reports; there had been 12,000 people arrested at a single protest in Washington, D.C., in May alone.

The festival was on a scorchingly hot weekend in the Hockley Valley. On the Thursday before it began, festivalgoers started drifting through town. Clouds of pot wafted from cars when the doors opened, and mickeys of lemon gin peeked from the back pockets of cutoff jeans. Hitchhikers wearing backpacks and bandanas strolled into Pike Creek. A few, carrying guitars, stopped for a while to busk in front of the IGA. Until Mrs. Gillespie lodged a complaint, that is, and Constable Wagner was obligated to wander down and suggest that they move on.

On Friday afternoon, Hetty and I were standing at the main intersection in Pike Creek, gnawing on Fudgesicles as we waited to cross the street. Two very cool guys emerged from the Market. One of them carried a bag of ice, which he stashed in a small cooler strapped to the back of his motorcycle parked at the curb. He threw a leg over the bike and was settling onto the seat when he spotted us. "Hey," he grinned, "do you chicks want a ride to the park?"

Hetty raised her eyebrows. She glanced at me, then looked behind us. She wasn't entirely sure if he was talking to us. She must have thought, as I did, that we'd been standing in the way of someone much older, someone—much hotter than us.

"Yeah, you two ladies. You're going out to the valley, aren't you? The Hawk is playing tonight. Hop on and we'll give you a lift."

Hetty pulled the Fudgesicle from her mouth. "Uh, we can't—"

The guy who had spoken adjusted his shades. He was obviously waiting, along with me, for Hetty to follow what she said with a reason. We can't go because—we have an appointment. We have to check with our parents. We plan to wash our hair tonight. Two girls have been viciously murdered around here and we never go anywhere with guys on motorcycles with dark glasses and long hair.

"Uh," Hetty repeated, "we have to be home by six." Chocolate melted rapidly off her Fudgesicle onto the sidewalk.

He now inspected us a little more closely. His eyes dropped to the dots of brown ice cream splashing around her bare feet. Perhaps realizing his mistake, he started his engine. "Well, too bad. It's going to be a blast. If you change your mind, maybe we'll see you out there."

They roared off, leaving Hetty and me feeling about six years old and knowing we had to find a way to go.

Hetty discovered that Mandy Green and Doug McCrae were headed out to the festival on Saturday afternoon. Doug offered to give us a lift; he said there would be plenty of room in the back of his dad's truck. I got Mom to drop us off at Mandy's house in town. She was not so sure I should be going to a rock festival. She'd seen pictures of what they were like on TV. Everyone was just so, well—uninhibited! But I was somehow able to convince her that Hetty and Mandy were allowed to go without any problem, so she caved in.

When Doug arrived at Mandy's, we climbed into the back of the open pickup. Doug started out on the highway. Traveling at sixty miles an hour, the wind twisted our hair into a million tiny knots but did nothing to cool us off, and our cotton shirts remained stuck to our chests with sweat.

Traffic was heavy at the festival site and we had no choice but to park half a mile away along a gravel road. After pulling our backpacks from the back of the truck, we trailed behind the long line of people swinging baskets and thermoses, clutching sunhats and leading dogs as they headed toward the festival gate. Once we were inside, we were met with waves of color; people occupied nearly every square foot of grass on the gradual slope that formed a natural amphitheater in front of the stage.

Doug pointed out a bare patch of ground toward the middle of the slope. We followed him, hopping over sprawled limbs, treading carefully around heads and jumping out of the way of the flailing arms of dancers as we made our way across the grounds. He stopped. "This okay?"

The small patch had looked much more significant from far away—like the missing piece of a puzzle. It now looked like the piece was only slightly out of place. But we didn't have much choice. Mandy spread out a blanket as far as the space allowed, staking our own small festival space.

Once we were settled, I leaned back on my elbows on the blanket. The sky was flawless and the sun was warm on my face. Hetty poured a lemonade. Doug lit a joint, took a drag and passed it to Mandy. She did the same and passed it to me.

Hetty cocked an eyebrow, wondering what I was going to do. This was more Doug and Mandy's thing than ours. But, hey, it was an incredibly mellow day. I took a toke, held it in my lungs and passed the joint to Hetty. Lying back on the blanket, I fought to suppress the tickle in my throat. It was no use. "Allergies," I quickly invented, sitting up, coughing out the word. "It's the goldenrod. It always gets to me like that."

Only Hetty seemed to notice. She giggled and also took a drag. She nudged me with her toes. "Hey, maybe we'll bump into those guys we saw outside the market yesterday."

"Maybe," I said, "but they probably won't recognize us without our Fudgesicles."

She laughed again, remembering how juvenile we must have looked clutching our ice cream as we walked in our bare feet down the sidewalk in Pike Creek. I sat up when Hetty brought out the lunch Ruby had packed.

"Cool, butter tarts!" Doug took two, scoffing the first one in two bites.

Through the smoke hovering in layers above the crowd, I spotted Eric standing with Jimmy and Miles to the left of the stage. They were talking to some guys I didn't know—two of them sat in the back of an open van surrounded by sound equipment, so I assumed they must have been members of another band. Malcolm wandered on his own a short distance away from them. He was talking, carrying on what looked like a pretty animated conversation—although from where I sat it sure didn't look like there was anyone close enough to hear. He drifted into the crowd, where I lost track of him and then forgot about him. I guess I became distracted by other things going on at the time.

Behind us, Ross Nash and Lyle St. Vincent leaned against the fence at the back of the field. They didn't mingle. At least not with anyone sitting on the grass. Instead they chewed toothpicks while admiring the motorcycles of several other guys who I had never seen before. These guys wore black jeans and cleated boots like Lyle and Ross. I didn't get why Ross and Lyle were there. They didn't even like music. At least, I knew they didn't like this kind of rock music. Watching them, I found something disturbing in the way they didn't sit down, the way they just leaned there with one foot up against the fence like they were waiting to take their turn at something.

Someone from behind the stage batted an inflatable beach ball above the crowd. It was kept aloft until it was inadvertently whacked over the fence. Less than a minute later the ball mysteriously bounced back again; Constable Wagner's head appeared and he grinned from the other side of the fence.

The only one hurrying anywhere was Maury, who was running around, carrying a clipboard, as he organized the lineup. He spoke with musicians clad in sunglasses, punctuating his words with the pipe in his hand.

Hetty and I watched two bands before we got up and wandered around. We discovered a sprinkler set up for people to cool off. Adam Brown and some other people we knew from school had thrown down a piece of plastic and were skidding across the wet surface. We both gave it a few tries until Hetty slipped and fell, bruising her butt.

It was when we returned to our spot that I first noticed the mood had changed. Ross and his friends were louder. One of them didn't like the length of the last drum solo and made a point of telling the band. He laughed stupidly when the guitarist broke a string. I guessed the bottle of Jack Daniels I'd seen them passing around had made a few circuits by then. Doug began packing the food back into Hetty's backpack. He seemed uneasy.

"What's wrong?" Mandy asked.

"Those guys with Nash, they're looking for trouble."

She glanced behind her. "We'll move as soon as we see an open spot."

Hetty stood up. "There!" She pointed to an area closer to the stage. "Oh, no, sorry, the beach ball was in the way. I thought it was open." She sat down again.

We didn't have a chance to say anything else because a new band had taken the stage. "Give me an F!" the lead singer shouted into the microphone.

People all around us responded with an enthusiastic "F" that probably could have been heard on Mars.

With the exception of a single gruff voice that came from the direction of the gate. "Hey—shove your F!"

This was followed by a small ripple of deep-throated guffaws.

Hetty and I, along with most people in the crowd, turned. It was the mouthier of Ross Nash's motorcycle acquaintances. He was sitting on his bike with his arms crossed.

The singer did his best to ignore him. "Give me a U!" he yelled.

The band was gearing up for "I-Feel-Like-I'm-Fixin'-to-Die Rag," a Vietnam War protest song by Country Joe and the Fish.

The crowd responded with a whopping "U" when, over by the gate again, "You suck!" the heckler shouted.

"Shut up, greaseball!" hollered someone from the crowd.

There were several more shouts, then a scuffle. When we could figure out what had happened, we realized a fight had broken out between a big bouncer type and one of Ross Nash's friends. The sound of the punches was what I remember most. It was horrible to realize the soft thuds were actually knuckles pummeling flesh.

Both sides had people quick to come to their assistance. All I recall of the next ten minutes was a bottle flying over my head and smashing against the side of the concession stand, Hetty's fingernails digging into my arm and her yanking me toward the front gate. We were rushing for it when Eric stopped me.

"Have you seen Malcolm?" He was breathless.

"I—yeah, about twenty minutes ago. He was walking around the stage not far from you."

"That's it? You didn't see him come this way?"

"No."

"Alright. Get out of here. You and Hetty, right now." Eric gave me a little shove on the back and took off.

We weren't the only ones looking for a way out. The mood changed drastically within a matter of minutes and the mellow crowd erupted into a chaotic, panicked rush. A bottleneck of people quickly built up to get through the gate as the fight not only continued, but grew. Police sirens screamed and suddenly uniformed men were spilling into the park. It all happened mind-numbingly fast.

Hetty and I were close to the entrance when I spotted Malcolm—Malcolm, with his long hair and shabby jean jacket, was grabbed roughly by two uniformed men. Despite holding his hands up to indicate he was innocent of whatever they might think he was guilty of, they forced him to face the fence. Malcolm attempted to turn around. He was prevented by one officer while the other frisked him for drugs.

I looked for Eric. I scanned the crowd for Constable Wagner, who knew Malcolm and would never have treated him like that.

"Move out!" a voice next to me shouted.

I felt Hetty tug my arm. I kept searching the grounds for Eric or Miles or Jimmy, someone who could explain to the police officers that it was just Malcolm and to be easy on him, he was ill.

"Come on, let's go!"

This time I realized the order was directed at me. A police officer grabbed me by the arm. He pointed toward the gate.

My first impulse was to wrench free. He had no right to touch me; I hadn't done anything wrong!

"That guy over there—Malcolm, he's a friend. He didn't do anything. Tell them to leave him alone."

Shouts, pounding and the sound of breaking glass caused us all to turn. Two of Ross's friends had jumped on the roof of a police car and were kicking in the siren. The officer with his hand on my arm yelled to another police officer, then turned back to me. His grip on my arm actually hurt as he shoved me forward. "Never mind about him. Just keep your mouth shut and keep moving!"

I couldn't believe it! He was treating me like I had something to do with the guys on the car. Like I was one of them!

"Come on, Emma." Hetty pulled me with her. "He just wants us out of the way of the fight."

I let Hetty lead me through the gate, and we joined the rest of the crowd making its way along the road. We reached Doug's truck. Ten minutes later, Doug and Mandy made their way through. We squeezed into the cab together and sat there, frightened and thoroughly stunned.

"What happened back there?" Hetty whispered. I noticed a gash on the back of her hand.

"I'm not sure," said Doug. "I don't know if Ross's punk friend started it or if someone jumped him."

Two more RCMP cars with sirens blaring roared past us. Hetty looked after them. "It wasn't just them. It's everything that's happened."

Doug started the engine. As we drove into town we went over the events, still uncertain how the whole thing blew up like it did.

"Did you find Malcolm?" I asked Eric later that same night.

Eric shook his head, no.

"But where would he go?"

"I don't know." This was followed by a sigh, like Eric was tired of keeping track.

There were three arrests for drunk and disorderly conduct that night, several drug charges laid, and at least one person, Ross's friend, spent the night in jail. Mom didn't say anything about it.

She didn't need to. She simply repeated aloud what Mrs. Bolton told her over the phone while looking at me, wearing her I-told-you-so frown.

The riot only helped to further fuel frustration and fear. People were desperate to place blame.

Mr. Crossley accused the police of being incompetent. Two days after the riot he challenged Constable Wagner as I was waiting for Megan outside the drugstore.

"Tell me, Constable," he said, stopping him not far from where I stood on the sidewalk, "what do you do in that cushy office of yours all day?"

Constable Wagner was taken by surprise. He didn't immediately have an answer.

"Come on, Jim," Mrs. Crossley urged her husband on. "Leave the police officer alone. Let's go."

"No, I pay my taxes. I want to know what I'm getting for my money. What are you doing down there? I think you're catching up on your sleep, that's what, 'cause I sure don't see any signs of police action around here. We've got a murderer walking around killing young girls and hoodlums rioting like this is Detroit. I want to know what you're doing about it."

I wasn't sure if it was Mr. Crossley's doing, but a week later two new staff members were added to the police force in Pike Creek. This allowed Constable Wagner to spend more time on the street. He'd walk up and down the main drag, visiting store owners and generally keeping an eye on the action.

A few businessmen, including Mr. Crossley, installed bars in the windows of their stores. The Pike Creek Market handled security in a different way. They simply posted a sign on the door stating that there were to be no more than three teenagers in the store at one time, and absolutely no long-hairs.

Standing in the window of his store, looking across the street at the security bars, Maury shook his head and sighed.

15

AFTER THE RIOT, Mr. Blane would not allow Ross Nash and Lyle St. Vincent to loiter on the sidewalk outside the pool hall. So, with nothing else to do, they became employed.

They both got jobs in Pike Creek's industrial park, two flat blocks before the highway passed the Dairy Queen. It was made up of a few modern concrete buildings including the Pike Creek Dairy and a yellow brick building that housed the presses for the *Pike Creek Banner*. Ross got a job at the presses, where he was learning to set the printing plates. Kitty-corner to the presses was a plant that produced plastic wrap and employed a number of my friends' fathers. Adjacent to this was a small garment-bag factory where suitcases and hiking packs were manufactured. Lyle worked at the factory, where he operated the machine that put grommets into the straps of the bags.

Lyle and his girlfriend were expecting a baby in January. They got married in late August of 1971. On the day of the wedding, the flat-black Dodge Charger—festooned with red streamers and purple plastic flowers—was left idling outside St. Mark's United Church while the ceremony took place.

It wasn't that we missed Ross and Lyle loitering in the doorway, their catcalls, their blundering opinions on whatever topic happened to occur to them as they observed the world from where they stood—but they had added a last dash of animation to the town. Sadly, Megan and I concluded, there was now none at all.

This struck us on Labor Day as we wandered down the street past the former Dairy Bar, the barred storefronts and now the empty space in front of Blane's Pool Hall.

Megan stopped at the intersection and looked wistfully around. "Remember when we were kids and our dads would give us a nickel to buy an ice cream at the Dairy Bar while they hung around General Seed? We were like six and five or something. Man, they wouldn't dream of doing that now."

It distressed us how the face of Pike Creek had changed.

Once September came, with Eric and me back in school, my mother announced that she could no longer sit in the house and simply read or she would go crazy. She too got a job. She worked a few hours a day in the craft store run by Katie's aunt. At home she would fuss over window displays, creating signs with stencils and choosing just the right doilies to set off Ruby's latest vase. Her housework began to suffer; our sheets were not always ironed and the silver tea set on the dining room buffet had its first brush with tarnish.

"Oh, pish posh," Mom said when I drew the state of the tea set to her attention. "I'll get around to it when I have time."

I had never known my mother to utter a procrastinating thought and it worried me. With everything else falling to pieces around me, there was something comforting in her particular ways.

Detective Mather had made only one trip out to Ruddy Duck since June. In the third week of August, more haggard and unhealthy than I'd seen him yet, he drove out to show us an updated sketch of the Shelburne girl's abductor—

apparently she had remembered some detail, a birthmark or scar or something. Detective Mather didn't seem convinced. He was not surprised the new drawing didn't jog any memories. After we shook our heads, he confided that it was probably farther from the truth than the first drawing, when the girl's memory had been fresh.

"Maybe the killer's moved out of the province," I told Megan. "Maybe he never stays anywhere very long, and that's how he avoids getting caught."

She gave what I said some thought. "No, he'll probably stay around this area."

"Why's that?"

Megan shrugged. "Okay, he blew that one in Shelburne, but overall he's had a lot of success around here."

It was a morbid but practical thought.

I was actually glad when school started again. The summer had been a bust. Any rejuvenation of our spirits had withered in the riot. So, for most of us, school brought routine back into our lives.

THIS WAS NOT TRUE for the Fritzes whose lives had been thrown into chaos with Malcolm's illness. Malcolm had not resurfaced since the day of the riot. He had not gone home or contacted any of his friends. He had vanished. When he was still missing a couple of days after the riot, I wished that I had never lost sight of him that day. I wished that when I'd spotted him being frisked by police, I hadn't allowed myself to be pushed forward. At least I might have known something or seen him leave with someone that could have given us a clue to where he was.

Malcolm's family was particularly worried because, wherever he had gone, he'd left his medication behind. It got rid of the voices in his head, but he couldn't stand the other ways it made him feel. He'd felt groggy and slow-witted, and his mouth was always dry.

Eric took Malcolm's disappearance hard. Even when Malcolm finally phoned his family at the end of August, Eric did not believe he was alright. He was living in Toronto, he told them, looking for a job. He did not say specifically where he was living, only that he was okay and he would call again soon.

Eric, Jimmy and Miles had worked on the highway all summer but Malcolm had been unable to hold a summer job. Now the three of them would be starting grade thirteen, and Malcolm would not be returning to school. On top of all the other confusion, Malcolm must have been feeling alienated from his friends. Dad explained this to me—the complexity of Malcolm's circumstances, the factors that were likely influencing his decisions—things that Eric must have already known.

Over the month of September Eric became increasingly difficult to talk to, and while my friends and I began socializing more now that we were back in school, he did things on his own.

I found it almost impossible to provoke an argument, let alone get him to do anything fun.

"I'll have you a game of Clue," I said, walking into his room and turning down Black Sabbath on his stereo.

"I don't feel like it."

"Okay, then how about a game of Risk?"

He looked up from the *Popular Mechanics* magazine where he lay reading on his bed. Eric knew I hated Risk because he always won. He seemed to think about it, but then he shook his head. "Naw."

Pushed into desperation, I snatched the magazine from under his nose. I paused in the doorway before peeling down the hall. He hadn't moved. "Aren't you even going to chase me?"

Flipping to his back, Eric stared at the ceiling. "There's no point. It was boring anyway."

My father was aware of the change in Eric's mood and was trying to help him in the best way he knew how. I didn't recognize this at first. I only thought I was being treated unfairly.

For some reason I had believed that the older I got, the fewer chores I would be assigned. But when I turned fifteen in August and in September was still cleaning the duck house, I mentioned this oversight to my father. Apparently I was mistaken.

"Whatever gave you that idea?" Dad laughed.

"Well, it seems to me that Eric doesn't do much around here anymore."

It was true that Eric's work around the farm had tapered off. Dad was feeding the cattle, shoveling hay into the trough through the trapdoor in the barn floor—something my brother had always done in the past. For the past several weeks, Dad was the one who had pulled our weekly load of garbage to the dump, past the duck house, through the woods to the other side of Fiddlehead Creek.

"It's only temporary," said Dad. "And until Eric is feeling up to it again, perhaps you can help out a bit too. He's got a heavy year at school, his last one, and a lot on his mind."

Jimmy made many attempts to cheer Eric up. The two of them made plans to see the movie *Gimme Shelter*. Jimmy drove out to the farm in his dad's new Thunderbird. Eric, of course, loved anything mechanical and normally he would have checked out the engine of the car. They would have discussed things like the horsepower and the number of cylinders and the revolutions per minute at great length—amazingly dull details that would make me nearly pass out from boredom. But this time Eric didn't ask any questions. Instead, as Jimmy tried to interest him in the car's features, he only nodded many times in a row.

"It's real nice, Jim," he finally said.

Jimmy was very enthusiastic about the car and I was sure that Eric had let him down.

"Yeah, I can't believe my Dad let me drive it. He's only had it a day. Are you ready to go?"

"Go?"

"To the movie. *Gimme Shelter*. You know, the Stones at Altmont. Jumpin' Jack Flash and all that. Remember?"

Eric shoved his hands deeper into his pockets. He was already on his way to the back door. It didn't appear to me that he had any intention of going anywhere. "Oh, hey, Jim, look, I've got a chemistry lab due. Can we make it some other time?"

Jimmy must have been disappointed, but he didn't convey it in his voice. "Yeah, sure, whatever you want." He drew a finger through the thin layer of road dust on the hood of his father's new car.

I had stopped to admire the car on my way back from the workshop. As Eric disappeared through the kitchen door, I found myself apologizing on his behalf.

"He's not himself," I started to explain. "I'm sorry he wasn't more excited about your new car, Jimmy."

"Hey, don't worry about it. I only thought it might help take his mind off it, that's all." Jimmy opened the car door. "Man, I can't even imagine having to deal with what he saw. I don't know how he's kept it in as long as he did. I mean, it's not like he saw it in a movie or something. And then there's this whole thing with Malcolm on top of it. That's been a real drag too."

Jimmy must have seen the worry on my face. "Don't worry, Emma, he'll get over it. It's just going to take some time that's all. And Malcolm, well, he'll turn up, I'm sure of it. He always has." He smiled a little. "I don't suppose you want to come to the movie with me?"

It was cold and I pulled my sweater a little closer around me. I hadn't even thought to put on a coat when I'd run up to talk to Dad in the workshop. I shrugged. Eric sure didn't do anything fun with me anymore. "Yeah, I would like to go. I'll get my coat."

Jimmy was in an up mood and it was great to be around someone fun for a few hours. He couldn't sit still when the Stones were performing onscreen. He drummed continually on the back of the seat in front of him. He had drummed all through "Sympathy For the Devil" when he suddenly stopped, turned to me and asked, "When did you grow up?"

I didn't know the answer. But I was glad he'd noticed.

"I mean, didn't you use to be a kid?"

"Yeah," I said, "I was. But I got my braces off."

He laughed. "Oh well, that must be it." He turned back to the screen and began drumming again. He stopped briefly. "Did you wear braces? I never noticed."

Eric was sitting at his desk with his chemistry books spread before him, making a paper-clip chain, when I arrived home. His lab notebook was open to a fresh white page. Nothing but the number one had been written in the margin. It appeared that was all he'd accomplished in the nearly three hours I'd been gone.

"You missed a good movie," I said.

"Yeah, well, that's the way it goes." He weaved another paper clip onto the end of the two-foot chain.

Wandering over to his desk, I glanced at the chapter assignment in his textbook. There were fifteen questions. "Wow, you keep this pace up and you might be finished by Christmas." When he didn't say anything, I slumped into the big chair. I thought it was time I said something. Somebody had to. So I told Eric that he should get a grip and not disappoint his friends. "Jimmy's a nice guy. He's only trying to help. Look, I know you're worried about Malcolm, and what you saw is probably impossible to get over, but everybody's trying to help. Maybe you could just try."

Eric looked over to where I sat in the chair. I had his attention. I leaned forward.

"You're going to have to get over it sometime. You can't just stop doing things forever. I mean, don't you miss flying? And playing your guitar? And by the way, when Dad gets sick of doing your chores for you, I sure don't want to get stuck having to do them too. I don't have a clue how to change a spark plug. And besides," I studied my hands, "it would really wreck my nails." I sat back.

Eric didn't reply.

"Hey, do you know what Jimmy asked me?"

He picked up his pencil and returned to his lab book. "No, what did Jimmy ask you?"

"He asked me when I grew up."

Eric jotted down a chemistry formula. "He doesn't know you still can't sleep without a night-light."

Okay, it wasn't much—but it was the best shot he'd thrown my way in some time.

"Yeah," I said. "Me and half this town. Anyway, it's only a little light. And you'd better not tell him."

Eric finally managed a half smile. He assured me that it really wasn't such a big deal.

THAT FALL WAS THE FIRST TIME in my memory we didn't eat Thanksgiving dinner together. Eric was invited to the Fritzes' along with Jimmy—and because the family was still unsure where Malcolm was or if he was all right, Eric didn't want to disappoint them. Carl was gearing up for the skating season. He spent the long weekend working overtime at the arena, where he stocked the concession booth and helped Mr. Dikkers ready the ice. And Mom was so busy preparing the Halloween display for the craft store that, amazingly, Thanksgiving seemed to almost slip her mind.

Throughout the month of October, the dining room table was covered with a heap of orange crepe paper and black felt. Silhouettes of witches and white floss for spider webs cluttered the buffet. On the Monday morning of the long weekend, I stuck my head in the doorway. "Do you want me to help you clear the table?"

"Huh?" A little bleary-eyed, Mom looked up from the outline of the ghost she was tracing. "Sorry, dear. What did you ask?"

"For Thanksgiving dinner tonight. Do you want me to help you move all that stuff?"

"Thanksgiving?" She surveyed the mess on the table. "That won't be necessary. There will only be the three of us. I was going to make a chicken, and I think we'll eat in the kitchen. We'll use the stoneware and the regular silverware tonight."

The regular silverware? On Thanksgiving? I seriously wondered if my mother was ill. I thought I'd better ask my father. I wandered up to the workshop, where Dad was building shelves for the seniors' home. He had just said goodbye to Mr. Fraser, who waved to me as he drove down the lane. Dad didn't answer right away when I asked him about Mom. He appeared preoccupied as he continued pounding nails. I asked if there was something wrong with him.

"Oh, no, sorry. It's just that Mr. Fraser's still keen on mining gold in Costa Rica. I guess I've never been much of a gambler. I'd like to see the prospector's reports, that's all. What was it you asked me, Emma?"

I sat on a stump in front of the roaring stove. I patted old Halley and again put the question to him regarding my mother.

To my surprise, he laughed. "Your mother's fine, Emma. She's just enjoying her new job."

"Enjoying? She worries over the tiniest little detail, and she spends so much time on it, it's like she's forgotten about us."

"People enjoy things differently."

I clapped my hands over Halley's ears to protect them from the momentary scream of the electric saw.

"And she hasn't forgotten about us, she's only been sidetracked—we're still very much on her mind." Dad smiled. "Trust me on this."

There was a cold snap at the beginning of November. On my way down the lane one morning I passed my mother's rose garden. It was as if the roses had been hit by the plague during the night; the heads of the flowers now drooped and the leaves had turned limp and black. Waiting for the bus, I lost the feeling in my toes despite continually stamping my feet. They didn't thaw until I got to school when, slowly, during math, a hot, tingly sensation told me they were coming back to life.

During the lunch hour we stood in the smoking area, chatting as usual. A brisk wind stung my cheeks and reddened my ears. To keep warm, I clutched my arms to my chest. I didn't know how Doug McCrae could just stand there with a cigarette wagging from his lips, wearing only a T-shirt and leather vest, acting like it was the middle of July.

It was unusually quiet walking up the lane after school. I looked toward the pond where the surface was undisturbed. I realized my father must have rounded up the ducks and geese and paraded them into the barn for the winter while I was at school that day.

At dinner I noticed that Eric's hands were already rough and chapped.

"You should wear gloves," I told him.

"You tell me that every year."

"So why don't you? I don't get it with you guys—what's so cool about not wearing gloves?"

"It has nothing to do with being cool. They get in my way, that's all."

Eric was watching the news while I did my homework in front of the television after supper. The telephone rang. Mom called Eric into the kitchen. It was Miles with the news that Malcolm had been found. He had been discovered in a park in Toronto early that morning. He'd been wearing only a light shirt with a T-shirt beneath it, jeans, and sandals with socks the night before when he'd lain down on a bench to sleep. The temperature had plummeted and Malcolm had died of exposure overnight.

I suppose, looking back, it was the news Eric had been waiting for. He knew it was coming, he just wasn't sure of the particulars, but there it was.

I spent the evening with Megan while Mom and Dad drove Eric to see Miles and offer Mr. and Mrs. Fritz their support.

"Wow," Megan said when I arrived. I followed her up to her room, where she sank into a chair. "This is so hard to believe. A person can die just like that? I mean, that easily? A big guy like Malcolm? Just by lying down and falling asleep when it's cold? Poor Malcolm. Poor Miles. His poor parents. What's with this place anyway? It's like we're jinxed. They should make a horror movie out of us. This just sucks so bad."

In retracing the last few weeks of his life, the police discovered that Malcolm had been living on the street since the day he wandered off from the music festival. He'd moved around a lot, hitching rides, bumming money for food, sleeping when he had a need to and where he could find a dry spot. Often this was in bus shelters, under bridges or, on milder nights, in a park. Only a couple of times did he check into a shelter, but there were complaints; he kept others awake with the rambling dialogue he carried on with the voices in his head.

People certainly remembered him—with his untamed beard and waist-length hair he would be hard to forget—but he avoided talking directly to them or making friends with others who lived on the street. He had refused help from social workers. He accused them of plotting against him. He knew their plan was to get him alone and interrogate him.

I asked Eric, "About what?"

"I don't know. About whatever. About the mission to Mars or his involvement in the Attica State Prison riot."

"Malcolm was involved in the Attica prison riot?"

Eric rolled his eyes. "Of course not."

It was all a bit surreal, Malcolm's death and the funeral. The service was very large, with a ton of Malcolm's friends, classmates and former teachers filling the church. His mother and father sat at the front, and although their eyes were swollen, they looked composed. I remembered what my mother said Mrs. Fritz had told her the night they'd learned of Malcolm's death. "I felt as though we lost him the day the doctors told us of his illness. And now I've lost my son twice. I never would have believed anything could be as painful as this."

Several people spoke in memory of Malcolm, but the one I most admired was Miles. I don't know how he held it together to talk about his brother.

"He had to do it," Eric told me after the service.

I couldn't imagine anyone heartless enough to force him into it. "Why?"

Eric shrugged. "He was his brother."

"Man," said Jimmy, shuffling his feet on the sidewalk, "I keep thinking I should call him up. I feel like it's been a long time since I talked to him and I should find out what he's been up to. That guy that was hanging around with us the last few months—that guy wasn't Malcolm. It seems like he's been gone for a really long time."

The four of us were silent as my father drove home after the reception. It was just too difficult to talk. In the dusk I looked past my emerging reflection in the window and then across the brown stubble fields. I thought of Malcolm standing in the doorway of the Hippie House when they'd first started The Rectifiers and how he was so cool. Megan had such a crush on him—any girl would have jumped at the chance to go out with him back then. Six months later he was sitting at our kitchen table, talking about the mouse running across the floor, the tsunami in Japan and how he was so worried about upsetting the greater scheme of things.

A frightening thought occurred to me—if I had not caught that mouse, if I'd let it go about its business the way Malcolm wanted it to, would things have turned out differently for him?

THE FIRST SNOW FELL during the second week of November, large soft flakes like dandelion seeds floating silently, melting on water and settling on the ground. With them, the weight of a memory—what he found one snowy December day the previous winter—descended on Eric. It seemed such a long time after the fact, but this is what happens—things that are too horrible to think about at the time can come back to you like that.

He didn't remember it in a dream or as a flashback or anything like that. It was the crunch of the snow beneath his boots as he walked back from the barn. It was the whirling snow around him while the rest of the world stood still. It was the silence most of all. Just like on that day. A sudden feeling of doom overwhelmed him, and by the time he had reached the house he was in an unusually anxious state.

Over the next couple of weeks, Eric lost weight, anxiety prevented him from eating. He rarely laughed, and even a smile seemed to cause him pain. I could call him any abusive name I wanted and he made no attempt to retaliate. That would take energy and he seemed to require all he had just to go to school and accomplish the routine things in his life.

It was snowing lightly after school one day when Eric and I arrived home at the same time. The house was empty—Mom was at work and Dad was in the workshop. Halley did not greet us right away, and she was not in her usual spot—the blanket by the kitchen door. We called her name several times but there was no response. I did a quick tour of the main floor while Eric checked upstairs. When we still didn't find her, Eric walked up to the workshop. My father had not seen her since letting her outside after lunch. He was certain he'd let her in again.

It was unusual for Halley to wander, and even more doubtful that she would now that she was so old. She was a very social dog and rarely let us out of her sight. Eric sent me down to the duck house while he walked around to the other side of the pond. He was exceptionally anxious when I met up with him again.

"She couldn't have gone far," he insisted. "She doesn't have the strength."

"Maybe she's in the barn."

I didn't know how she could have possibly got in the door, the latch was so stiff, but we checked it out anyway. We walked through the barn together. Eric lifted the trapdoor through which we dropped hay into the cattle trough below.

"Do you suppose she could have somehow got in with them?" I asked.

Eric dropped the trap. "Only if the door was open to the barnyard."

It was very unlikely she would be in with the cattle—Halley didn't like to be around them in a space as confined as that. Despite this, entering through the barnyard, we pressed our way through the frozen muck into the basement of the barn where the ceiling was low and the room steamy. A few cattle noted our presence with low, mildly disinterested sounds.

I was certain Halley couldn't have gone far. I was also certain she'd show up. She always had in the past. "I'm going back to the house," I told Eric. "Mom asked me to start supper tonight."

Eric threw his hands in the air. I wasn't sure if he was frustrated with the search or with me for abandoning it.

"She's probably tracking a rabbit in a field somewhere. She'll be back," I told him.

Eric didn't follow me. I returned to the kitchen, where I began peeling potatoes. Within half an hour, Mom arrived home and my father returned from the workshop. Dad went down to the basement, sent by Mom to retrieve a jar of pickles. I had just finished setting the table when I heard a familiar clip-clop on the wooden stairs.

"Look who I found," Dad chuckled, emerging from the basement behind Halley. She rushed over to greet me, madly wagging her stubby tail. She was panting and slobbered heavily. "She locked herself in the pantry. She must have been snuffling around and knocked the door closed again."

It had happened once before. Poor Halley, she was beside herself. The way she panted in her panic, it didn't take long for her to turn the small preserves room into a sauna. She must have been sweltering down there.

"Halley, you goof." I gave her fresh water and tried to get her to calm down.

Dinner was nearly ready and Eric still had not returned. We sat in the living room waiting, although not impatiently; Dad was reading the newspaper and Mom was leafing through a magazine.

I did try calling Eric's name out the door but there had been no response. "He was worried," I explained. "He must be searching every corner of the farm."

But none of us were aware how worried Eric actually was. Although, when I tried to trace it all back to one incident, I realized it was much more than concern for Halley that led to what happened next. It was all that had happened since the previous December. It was the horror of discovering Katie—resurfacing. It was the helplessness, the guilt Eric wrestled with as he blamed himself for an inability to prevent Malcolm's death. He was already haunted by two ghosts; he couldn't handle another in Halley.

My father heard the engine first. Of course it was not surprising that he would be the first to recognize the sound of his own plane. He dropped the newspaper in his lap and listened, as if, initially, he doubted the reliability of his own ears.

It took me a minute to clue in. I was used to hearing the Maul Rocket, but never, it occurred to me, while Dad was sitting in the same room.

"That sounds like your plane," my mother commented, the obvious also not registering in her voice right away. This was followed by "John!" a moment later when it had registered and Dad was already on his way out of the house.

My mother and I tore after him. The sound of the engine became very loud as soon as we were out the door. The Rocket had just cleared the woods at the end of the airfield by the time we'd passed the barn and reached the hangar. There was no point jumping up and down and yelling. My father knew Eric would not hear or respond. Although that didn't stop me from doing it.

There was not much we could do—in fact, there was nothing we could do. My father paced before the hangar while Mom and I stayed back, watching the plane circle over Fraser's fields. Eric did not have his license yet, and so, of course, he had never flown the plane alone. I couldn't imagine what was going through my brother's head that he would do such a thing.

The sound of the engine receded as the Maul Rocket disappeared from sight. Dad stood still now, with his hands in his pockets, staring off to where his plane had last been visible in the sky.

Mom ran to the workshop, where she called Uncle Pat. Not that there was anything he could do either, except that perhaps she felt that none of us were in a frame of mind to make a sensible decision. My uncle would remain level-headed enough to know what to do.

Uncle Pat arrived within minutes, but it was a long twenty minutes more before the familiar sound of the Rocket returned. This time my father and uncle flagged him with both arms, hoping Eric would land. The plane began to lose altitude. It appeared that Eric planned to come in. As he descended over the woods beyond the field, the wings of the plane tilted from side to side as though Eric was having difficulty maintaining control. My father locked onto it with his eyes, willing it, I believed, not to go down.

Eric cleared the trees. He was now over the field and the Maul Rocket was almost on the ground. One wheel touched down before the other, the plane dipped sharply to one side and a wing grazed the frozen ground. A six-foot section at the tip of the wing crumpled as the aircraft swerved.

"Oh my god!" my mother cried, releasing her hold on me. Along with my father and Uncle Pat, she ran toward the damaged airplane. Veering off toward the fence between the airstrip and Fraser's field, it came to an abrupt stop.

I followed, hanging back a little, afraid of what I might see. My father pulled at the door and bent down inside the plane. By the time I was close enough, I could see Eric was bleeding from a gash where he had hit his forehead on the instrument panel. His head fell forward and he seemed disoriented, confused, unaware of what he'd done. "I couldn't find her," he told us. "I thought I might be able to see her, or at least some kind of a sign."

Was he completely wacko? Whatever made him think that from three thousand feet in the air he could pick out a small white dog on fields and woods blanketed in snow?!

Dad released the seat belt before putting an arm around my brother's shoulder. "Never mind. Halley's just fine. She was in the house all along."

Between them, he and Uncle Pat helped Eric out of the cockpit and onto the ground.

Eric was unsteady on his feet. He leaned against the plane while Mom dabbed the cut with her apron and wiped away the blood running into his eye. Uncle Pat returned to his truck and drove it onto the airfield.

I'm not sure what came over me as Eric hobbled toward the vehicle, except that I had a sudden and horrible vision of me, sitting at a Monopoly board with a pile of money in front of me, all alone.

"You idiot!" I lunged at him. "Why would you do that?!" I whacked him hard. And then, since nobody else was going to say anything, I added, "Look what you did to the plane!"

Dad took hold of my shoulders. "Come on, Emma. Your brother's going to be okay. Go help your mother look after Halley while we're gone."

16

Eric took quite a knock on the head in his brush with disaster, but that may have been what roused him from his despondent state. Whatever it was, I realized why my father had not made an issue out of what he'd done to the Maul Rocket at the time. He knew that when Eric eventually did come around, he would be hard enough on himself. The sight of the crippled Rocket left him with a sick feeling, and until the aircraft was taken away to be repaired, Eric could not go near the airfield. He insisted on paying for the damage, but my father told him he would rather see him work hard at school than take on a job to pay for what he'd done.

"You're looking at university next year. We don't want to jeopardize your chances. However, if you insist on making it up somehow," Dad tossed a wink in my direction, "the sunroom needs painting, the linoleum needs to be replaced in the kitchen and the windows all need a coat of stain. When your head has recovered, of course."

Eric rolled his eyes. He told me later it would be a whole lot easier if he just went out and got a job. That way he could pay off the airplane and the debt would be settled. Dad's approach might seem casual, but it could have him painting and nailing for the rest of his life!

I was sewing for the drama production again that year. The school was putting on the rock opera *Jesus Christ Superstar*. I loved the music, but the costumes were not much of a challenge, at least not compared to the Victorian gowns of the previous year. I figured I could go a little crazy with King Herod's robe, so that's what I opted to sew.

I was also working on a black velvet outfit for the Christmas dance: a pair of pants and a bolero vest. Ruby had taught me some tricks to match the grain and keep the soft pile intact. But on the day of the dance, as I pondered the finished outfit on my dress form, it occurred to me that trimming the vest in gold braid would give it a festive touch. I had the afternoon to do it—that is, if I could get into town to buy the braid.

I stuck my head into Eric's room. "Will you drive me into Pike Creek?"

He was sitting on his bed, strumming quietly, working out the chords to a new Led Zeppelin tune, "Stairway to Heaven." Eric continued to play. "Jimmy's going to be here in a few minutes. We're going to the rummage sale at the church. You can come with us if you want."

Perfect. I returned to my room to turn off the sewing machine.

The rummage and antique sale was held in the basement of St. Mark's Church. It was an annual event to raise money for Santas Anonymous. Eric and Jimmy liked to go for the old radios and electronic equipment. They always found something that interested them.

Jimmy arrived at Ruddy Duck in his dad's new Thunderbird. On the way into town Eric commented on the acceleration, inspected the dashboard and asked a bunch of questions about the engine before saying, "Your dad sure is letting you drive it a lot."

"I know. I don't get it. I used to have to beg two days in advance if I wanted to borrow the Olds. It's weird, but my parents have been really laid-back about everything I do lately." Jimmy paused before adding, "I figure it's Malcolm. I suppose I should take advantage of it. I don't expect it can last."

Eric and Jimmy dropped me off in front of the fabrics and notions store in Pike Creek. We made arrangements to meet at the church an hour later.

It didn't take long for me to choose the trim; I already had a gold braid in mind. I had seen it earlier in the season and was thankful there was still enough on the roll. I stopped to rummage through the bin of remnants and marked-down notions. There was a remarkably gauche, twisted, silver and orange braid that would only appeal to someone completely insane. Or someone who was making a costume such as King Herod's robe. The whole roll was fifty cents, which said a lot about how popular it had been.

I still had plenty of time to kill before meeting Eric, so after leaving the fabric store I dropped by the drugstore to visit Megan, who still worked on weekends. She was allowed to take a coffee break. We sat in the back storage room. I leafed through a *Vogue* magazine while Megan moped. It turned out she'd broken up with Duncan the night before, or it could have been the other way around. At first she wouldn't tell me when I pressed her for details. "We're just not compatible." is what she said.

Alright. Since she didn't want to talk about it, I attempted to take her mind off it. I pulled the braid from the paper bag. "What do you think of this braid? Isn't it perfect for my black vest?"

Megan sat forward. "Okay, one thing—he's got this really annoying habit of chewing his ice. How can he expect me to pay attention to a movie when all I can hear is chomp, chomp, chomp?"

I returned the braid to the bag. "Yeah, well, I can see that might be a problem."

"And he hardly ever phones when he says he's going to. He's always at least fifteen minutes late. And get this—he puts ketchup on eggs!"

I closed the magazine in front of me. I was now sorry I'd asked. All I really wanted to do at that moment was get home, not hear every little thing that was wrong with Duncan. "Uh," I stood up, "I've got to get back to the church. I have to meet Eric. Call me when you finish work and we'll make arrangements for tonight."

SHE NODDED ABSENTLY as I left.

I went on to the church. Eric and Jimmy were playing with an old phonograph. They were too absorbed to even notice me, so I wandered around the room. I checked out the table with Mrs. Chisholm's crocheted baby bonnets and poodle toilet-paper covers. Mr. Dikkers had a booth where, for five dollars, he would burn your name into a piece of wood. And Rose's mother had a table with pincushions that resembled overstuffed miniature chairs. I looked at them closely. They were unquestionably tacky, made of foam-stuffed tuna cans covered with scraps of fabric and lace. Rose sat next to her mother looking a little humiliated and entirely bored. I felt sorry for her. Not so much for having to spend her afternoon sitting in the church basement, but for all the tuna casseroles she would have been forced to eat. I bought one of the pincushions.

Rose raised her eyebrows and shook her head. She waved her hands like it wasn't really necessary. I wondered if it had something to do with supply and demand; the more pincushions that sold, the more tuna casseroles she would have to eat.

"It makes more sense than sticking pins and needles in my jeans."

Rose's mom laughed. "I'm sure that can get a little dangerous. There you are, Emma. Enjoy."

I sidled up next to Eric. "How long are you going to be?"

"Look at this," he said, turning over a cylinder. "This is Mario Lanza. Listen."

Cranking the phonograph, he let the cylinder turn. A thin, scratchy voice that hardly sounded human emanated from the speaker.

"Yeah, it's cool. But how long are you going to be? I've got to get this vest finished before tonight."

"Hey, Eric," Jimmy called, "check out this accordion amplifier."

Ohhh. I sank down on the linoleum steps. This was so incredibly dull. I didn't know how most of this stuff could even be called antique. It all looked like just a bunch of junk to me. I had a thought. I suddenly remembered that Mom was working at the craft store and would be off at two o'clock. I went back to talk to Eric, who was down on his knees, studying the amplifier. "I'm going to catch a ride with Mom."

"Huh?"

"I'm going to go home with Mom, so don't worry about me, okay?"

"Yeah, yeah. Okay."

I knew when they were about to leave he'd suddenly wonder where I was, but I figured at some point this conversation would rise from his subconscious brain. I left the church with Rose, who had been granted a half-hour break.

She lit a cigarette as soon as we were out the door. "Oh, man, fresh air. All that junk and old people yakking at each other is giving me a headache. But it was the only way I could get the car for the dance tonight. My mom drives a hard bargain. Hey, Emma, are you going to the dance tonight?"

"If I can get home and finish my vest."

Rose was headed to the Pike Creek Market to buy a Coke. We said goodbye and I started toward the craft store. I was about to step from the curb when a van stopped at the corner. It was Mr. Fraser. He signaled for me to open the door.

"Hi, Emma, where are you off to?"

"Actually, I'm on my way home."

"Are you meeting someone or can I give you a lift? I'm headed back to the farm."

"I was going to get a ride from Mom. She finishes work in half an hour." But if Mr. Fraser was driving out to the farm right then, it would mean I wouldn't have to wait. "Would you mind?"

"Not at all, hop in."

I climbed in with Mr. Fraser, who smiled and pulled back onto the road. "So you were at the rummage sale?"

"Yeah, I was waiting for Eric," I arranged my bags in my lap, "but he was taking too long."

"What's the hot item this year?"

I told Mr. Fraser about Mr. Dikkers' wood-burned signs and the craft booths and who was selling what. "There's a lot of antiques, too."

Mr. Fraser smiled again "You mean old junk. And I bet there are a few old people, too."

"Yeah," I said, "there were some of those."

There was a lot of creaking and sliding around behind me. I turned around. Although they were empty, the back of the van was stacked with crates to transport chickens. I was familiar with the smell—it was the same stuffy animal smell that bombarded me as I opened the door to our chicken roost in the small room in the corner of our barn.

"How's your brother doing? Is he on the mend? Your dad tells me he had a little accident with the plane."

"He's okay. The bump on his head has healed." And for some reason I thought of how decent Eric had been to me since his accident. "But I think his ego is still a little bruised."

Mr. Fraser chuckled. "Well, we all do things we'd rather forget from time to time."

We were now on the highway heading out of town. I was thinking that I would have to phone Ruby and ask her the best way to attach the braid. It couldn't be sewn by machine, it would crush the fabric. I imagined it would have to be done by hand. If I had enough left over, I could trim the hem of my pants. Actually, that was a great idea. I wished I'd thought of it earlier so I could have bought enough for sure. But if I measured what I'd need quickly when I got home, I could phone Mom and ask her to pick up more.

"How are you enjoying school this year, Emma? What grade are you in?"

Or Megan—I could phone Megan if Mom had already left the craft shop. I was sure there would be enough braid; it looked like there were at least a couple of yards left on the roll.

"Emma?"

"Huh? Oh, sorry. School—I'm in grade ten."

"Grade ten," mused Mr. Fraser. "That must mean you're— what—fifteen or sixteen now?"

"Fifteen."

Mr. Fraser let out a low whistle. "Fifteen already, my how the time goes."

"Yeah."

Mr. Fraser turned off Highway 9 onto 25. It wasn't the most direct route—it took us through Marsville—but it was an alternate, and perhaps a little more scenic, way of getting to the farm.

I began to think about Megan and how she'd got her license in September. I was hoping Aunt Alice would let her drive us to the dance tonight. We were getting really tired of depending on our parents. It was beginning to cramp our style. It was embarrassing having them sitting there, waiting for us wherever we went. And what if one of these days I met someone and he wanted to drive me home? Was I going to have to explain forever that he couldn't because my mom or dad or uncle was waiting in the car?

Mr. Fraser was quite a slow driver. There was very little traffic on the road, yet, according to the speedometer, he kept exactly ten miles below the speed limit. He slowed down even more for a minor pothole. I looked at the speedometer again.

He saw me do it. "You can't be too cautious along this road," he told me. "I've had deer jump out of nowhere and almost gone off the road."

I nodded, although I really did wish he'd speed it up. At the rate he was going we would be lucky to make it home before dark.

"Would you like a corn chip?" he asked, pulling a glove off with his teeth. Before I had a chance to answer, he bent forward and reached an arm beneath my seat. I had to bunch my legs against the door to allow him to get under it. He was practically in my lap as he rummaged around for whatever it was. I really wished he'd just asked me to pass it to him. It was a small space and I didn't like the feel of his hand against my leg. Finally he dragged a crumpled bag of corn chips out and offered me the open bag.

I shook my head.

"You're sure? It would put some meat on those bones."

"No thanks," I said, resenting a little that he figured I needed meat on my bones.

But I was very sure I didn't want any chips. I just wanted to get home now. I didn't want to take the scenic route and I didn't want teatime along the way. Was it my imagination or was he going slower still? I didn't want to risk looking at the speedometer again in case he thought I was getting impatient—which I was. But then he might think I was ungrateful as well and dump me out on the street. I didn't know how much luck I'd have getting a ride after that because we hadn't passed a car since turning onto Highway 25.

"So, how about a boyfriend, Emma?"

"A boyfriend?"

"Yeah, a good-looking girl like you must have one."

It was kind of a nosy question, I thought. I mean, coming from somebody who I didn't really know all that well. But he was an okay guy otherwise, so I allowed him some slack. Some people truly don't know when they're being impolite.

"No, I don't. Not right now anyway."

"Oh well," he said, between mouthfuls of chips. "There'll be plenty of time for that. Don't you worry."

But I wasn't worried. He was the one who brought it up!

It began snowing—fat flakes flew at the windshield, melting as soon as they hit the glass. Mr. Fraser flicked his windshield wipers on at the intermittent speed. After a while I could see the intersection where we were to turn. But with the snow, and us traveling less than thirty miles an hour, and the way the windshield wipers were sluggishly beating time, it seemed that the whole world had slowed down. I calculated it would be hours before we got to the intersection ahead. I looked over at Mr. Fraser. He looked back at me, popped a chip in his mouth and smiled.

"Who was your friend back there?"

"Back where?" I wasn't sure who he was talking about.

"At the church. Who were you talking to before I stopped? Was that one of your friends?"

Oh, Rose. "No—I mean, yeah, I guess she is. She's my cousin Megan's friend. She's older than me, but I guess she's mine too."

"Ah."

The snow was coming at us faster now, in thick, feathery tufts. Mr. Fraser turned the speed of the windshield wipers up. Suddenly he began to brake. He couldn't already be slowing down for the intersection, it was still too far ahead. It almost looked like he was planning to turn into what appeared to be the back lane to a farmer's field. The tractor tracks led through a wall of spruce on either side. It didn't alarm me. If anything, I was annoyed because it would mean a delay. I thought perhaps he had to deliver the chicken pens or something. That he had an appointment to keep on the way back to the farm. My father always had errands, promises he'd made to drop by and help someone out.

A car came to a stop at the intersection ahead. Mr. Fraser made a left turn into the tractor lane, drove a few hundred feet and stopped. He turned off the engine. Snow quickly began obliterating the windows. He turned to me. "This will only take a minute."

What will only take a minute? What was he doing? We were parked in the middle of nowhere, it was snowing and I wanted to get home.

Mr. Fraser reached for something behind his seat.

Just great. I really wished he hadn't bothered to pick me up if he knew he was stopping to help somebody. That meant they'd have to show their appreciation and he'd be forced to stay for tea afterwards. He'd try to get out of it by telling them I was waiting in the car, but they'd only insist on me coming in too. That was always the way it worked. I'd been through it enough times with my father. It looked like I was never going to get home!

Mr. Fraser turned forward again, bringing with him a roll of binder twine. As he turned, his elbow caught the open bag of corn chips he'd set on the center console. It fell, scattering chips over his lap, my lap and the floor. Mr. Fraser swore. It surprised me. For one thing, it seemed a tad of an overreaction considering they were only chips. But it was also very uncomfortable hearing that kind of language from someone nearly as old as my father, particularly in such a confined place. I hurriedly bent to pick them up. I reached to open the door, intending to brush them off my lap.

"Leave the door!" Mr. Fraser snapped.

I thought he must have had a reason—the hinges were not secure and the door would fall off or something. I took my hand away from the handle.

A sudden knock on Mr. Fraser's window made me jump, although it seemed to startle Mr. Fraser more than me. I could make out the dark profile of someone's head through the build-up of snow on the driver's side. Mr. Fraser rolled down the window. It was Mr. DeSousa.

"Hi, Grant." Mr. DeSousa leaned forward. "Is everything alright? I saw you turn off here and thought you might have run into some car trouble."

Mr. Fraser appeared a little flustered. Waving the binder twine, he opened his door. "No, it's that tailgate." He stepped from the van into the snow. "The latch keeps popping open. Drives me crazy. I just stopped to tie it in place."

Mr. DeSousa smiled and nodded. "Looks like we're in for a real blizzard. They say we're going to get ten inches in the next twelve hours."

"Is that right?" Mr. Fraser rounded the van. I could hear his muffled voice as he tied the tailgate in place. It struck me that it may have been driving him crazy, but I hadn't heard a thing. But then I'd had my mind on how I was going to get the rest of that braid.

Mr. DeSousa noticed me, stuck his head farther in the van and winked. "Hi, Emma. Hetty's all excited about the dance tonight."

I smiled back.

He stood up. "Well, Grant, I won't keep you. Glad everything's alright." Mr. DeSousa returned to his car, backed onto the main road, waved and went on his way.

Mr. Fraser stamped the snow from his boots, climbed back into the van and closed the door. The impact dislodged the snow clinging to the windows and it was suddenly much brighter inside. He sat for a moment. "Well, I guess we'd better get home before this blizzard really hits." He also backed out of the lane and onto the main road.

Surprisingly, despite the weather becoming wilder, he now began to drive much faster than he had for the first part of our trip. But I was thankful for that. I was anxious to catch Mom or at least Megan before they headed for home.

A WEEK LATER, Eric and I pulled the toboggan past the hangar and the duck house, and down the lane that ran through the woods. We didn't go as far as where the Hippie House had once been. Where the lane turned the corner we cut off onto a narrow path. It took us to a part of the woods where Dad had sent us to collect our Christmas tree.

The snow was deep, soft beneath with a thin, shiny crust. Eric was wearing snowmobile boots that tied just below his knees. I followed close behind him, stepping into his tracks. The powdery snow worked its way into my boots and I wondered if there'd be a time in my life when I'd get through a winter without wet socks.

I stopped to scoop up a glove full of snow from Eric's newest footprint. I tried pressing it into a ball but it crumbled like fine ash.

"Don't bother," Eric said without turning around.

How did he know what I was planning?

"I already tried. It's not wet enough."

"Hey, were you going to throw a snowball at me?"

"Yeah, if I could make one." Eric turned. "And I suppose you were going to huck yours at a tree."

I threw the handful of powder at him anyway. A slight wind caught it and blew most of it back in my face. Eric laughed.

Dad had already tagged the seven-foot pine he wanted us to cut down. He had cultivated this lot and he pruned the trees every year. I was sure he already knew which trees we'd be cutting for the next ten Christmases. Eric began to saw the base while I stood out of the way.

"Timber!" he shouted, stepping back.

We waited. The tree remained stubbornly connected to its stump. Stepping forward again, Eric gave it a shove with his foot.

"Timber," he repeated, sounding a little less confident.

Seconds passed. Finally, obediently, the tree fell with a whomp.

Eric lifted the base, I grabbed the top and we maneuvered it onto the toboggan. It left my gloves sticky with sap.

We hauled it back through the woods and along the lane. In the woods, the weight of the tree on the toboggan carried it away on the icy surface, but once we reached the lane it was trampled well enough that we were able to regain control. We passed the hangar and had just come around the corner next to the barn when we spotted Detective Mather's car. He was leaning against it, talking to Dad. Seeing us approach, he smiled warmly. There was something different about him. He wasn't pacing. He was just leaning there, looking almost relaxed.

"Eric, Emma, Detective Mather has something you'll want to hear," Dad announced. "Let's go inside."

Once we were seated in the living room, my father leaned forward with his hands clasped before him. His voice was sober as he told us about Mr. Fraser's arrest. He then stood up and while he gazed out the window, Detective Mather took over, filling us in on some of the details of the crimes. As he explained things to us, Eric blinked at the detective. But I could not concentrate on anything that was said after Dad announced the name. I was paralyzed by the thought of what had come so close to happening. I was embarrassed at how gullible and stupid I had been.

So I simply stared at the floor, too numb to cry, as the detective spoke. I could think of nothing but how Mr. Fraser, had meant to kill me that day of the rummage sale. He'd pulled his van into the farmer's field because he'd meant to rape and kill me like Katie. Mr. Fraser, our neighbor. Mr. Fraser, who I had known since we had moved to Ruddy Duck when I was seven years old. He'd brought us chickens and he'd shared duties with my father, repairing the fence that separated our properties.

With a sudden pang of both anger and sadness I understood better than anyone else why Katie Russell had stepped into the van so easily that November night.

The arrest was nothing to celebrate, I heard my father explain somewhere in the distance. It was nothing any of us could have known about either. It was something that we would have to absorb and, maybe someday when we were older, comprehend.

Detective Mather explained some of the particulars. Part of the evidence linking Mr. Fraser to Katie was some feathers from a specific type of chicken. When I heard Detective Mather say this, I remembered what he'd said many months before. "There are certain things that we don't tell the general public. These are details about the crime or the crime scene that only the killer would know." Only the Frasers and a handful of farmers in neighboring counties owned this particular breed. The girl he'd abducted in Shelburne had also picked up on the odor in the van. I believe it was something similar that tied him to Fiona. I don't know that I ever really heard.

I never told anyone but Megan about my ride with Mr. Fraser the Saturday before he was arrested. There was no point. Mom would never have let me out of her sight again. But for many months to come I got a chill every time I thought about it and what could have happened to me. Megan was so angry with me I thought she might spit. How could I have been so clueless after all we had discussed? After all the scenarios we had created, working out the details of how we should react. How could I have just sat there like a dimwit when he turned off the road?

After asking these questions, she'd glare at me, waiting for an answer.

But I didn't have an answer for any one of them. Finally I told her that it was possible I'd imagined the whole thing. Maybe Mr. Fraser really did have a broken tailgate and he'd been driving slowly because the visibility was poor.

Megan frowned at me like I was trying to pull something over on her. But eventually she said nothing more.

AND SO IT WAS OVER. But really it was only the beginning of a more reserved chapter in our lives. Six months later, Mr. Fraser was found guilty of murdering Katie Russell and Fiona Young. When the trial ended, Dad and Uncle Pat helped an emotionally crippled Mrs. Fraser auction off the equipment and put the farm up for sale.

It was a warm May evening the following year when Mr. Fraser left Pike Creek and all that he was responsible for for good. And there was a lot he was responsible for—I don't think he left one life untouched. Megan and I were waiting at the main intersection as the sun settled behind Blane's Pool Hall. Ross Nash had taken up his old position outside the door. An unmarked blue sedan turned the corner.

"Look!" Megan pointed. "Emma, it's Mr. Fraser."

I strained for a glimpse of him after the car turned. But I could only make out the profile of three heads in the backseat. It was possible it was him, but I couldn't be sure. Mr. Fraser had been shuttled between Toronto and the county courthouse over the course of his trial. He'd been sentenced that morning.

"Yup, there goes the creep," Ross said from behind my back. "Off to the big house."

I turned around and looked at Ross. He pulled a pack of cigarettes from his shirt pocket, but hesitated before taking one. He held it toward me instead. "Want one? You're old enough now, aren't you?"

I shook my head. But then I changed my mind. "Yeah. I'm old enough." I walked over to where Ross stood and helped myself to a cigarette. He flicked a lighter. I inhaled as smooth as silk when he held the flame to the tip.

"Emma?" Megan said, blinking at me.

"What?"

"Uh, the streetlight. It's changed."

I thanked Ross, stepped from the curb and began to walk. As I did, I took one more perfect drag to be certain that I could. Once I was on the opposite side of the street I tossed the cigarette in the gutter and squashed it with my foot.

Megan walked quickly next to me. "God, I'm glad he's gone. Just knowing he was still around gave me the creeps."

The drop-in center never reopened. It became only a memory and a storage space for cast-off hockey equipment again. Many years later, after Mr. Dikkers had retired and my cousin Carl maintained the arena on his own, he hauled away what was left of the stage, took down the spotlights and painted over the graffiti. He would rent out the large room to various organizations for special functions, but these were groups with specific purposes and they paid for use of the space.

We were never quite sure what happened to Mr. Gillespie. He seemed to simply disappear. One rumor had him in Alaska, working as a chef in a mining camp. Another had him riding the Canadian National Railway, cooking short-order meals for passengers on the train. It's possible that he did go to North Dakota to open a new Dairy Bar like Eric said—but that would be only a guess.

The Dairy Bar sat empty for a year before it finally sold to some businessmen from Toronto. After that the building was renovated—the curved exterior walls were squared off and the white stucco was replaced with brick and glass. A new restaurant opened. Something Sophisticated, it was called. Many people said Pike Creek was long overdue for a decent place to eat out, but Megan and I felt differently. There was nowhere to go after school where Mandy Green could fire chips at Doug McCrae because he criticized her hair.

Admittedly, we were too old for that anyway.

Donny Russell continued to wave to me in the hall at school, but eventually his acknowledgments turned to little more than a nod. I would always be a reminder of what had happened to his sister—I guess he knew that. No matter how much time passed.

Eric, Jimmy and Miles all went to university in Toronto the following year. On an August day before he left, I sat on the chair in his room and watched my brother pack. Halley lay beside me, sleeping. She didn't do much else anymore, although she still rolled over to get her tummy patted, pawing at me when I stopped.

I hated seeing Eric's room so empty. His empty drawers and closet. All the stuff that was necessary or important to him in his suitcase with only the little-kid stuff left on his dresser, the model airplanes turning from the ceiling, and the posters of Cream and Jim Morrison on the walls.

"Are you taking your posters?"

Eric shook his head. "No, they can stay. Besides, Cream broke up in '68 and Jim Morrison's dead."

This was somehow comforting. Not that Cream broke up or Jim Morrison was dead, but that on top of everything else I wouldn't have to stare at his empty walls.

"How about your guitar?"

I was trying to sound brave, like I was helping him out by suggesting things he might need. But as soon as I said it I had to bite my lip to stop it from vibrating.

Eric picked up his guitar and played a few chords. When he stopped, he stored the pick beneath the strings at the top of the neck. He continued to look at the guitar in a reminiscent way—I thought perhaps he was thinking of Malcolm. I know

I was. He lay it on his bed again. "No, I think I'll leave it here. It's too likely it would get damaged. And besides, I'm not going to have time."

I had never felt so empty and abandoned. It hurt deep down in my stomach and a tear rolled down my cheek. Eric must have seen it.

"I'll tell you what—how be you keep it in your room? Then if Carl comes over I don't have to worry about him sitting in here and wrecking it or getting it all out of tune."

Lifting the guitar by the neck, Eric passed it to me.

I accepted it in my arms like I would a baby. I carried it to my room, placed it carefully in the corner next to my sewing machine, flopped on my bed and cried as though it were the end of the world as I knew it.

It was true that with Mr. Fraser's conviction the immediate threat to our lives had been removed. But the experience had cut deep and the inherent trust in the world we had known as children was gone.

Megan and I continued to be leery if we were stopped and asked for directions. We never walked alone at night again. We never got in a car if we didn't know the driver. Only once, a year later, did Hetty suggest we hitchhike somewhere—I think it was to see a band play in Shelburne.

"Are you out of your mind?" Megan responded. "Remember Katie Russell?"

Hetty rubbed her forehead in an apologetic way, as if she had temporarily lost her sanity and forgotten. Yes, of course we remembered Katie Russell. How could we ever forget? There was a twelve-by-sixteen-foot scar on the ground next to Fiddlehead Creek to remind us.